Also by Susanne L. Lambdin

A Dead Hearts Novel Series:
Morbid Hearts
Forsaken Hearts
Vengeful Hearts

Coming Soon:
Defiant Hearts
Immortal Hearts

MORBID HEARTS

MORBID HEARTS

A DEAD HEARTS NOVEL

by

Susanne L. Lambdin

WYVERN'S PEAK PUBLISHING
An imprint of The McGannon Group, Ltd. Co.

Published by Wyvern's Peak Publishing
An imprint of The McGannon Group, Ltd. Co., 2014

Morbid Hearts
by Suzanne L. Lambdin

Copyright © Suzanne L. Lambdin, 2014

Morbid Hearts / by Suzanne L. Lambdin – 1st ed.

Summary: After the Scourge, Cadence and her Fighting Tigers guard the border of Pike's Peak. During a routine patrol, an aircraft crash brings news of the outside world, along with enemies old and new.

1 2 3 4 5 6 7 8 9

ISBN-13: 978-0-9854088-9-3

www.DeadHeartsNovel.com

www.WyvernsPeak.com

In memory of my brother, Sterling.

Chapter One

*T*hin white clouds trailed across the sky, blending with the smoke of a failing jet engine.

Cadence and her Fighting Tigers sat on a rocky outcrop in the Garden of the Gods, tracing the plane's path from the east over the ruins of Colorado Springs. Trembling with violence and descending fast, it was a spinning top of flames and smoke, spiraling out of control. An angry beast before its death, the jet roared its final cry.

The explosion was deafening, echoing through the red rocks with a sonic boom. Wings and chunks of the fuselage split, showering fragments of metal in every direction. Through the smoke, Cadence spotted a lone survivor falling to the ground under the twisted lines of a folding parachute. The pilot plummeted toward the earth.

Cadence and her team stood up. Dodger, the leather coat and dirty jean clad scout for the Fighting Tigers, gave a loud whistle. Standing next to the fifteen-year-old was his best friend, Smack, a twelve-year-old freckled tomboy, sporting reddish-blonde braids and a different color for every one of her cracked nails. The two jumped about like it was Christmas morning. Cadence couldn't blame them. Six months of patrolling this area hadn't witnessed a single incident.

"Damn fool. If he keeps that up, he's not going to be able to straighten the lines in time," said Highbrow, in a voice too old for seventeen.

Tall and lean, with wavy brown hair and a light tan, Highbrow was an average-looking teenager, except for his combat boots and faded, green Army coat. He wore the team's signature orange beret, with the Fighting Tiger's team patch stitched on the side. As her second-in-command, Cadence valued Highbrow's opinion above all others.

"I give him thirty seconds or less to get those lines untwisted and get that canopy under control or he's a goner," said Highbrow. "Why doesn't he break away and deploy his reserve?"

"Maybe he's injured," Cadence replied. Paying more attention to the imperiled pilot than her own feet, she stumbled on a rock.

Highbrow caught her, locking eyes with Cadence for a moment. His dark brown eyes sparkled with flecks of gold, emanating concern. She felt her heart quicken a beat before yanking her elbow free.

"I'm fine," she huffed. She smoothed back a tendril of her brown hair and returned attention to the pilot. "Has he got a chance or not?"

"He'll hit the ground and splat like an egg." Highbrow tightened the strap of Cadence's AK-47. "Pay attention. You don't want to drop your weapon." He glanced at the rifle and flipped the safety lever. He lifted her chin until their eyes met. "Remember, I just put your safety on."

"I will, I will. Stop distracting me." Cadence pulled away from Highbrow. "The pilot might make it and land on our side of the fence."

Green eyes bright with anticipation, she glanced toward a twenty-foot electric fence that cut Manitou Springs off from Colorado Springs. The fence was put up in sections around the Garden, blocking all roads facing the city. The largest sections housed generators, supplying electricity from Manitou Springs to Pike's Peak. Patrol teams checked the fence and generators daily, making necessary repairs.

Highbrow caught his breath and looked upward. Cadence felt her stomach lurch as one of the parachutist's cords snapped, and then another, causing the chute to collapse on one side. Sunlight glinted off of the pilot's closed helmet as he pulled at the cords in desperation, trying to control his fall. There wasn't much hope.

"Deploy, deploy," said Highbrow with a grim hush. "What if he drops beyond the perimeter? We can't cross the fence for any reason. You know the rules, Cadence."

"Get ready!" shouted Cadence. "We can't let him get away from us. No matter where he lands, we're going after him. He might be carrying something important."

"This could be our lucky day," said Blaze, dripping with sarcasm. "I hope he has cigarettes." Blaze always dressed in black and was never without thick eyeliner, further accentuating her bleached-white and purple-tipped, cropped hair. Knee-high boots completed her look, as fierce as her sarcasm.

"Luck has nothing to do with it," interjected Freeborn. "This is an act of God."

Cadence always counted on Freeborn to be the realist, which meant she was often a perceived as a downer. She was the patrol's guard—tall, reliable, and tough. Freeborn was a sixteen-year-old full-blooded Cherokee, and the only Native American at Pike's Peak. It was rumored that survivors from the Cherokee Nation had moved north into Canada, but Freeborn remained. Cadence picked her to join the Tigers due to her resilience and bravery. Freeborn carried her father's old shotgun instead of a high-powered rifle.

"Zombie," said Smack, chewing a wad of bubble gum and popping a sticky, pink bubble.

"You don't know if he's infected," said Dodger, tugging at his beret to scratch the top of his head. Smack stuck out her tongue at him, and he frowned. "What's that for? Everyone in the world isn't infected."

The girl laughed. "You are. With lice. Ha!"

Cadence ignored the pair and watched the pilot as a sudden gust of wind changed the direction of his fall. Like a miracle unfolding before them, the remaining lines of the parachute untwisted. The canopy spread wide except for one side, leading the survivor toward the tall rocks. Cadence started forward at a trot, with Dodger and the three girls following close. Highbrow remained on her right. Whisper, the sixteen-year-old dreadlocked teen, known for his silence and deadly accuracy as a sniper, supported Cadence on her left.

"He's in the wind now," said Highbrow. "Hurry!" He moved ahead of the group, never slowing his pace. "I think he's going to hit the fence!"

"This is horrible!" Smack cried out.

She and Dodger ran inseparable bickering about whether or not the pilot would drop on their side of the fence or smash into it.

Cadence and her team ran under a rock archway, following a road leading into the Garden. She caught up with Highbrow, jumping over large cracks in the pavement. The pilot was drifting a hundred feet above when the canopy collapsed again. He must have known his fate, as he managed to unfasten his backpack and drop it on the Tigers' side of the fence.

Blaze and Smack darted toward the backpack. Dodger walked behind them, dragging a long stick he found. The thin form of Whisper stepped in front of Cadence, lifting his M24 rifle, watching the falling man through the scope. Cadence, Highbrow, and Freeborn watched the pilot's death spiral, ending with an abrupt slam into the fence.

The impact produced a loud explosion followed by a series of zaps and sizzles as thousands of volts of electricity surged through the pilot's body. A shower of orange and red sparks flew from his frying flesh. The pilot jerked and thrashed with unyielding violence and horrific screams.

No one flinched. They had seen worse.

The report of Whisper's rifle put an end to the pilot's suffering. The bullet pierced the man's forehead. The body transformed into a black lump, baked through. Wisps of smoke trailed upward from the charred remains while the fence continued to hum and sputter like a happily fed monster. After a while, it also grew quiet.

"Nice shot," said Highbrow. Whisper nodded.

"Let's get him off the fence," Cadence urged. "Without a doubt city crawlers heard that explosion. I want him down before zombies get here."

Cadence scrambled down an embankment, sending rocks and pebbles rolling. Freeborn kept pace with Cadence. It was her job to keep the team leader safe, and she didn't slack in her role. By the time they reached the fence, both girls were sweating and breathing hard.

"Like I said, it was fate," said Freeborn. "There is no shame in his death."

Cadence said nothing. When the Scourge had broken out almost a year ago, everyone questioned their faith. Cadence couldn't bring herself to blame God for the virus or for the millions who died. The virus killed many people. It wasn't God's fault. Neither was the pilot's death.

Clotted to the fence, the pilot looked like overcooked bacon. The shredded canopy of his parachute lay on the other side of the fence. The only recognizable piece was an Air Force patch stitched onto the sleeve of his smoldering jacket. Cadence thought it odd that the patch remained in pristine condition. She wanted to rip it off; however, getting electrocuted was not high on her list of stupid things to do, so she left it alone.

Highbrow stood beside Cadence. "Think he came from the Air Force Academy?" He picked up a stick and nudged the crispy corpse. "Damn shame. I would have killed for some news from the outside world."

"No one is left alive in the city, Highbrow," said Cadence, "and the Academy fell months ago." With morbid fascination, she studied the unrecognizable features of the pilot. The helmet had melted into his head. She looked away with effort. "If survivors in the city tried to contact us, Garble would have picked it up on the radio. But we haven't heard anything in months, from anyone."

Colorado Springs was a dead city, or rather a city for the living dead. Cadence figured it to be the same way everywhere. Noise and odor of burning flesh guaranteed to arouse the interest of the zombies. The fence would hold as it always had, but if thousands ever rushed it at the same time, she believed it would spell disaster.

"You're assuming anyone left alive is transmitting over the radio. Maybe they have no way to communicate with the outside world," Highbrow said as he wiped a hand across his face. "I'm not sure how we're going to get him off the fence. The way he was struggling . . . I'm not sure we should get that close. Those are the rules, right?"

"Smack was right," said Freeborn. She tugged off her orange cap. "The guy was infected. That's why he didn't deploy his reserve. Whisper wasted a bullet trying to be merciful."

"Zombies can't fly planes, Freeborn," Highbrow said, not buying her explanation. "Stop acting like God planned all of this ahead of time. It was an accident, plain and simple."

"I saw what I saw," said Freeborn. "He didn't eject from the plane on his own. He was thrown out. His chute opened automatically. The plane was probably on autopilot until he pushed something wiggling about up there and blew the damn thing up."

"It was obviously engine failure," said Highbrow, angry.

"Yeah, well, he's dead now, so we can't ask what happened." Freeborn acted as though she won the argument since Highbrow said nothing further. "I'll get him down, Cadence."

Freeborn used the butt of her shotgun to knock the charred corpse off the fence. When it impacted with the ground, an arm broke off the torso. No one made a sound. Cadence looked over to Blaze and Smack as they carried the pilot's dropped pack between them. Dodger followed behind them, still dragging his stick. They came over and stared at the remains.

"Check it out," said Cadence. "Maybe there's some form of identification. A wallet, or an ID card. I want to know where he came from and who sent him."

"I want his watch," Smack said. She glared at Dodger as he approached. "I called it first, so don't get any wise ideas."

Dodger let out a soft whistle. "Touchy, touchy."

"The Captain gets the watch," Cadence said, before an argument broke out. Even from where she stood, Cadence could tell the watch was in bad shape. "If there are cigarettes in the pack, you can have those instead. Use them to trade."

"Are you serious?" asked Smack, excited. She and Blaze dropped the backpack at their patrol leader's feet. "It's heavy. Must be good stuff inside. Can I open it?"

"No. That's Highbrow's job."

In a few months, Cadence would turn eighteen and be inducted into the Freedom Army as a soldier, leaving Highbrow to take command of the Fighting Tigers. Understanding the success of the team was a direct result of time spent together in the field, Cadence had appealed to the Captain to add a seventh member of the Fighting Tigers. By rule, there were to be six members per patrol team. He agreed to let her train Smack as a replacement member. Though Highbrow was skilled enough to choose his own recruit and could fully train someone new, Cadence liked Smack and wanted her to be a Tiger. It was the first time a seventh member was allowed to join a patrol team.

"Don't be so disappointed, guys," Cadence said, grinning. "The pilot fell on our side of the fence, so we get to claim whatever he has on him. I'll make sure Highbrow gives you something good. Okay?"

"Rules suck," said Smack, spitting out her bubble gum.

Chapter Two

The Fighting Tigers arrived at Base Camp located at the foot of Pike's Peak. They parked their ATVs in the former tourist lot and headed toward a large stone building, the pilot's backpack in hand.

Two smaller buildings serving as garage space and a storage shed stood nearby. Parked outside the garage were an Army-green Harley Fat Boy and a Hummer with a flat tire. A limping mechanic walked out of the garage. Eighteen, blonde, and muscular, Wrench was cute by most standards. He could fix anything mechanical, awarding him his nickname. His blue eyes twinkled as he spotted Cadence, and he didn't bother hiding the fact that he liked her. Cadence was fond of Wrench, but she was committed to her Freedom Army boyfriend.

Other teens wearing grease-covered overalls joined Wrench. Their apparel was the trademark for anyone in the pit crew, and their main task was to keep machinery and vehicles running smooth. Fixing flats on military Hummers was easy compared to the broken axles, busted gaskets, blown transmissions, and shredded serpentine belts that Wrench normally dealt with.

Cadence waved at him. Wrench and the boys waved back.

"And they call me a flirt," said Blaze, trudging behind her leader. "He's not that good a kisser, in case you were wondering."

"Doesn't hurt to be nice," Smack said, butting in. She waved back at Wrench with a grin on her freckled face. One of the boys perked up, beaming, until Wrench pushed him forward.

9

Cadence entered the larger building and found Sarge seated behind a desk, his attention directed on a large map spread out in front of him. He was a former Marine, in his forties, with a square jaw and a head the size of a watermelon.

Two Freedom Army soldiers in light blue berets stood at attention beside the table. Corporal Garble sat behind Sarge at another desk, fiddling with the shortwave radio, turning switches, and grimacing when static filled the room. Next to the radio was a radar unit that had been taken from the city airport and worked on rare occasion. This was not a good day for the radar to go down. Cadence glanced at Highbrow in alarm, and he turned toward the doorway where Smack and Blaze stood holding the backpack between them. The rest of the team waited outside.

"We brought the Captain something we picked up at the Garden," Cadence announced. She pointed at the backpack when Sarge decided looked up at her. "This comes straight from the Air Force. Garble, did you by chance pick up a jet on your radar?" The corporal shook his head. "Well, that doesn't mean it wasn't there. We did see a jet and this is the pilot's backpack. I want the sighting listed as confirmed. We have proof."

Sarge scowled. "What proof? Did you bring the plane or the pilot?"

"The jet blew up," Highbrow said. "Unfortunately, the pilot's chute tangled and his reserve failed to deploy. He dropped the bag before hitting the fence."

"Yeah?" Sarge was unimpressed. "You claim the jet blew up over the Garden? Where, precisely?" Cadence leaned in and pointed at the map. "And it was American? You're sure?" He glared at the corporal. "Why didn't you pick this up on radar?"

"The radar isn't working," Garble said. "Sorry, Sarge, but I didn't see a thing."

"Then it's unconfirmed. Drop the bag and scram." Sarge looked back at his map.

"Just because Garble didn't see it on the radar, doesn't make it a phantom jet," said Cadence, refusing to leave. A confirmed sighting meant they would receive extra rations. "There was nothing left of the jet. We buried the pilot before the zombies could get him and came straight here. This is a big deal, Sarge. There's been no activity in the air for months. I wonder where he came from, don't you?"

"And where he was going," Highbrow said. "Maybe the government didn't fall. Maybe the president is still alive. Maybe—"

"Maybe you can zip it."

Sarge glared at Highbrow before his beady eyes transferred to Cadence. Neither were among his favorites.

"Only you Tigers would come in here with a story about a fighter pilot whose plane blew up, and who just happened to toss you his backpack before he crashed into the fence." Sarge frowned. "Is that why the electricity went down in Sector 10?" With a snap of his fingers, he pointed at Garble. "I want that generator back up and running in one hour. Is that clear? Put Lieutenant Destry on it and send out a patrol of real soldiers, not teenagers."

Garble nodded and made the call.

"Pity you didn't bring the corpse in," said Sarge with a growl. "No, you bring me a backpack and a lame duck story. You kids would say anything to impress the Captain, thinking he'll feel obliged to let you join the Freedom Army. Frankly, your story reeks."

The grunts of disagreement and shuffling of feet behind Cadence invited a threatening glare from Sarge. Cadence didn't like him. Never had, and never would.

Sarge served in Desert Storm and spent several years in Afghanistan. He had been on leave, visiting his wife and three kids in Texas when the Scourge broke out. His family didn't survive the journey to Pike's Peak.

The first case of the virus surfaced in New York City on the first of October. Within three weeks the virus went global. War was inevitable, but it wasn't the next World War everyone expected. Survivors, in every city, town, and village around the world fought against the infected that had multiplied at an insidious rate. By mid-November, no country had a government intact, a military or living population. News from television and internet was terminated. Cell phones no longer worked. All forms of communications were obsolete, except for shortwave radios. No one had contacted the camp in ages.

There was never a question about how many had survived for Cadence. Everyone she knew had either been eaten or killed fighting zombies. Anyone able to get through the zombie hordes alive, made it to Pike's Peak. At the top of the mountain a large camp had been set up where the survivors and their families lived in RVs and permanent structures. Headquarters was established in the former tourist cabin, and a hospital and school were operational as well.

The Captain seldom left his post from his overlook on the mountain. Like Sarge, he served in the armed forces but most of his unit was wiped out in the first week of the Scourge. The Captain arrived at the Peak with a handful of soldiers from his original unit. He made do with what he had and began to set up camp. As far as they knew, it was the only camp of its kind.

Cadence remained silent as Sarge pushed back his chair and stood, releasing a wave of repulsive body odor in her direction. He was short and stocky, with a thick neck and oversized biceps, not unlike a bulldog. She tried to maintain a blank look. *Bathe much?* she thought. She wasn't sure which was more offensive, his smell or lack of trust.

"Open the bag, Highbrow," said Sarge. His voice was deep and rough.

The sergeant sat on the corner of the desk while Highbrow knelt beside the backpack to do his job and search inside for what they had found. Being cautious, Highbrow wore leather gloves, biker goggles, and a red bandana pulled over his face.

"You think something in there's going to bite you, boy?" Sarge expelled a coarse laugh.

Garble snickered. His lanky black hair hung slick and greasy, while his yellow beret stuck out of his back pocket. Yellow denoted those serving in Communications. Garble wasn't a bad sort by nature. He could fix anything with gadgets, wires, and electronic components. The malfunctioning radar proved a fluke. He got computers working again which were used for research and scheduling.

Highbrow opened the backpack. Cadence stood behind him, pistol in hand, prepared to shoot anything moving around, gaping at her with red eyes. Severed heads had been found in coolers left behind at abandoned campsites, and had once been found in a freezer at a destroyed gas station. Highbrow yelped with excitement as he revealed a folded American flag, a revolver, and a box of ammo. Completing the inventory were two candy bars, clean socks, disinfectant spray, and a locked, black metal box. The top of the box fashioned a worn Grateful Dead sticker, which seemed fitting.

"Give me the black box," said Sarge. He always sounded gruff, no matter his mood.

"Sarge, the pilot made it a point to drop the backpack so we could reach it," Cadence said, not caring if she spoke out of turn. "It seemed odd to me. We haven't seen any planes since last winter. Maybe it's a coincidence, I don't know. He was in the right place at the right time, though. I know he saw us."

"I see," growled the sergeant. "You kids think everything that happens to you is some kind of government conspiracy. Well, I don't believe in conspiracy theories, magic, or fate. But I do believe in luck. You got lucky today, Cadence. That's all."

"So you believe me then?"

"Oh, I'm going to check your story." Sarge snapped his fingers again. "The soldiers will dig up the body and bring it back here, something you should have thought to do. If they find any pieces of the wreckage, they'll bring that too. Then we'll determine if it's a confirmed sighting. Until then, get out of here and stop bothering me."

"Don't we get to keep anything from the backpack?" Cadence kept her cool, but not without effort. "Highbrow took a few items off the pilot's body."

The marine's eyes lit up and he held out his hand, snapping his fingers, making it clear he wanted all the evidence to be handed over. Highbrow showed the items he had salvaged.

"A watch, a pocketknife, and a wallet," said Highbrow. "Check out the military ID I'm sure it will confirm he's Air Force. Besides, I would like to know his name."

Sarge took the items from Highbrow and laid them out on the table. He picked up the pilot's wallet and rifled through the contents, removing the military ID and a driver's license. Both cards were burned and the plastic coating bubbled from the electrical heat.

"His name was Lieutenant Joe Strong," said Sarge. "Looks like your story might just pan out, Cadence."

Cadence stared at Sarge, thinking his brain was small as a walnut.

"There are a few more things in the outer pockets," Highbrow noted under his breath. "Socks, photos, a pack of gum, candy bars, and a stick of deodorant, which apparently no one around here uses."

"I'd give the watch to the Captain, it's a Rolex, but it's worthless. Shame. It was a nice one," said Sarge. "The flag stays here, but the Tigers can have the gum. Little girls love chewing gum, don't they?" He laughed hard, along with his soldiers, and then stopped to peer at Cadence with a more critical eye. "Have you looked in a mirror? You have pieces of fried skin on your baby beret. If you ever hope to replace that orange cap with a blue one, you'd better start presenting yourself ship shape."

"I tell you about a downed fighter pilot and you give me gum," Cadence said, not masking the anger in her voice. "I take my job seriously, Sarge! The Tigers are the best patrol on Pike's Peak and you know it!" She yanked the orange cap off her head and brushed off the charred skin. "What about the rest of the stuff? You got any use for it or can we have it?"

"Keep it. The black box goes to the Professor. If there's anything special inside, the Professor can sort it out. What's the matter, Cadence? You need a pat on the back?" He reached out a hand, but she flinched and he laughed again. "How 'bout I stroke your ego? You and your Fighting Tigers did good."

His compliment came too late.

"Got something in there for me, Cadence?" asked and eager Garble. He looked at the backpack. "Can I have one of those chocolate bars?" He smiled wide, revealing a missing front tooth.

Sarge swatted him away. "The answer is no, Garble. Stop your whining. The girls get the candy bars." He leered at Blaze and Smack who were beaming with joy. "You twits can take what you want, but leave the revolver. It's a Smith & Wesson and it goes to the Captain. Anything good always goes to the Captain. Or me."

The general rule was that one item could be kept by any member of a scouting party when they brought in recovered items and supplies, as long as it was cheap or readily available. Cadence thought the rule unfair, but there wasn't anything she could do about it. Everything else went to the officer on duty, who took everything to Sarge. Important things such as weapons and jewelry went to the Captain, to keep or dole out to at hid discretion. The flag went to him without question. The American flag represented what they fought for and it would be flown at the top of the Peak, with a dozen or more flags found over the past eleven months.

"Take your team and go get some chow," said Sarge. "We're through here."

Sarge turned to Garble. The corporal was making frantic attempts to clear the static on the radio. The tough sergeant sat in his chair, leaned toward the radio and smirked as Garble turned up the volume.

Cadence and Highbrow hung by the doorway, glancing at one another as a woman's voice came in clear amidst intermittent static.

"*. . . we're approaching Colorado Springs, but the main group is an hour outside Denver . . . highway cluttered with vehicles . . . crawling with zombies. There's no way through. Hank is finding another way. What is your position? Over.*"

Crackle and fuzz followed. Garble chewed a dirty fingernail as he turned a dial, tuning in. Another voice, male, answered.

"*I'm looking up at a twenty-foot tall electric fence. This is unbeliev-able, Marge. They've got a fence that runs around Manitou Springs and winds into the mountains. It's active, so we can't cut through until we find a downed section. I'll try to contact whoever is in charge at the camp and make nice. Call me when you arrive. Logan out.*"

More static followed and then silence.

"Scavengers." Sarge pointed at Garble. "Patch me through to the Captain. He needs to hear this. I want all units on patrol. That means you, Cadence. Fill up on food. Supply your sniper and guard with ammo, then get back out there. I want to know how many there are and where they're coming from. You should be able to get a visual on any caravan coming down Memorial Highway. Send word back the moment you do."

"I need a radio for that," said Cadence. Sarge seldom offered any team the means to maintain contact when on patrol.

His face turned bright red, and he yelled. "You think I'd give you something as valuable as radio? Forget it! Get out there and do your job. You see something, send one of your little girls back to report it. These people are dangerous and mean to take what we have. That's not going to happen on my watch. This Logan character is already here and scouting the area. This is a Code 4. If you see anyone suspicious, shoot first and ask questions later. Got it?"

"Got it," said Cadence.

Leading the Tigers to one of the smaller buildings, Cadence held the door for her team and followed behind them. The shed was filled with weapons and boxes of ammunition. Most of the weapons came from the National Guard, while a portion came from city gun stores and private owners. All types of hand guns, rifles, swords, knives, and even crossbows stocked the shelves and walls of the building. The team stared at the weapons like they had hit the jack pot.

"Those were scavengers on the radio," said Highbrow. "But it makes little sense that they'd use a radio. They have to know we can pick up chatter. Maybe it's a diversion. It's possible they mean to attack."

Cadence glanced at the door. "I don't care about the rules. We're not going out there unarmed." Highbrow looked surprised. "Take what you want and can handle carrying. Everyone is going armed, with enough ammo to last us a few days. Grab one of those .44's and a holster. Get me one, too." She paused as she came upon an elegant, battle-wrapped katana hanging on the wall. "Hello, beautiful."

The Tigers thought Cadence nuts for the hours she spent practicing swords with Dragon, the second-in-command of China Six. Hand-to-hand combat with a zombie was nobody's idea of a good time, but China Six prided themselves for being modern-day ninja and they prepared for every scenario. Cadence enjoyed training with them and because of it she knew how to handle a sword.

"Blaze! Smack! I suggest you each get an automatic rifle," said Cadence, strapping the sword across her back. "Hide them under your coats. Blaze, if you want a crossbow then take one. Dodger, I see you eyeing that M4 Carbine. Keep it hidden. You'd better pack a pistol, too."

"It's about time someone recognized we have mad fighting skills," said Dodger, stuffing a 9mm into his coat pocket. Lifting the M4 from the rack as if it were Excalibur, he slipped it under his oversized coat, turned around and grinned.

Whisper handed Dodger ammo for his weapons, and packed a sufficient amount for himself along with several magazines. He sheathed single rounds into the breast pocket of his worn parka and picked up a hunting knife.

Teams could keep swords, bows, axes, crossbows, and knives, but not guns. Cadence assumed Sarge had come up with the ordinance rules. If she had her way, everyone would be armed. She knew the boundaries she was crossing and was willing to take responsibility for her actions.

"This is a bold move, Cadence," said Blaze. She shouldered a crossbow before grabbing the last two AK-47s off the rack, passing one to Smack. "In two months, you turn eighteen. We'll get off with demerits if we're caught but the Captain will give you lashes, just like Thor."

"This time it's different," said Cadence. "Scavengers have reached the fence and Sarge has issued a Code 4 alert. When things heat up, nobody will care if the Tigers are armed. In fact, the Captain will be glad at least one team is ready for anything."

"All right guys, listen up," said Highbrow. "We don't want to draw any attention when we get outside. Straighten up, act normal, and move out."

Cadence looked out to make sure it was clear. The team lined up, and Highbrow checked to be sure weapons were hidden, sending them out one by one. He glanced at Cadence before exiting. Cadence followed the Tigers through the parking lot, passing several military trucks and approaching a row of colorful four-wheelers. Each Tiger took their pick and turned to Cadence for her signal.

"Finally," said Freeborn, starting up her engine, "we get to see some action." With the orange beret worn low on her brow, she looked tough, but it was the eagle feather at the end of her braid that gave her the look of a Cherokee warrior.

Cadence mounted last. The corners of her mouth turned upward as she motioned them forward. The Fighting Tigers, for the moment, wore goofy smiles. It shouldn't be enjoyable to go on patrol, but sometimes in their crazy, upside-down world, killing zombies could be, well . . . fun.

Chapter Three

Cadence and the Tigers trekked east through the burned ruins of the once beautiful and historic town of Manitou Springs. Zombies had been cleared out months ago. Except for the occasional hot springs bath or a fresh water run, it was a ghost town. The rumbling of the four-wheelers echoed through empty stores and houses with vacant, blackened windows.

Cadence spotted movement in an upper story window.

It was a grand old house on a hill that caught her attention, dead expect for that one flicker of movement. With her attention focused on the gutted shell she didn't realize her vehicle was careening toward Highbrow's, until she slammed into his back tire with her front. He swerved, hitting the bumper of an old truck, sending him flying through the air.

"Highbrow! I'm so sorry," shouted Cadence, pulling alongside Highbrow's sprawled body.

Jumping off her ATV, Cadence knelt beside her dazed teammate. The team circled the two, seeing that Highbrow wasn't injured other than a few cuts on his face. Exerting her frantic mother instincts, Cadence checked him over and sat him up to examine his head, spine, and limbs. Highbrow laughed at the fuss.

"Glad you weren't driving a car." Highbrow didn't complain when Cadence hugged him. She was up on her feet soon, offering her hand to help him. "See, boss. Nothing broken. What distracted you this time? You see something?"

"Could be nothing. Could be something."

Highbrow grinned. "Hell, Cadence, you're dangerous when you're paying too much attention to the wrong thing. You gonna check it out?"

"Both of us are going, you know the rules." Cadence spun around, finding her team parked and awaiting orders. "We're going into that house to check around. Blaze and Smack, watch the road. Dodger, make sure my team stays safe." The teen nodded. "Whisper and Freeborn, keep your eyes on the house and warn us if you see anything suspicious. As quiet as this place is, we'll hear you." She put a hand on Highbrow's arm. "You ready for this?"

"God, I love it when you're all tanked up. Yeah, I'm ready."

Cadence gave a gentle shove and pushed her second-in-command forward. She drew her .44 from its holster and started up the grassy slope, passing a set of railed stairs that were long blown to pieces. A light breeze swirled and dead leaves marched around the blackened ground. Listening for anything suspect, Cadence paused on the porch and glanced back at her team.

"Paranoid much?" teased Highbrow. He lifted his pistol, grimaced, and lowered it again. "I think you broke my elbow. It hurts." She ignored him. "Okay, not broken, but it still hurts."

"Shut up," said Cadence, with a hiss. "I saw something on the second floor. Front room, third window from the left. Stay behind me, I'll go first. Keep your eyes open, and don't rush. Listen, watch, and then make your move."

"Wow," he said, trying not to laugh. "You really are paranoid."

"It's business, so keep it tight. Let's go."

Once inside, Cadence kept close to the railing of the staircase as she ascended toward the second floor. Midway up the stairs there was a large hole, dropping into a dark basement below the first floor. The abyss consuming this section of stairs required Cadence to stretch beyond what was comfortable to reach the next solid step. Highbrow had trouble crossing the pit. She turned back and frowned, catching him rubbing his sore elbow. He offered a shrug to apologize, but the bruised elbow was slowing him down. She froze, hearing a sound in an upstairs room. Putting a finger to her lips, she crept up the stairs. With her weapon trained and ready, Cadence stalked toward the corner room.

Outside the bedroom door, she heard rustling. A raccoon or large squirrel crossed her mind. Anything was better than what she expected to find. A zombie must have gotten through the fence. She would report it to Sarge, after she killed it. The soldiers, not the patrols, would be held accountable for any breach. Drawing a deep breath, she counted to ten and walked through the door.

"Holy!" Cadence stared at a small, dirty girl sitting in the middle of the room, clawing at a torn and ragged doll. Her dress was spotted and soiled. "What are you doing here, princess?"

The child was filthy and smelled of death. No matter the age of a zombie, they always smelled of week-old trash sweltering in the trunk of a car on a midsummer day. When the little monster turned to bite at Cadence's ankle, she popped two rounds into the kid's head without hesitation. Blood oozed from the wound. Zombie blood didn't spray like human blood, nor was it a bright red color. It was akin to thick black pudding, dripping from a spoon. She hated when it covered her boots.

"Gross!" Cadence tried to shake off the blood. The thick, black ooze plopped in gooey drops to the ground. "Highbrow, get in here! I shot a kid!"

He answered after what seemed like an eternity of silence. "Zombie or scavenger? You shoot it twice in the head?"

"Of course," said Cadence. "Get in here."

Not wanting to touch the dead girl, Cadence used the toe of her soiled boot to nudge the body. It didn't move, but something about the child's face touched her. She had been beautiful in life, and in death she held onto her doll as if it meant the world to her.

"Don't stare at it," Highbrow said, entering the room. "Shoot it in the head again and give it a hard kick to double-check. Don't worry. If it bites you, I'll pop two in your head."

"Jerk," she said.

Cadence looked around the room and spotted a tall, metal lamp in good condition. She used it to push the body over onto its side. The zombie was dead. Really dead. She stared at the child realizing something was wrong with its mouth. The tongue had been chewed off long ago. Not pretty. Cadence figured the kid had been dead a few months. Someone should have noticed her, yet no one had. Her skin was pale and dry. It was already flaking and her neck and arms were peeling like a reptile.

"I wonder why she wanted the doll. They can't think. Why did she want it so bad?"

Her morbid fascination with staring at corpses always freaked her team out. Cadence did not try to hide her curiosity, but Highbrow avoided staring. He never liked to look.

"I'm sorry I took so long to get in here," said Highbrow. "Due to someone's awesome driving skills, I had to cross the Royal Gorge in the stairs using one arm for balance. I almost fell through the hole."

Cadence shivered. Not out of concern for Highbrow, but because she couldn't stop staring at the gruesome little corpse holding the doll. "What's she doing here, Highbrow? She's alone. How did she survive so long without being noticed?"

"Left behind. Forgotten. We missed one when we cleaned this place out. So what? There are always a few you find later in a clean zone. It's how it works, you know that."

"She shouldn't be here. Someone wasn't thorough." Cadence forced herself to look at Highbrow. "There shouldn't be any zombies in a clean zone. We need to check the rest of the house. Tell the others we found one, and to be careful. Where there is one, there are others."

Highbrow smirked at her. "You shot her twice. I think they are aware."

"Tell them anyway. Follow protocol," said Cadence.

Protocol required that when killing a zombie one must deliver two shots to the head, and always double-check a kill. Remove the brain, and it's considered a sure kill. Protocol and security fences were the two main components of everyone's safety. Cadence would do her part to maintain the integrity of protocol, but she was angry that maintenance teams were slacking on fence repairs. The integrity of the fence was crucial to survival, especially now that another zombie was found in the clean zone.

Highbrow searched the entire house, and searched twice to be thorough, but no more zombies were found. He located a stash of canned food in the kitchen, and using an old curtain as a makeshift bag, he hauled the goods over his shoulder like a proud fisherman bearing his catch. Cadence followed him out and watched as Highbrow distributed the cans to each team member.

Highbrow dropped a can as Cadence grabbed the shoulder of his jacket and pulled him away from the others. Sometimes she was melodramatic, but he loved it.

"We need to get word back to Sarge. Seems we have a bigger problem than scavengers. Might be one lone wanderer, but I'd rather not chance it." Cadence had a fierce look in her eyes. "Sarge said he's sending a team to dig up the dead pilot. Tell him to have a squad check this area too. I'd do it myself, but I don't want to leave the team. I'd really appreciate it if you went in my place."

"Why me?" Highbrow held back what he really wanted to say. "Why not send Dodger or Blaze?"

"Because Sarge won't listen to the others," Cadence said. "I also know you'll get there and back without any trouble. I know it's a pain, and I appreciate it. Make it fast, though, I still need you here."

"That puts Whisper in my place as second when I leave. He'll have your back, as will Freeborn."

"If I thought for one second someone didn't have my back, I wouldn't have them in the Tigers." Cadence grasped the bear tooth necklace under her collar. Every Tiger wore one. The necklaces were made by Freeborn after she had saved Smack from an angry bear—it was a symbol of their team and of their care for one another. "We have the best team on the Peak. I can think of at least a dozen times when one Tiger has risked their life to save another. We'll be okay," Cadence reassured.

"I know. You're right. You saved mine a time or two, but I still don't like being away from the team. Or you." Highbrow rubbed the tooth through the material of his shirt. "I know how you feel about the Tigers. Just don't think they can do the impossible, okay? Keep your head about you. You have to rely on your own fighting skills, so play it smart." He lowered his voice. "And keep your eye on Dodger. I've always had my doubts about him. Dodger is in this for Dodger, and no one else."

"We'll be fine. I trust Dodger."

Highbrow knew Cadence was stubborn. She wanted to believe the best about everyone, but he knew Dodger's background. "Dodger didn't get that name for standing his ground. We attended the same private school. He was always getting into trouble. A few months into the first semester, he was expelled for stealing. Stealing my comics. Meeting up with him again at the Peak wasn't something I'd counted on. When you picked Dodger to be on our team, I wanted to tell you. You asked some kids to get you a pair of binoculars, and he's the one who came up with them. Do you know where he got them?"

"I don't care. He's not the same kid you knew in school. None of us are the same. Until Dodger proves himself unworthy, he has my trust same as you, Mr. High and Mighty." Cadence laughed softly and slipped her fingers around his arm, pulling him close. "Being able to dodge the bad guy isn't exactly a bad thing. You're the one I'm worried about. You won't have us to protect you."

"Well, he didn't steal your stuff," said Highbrow. "He's also the reason I got stuck with my stupid nickname. Nightshadow knew who I was, of course, but Dodger had to make sure everyone knew we went to St. John's Academy together. You were there. It was the day we met."

"Nightshadow could have given you a worse nickname." Cadence let out a sigh when Highbrow scowled.

"I've told you how I feel. I don't want to see you hurt or killed."

"Nor do I," she said, squeezing his arm before she released him. "Now get out of here. Report to Sarge and bring us back a radio, too. Steal it if you have to." She laughed when he looked alarmed. "Sometimes rules have to be broken. Dodger took those binoculars directly off of Sarge's desk and he never missed them. You want me to send him in your place?"

"I'll let that insult slide this time. You want a radio, I'll get you one." Highbrow pulled his bandana over his face. His voice was muffled when he spoke. "Should be dark when I return."

"Keep safe. And take my four-wheeler."

Highbrow walked over to the four-wheeler, gave her a mock salute and cranked up the machine. He caught a glimpse of the team in his rearview standing outside of the house as he raced toward Headquarters.

Arriving at camp without incident, Highbrow walked into the main office and found Garble at the radio listening to the Captain giving orders to teams in the field. They were preparing for an assault. Things could change as soon as the Captain made contact, but Highbrow had never met a scavenger who wanted to play by the rules. A tall, pimpled soldier held an automatic rifle and stared from a window while another was cutting an apple. A handheld radio, once outdated but now a necessity, rested on the table beside the apple slices. Highbrow made that radio his target. He addressed the corporal without being asked to report.

"Garble?" The greasy-haired whiz turned from the radio and lifted his eyebrows in inquiry. "Cadence killed a wanderer in Manitou Springs. It was a kid about eight years old, but she didn't look recently turned. Her skin was peeled leather."

"Are you kidding?" Garble's face lit up. "You Tigers are getting all the action today. No one else has reported seeing any zombies."

"Damn thing was clawing at a doll. Acted like she wanted it real bad. You have to admit that's weird. Ever hear of a zombie playing with a doll?"

"I haven't recently," Garble replied with a snide tone. He acted like Highbrow was joking. Highbrow stared at him, expecting more. "Look, kid. There haven't been any zombies, as you call them, in Manitou Springs in over two months. I suggest you drop it. Sarge is out dealing with another electric fence that went out in Sector 22. If you're so worried about a kid zombie, go tell the Captain yourself. I need to keep my ear to the horn."

"Fine, I will, but I want that handheld. If we find more, I want to be able to report it without driving five miles." Highbrow pointed at the radio on the table. "Just give me a nod, man. That's all I need." Garble nodded. Highbrow pocketed his target. "Thanks, Garble. This is between us."

"No playing around, Highbrow. No prank calls. I mean it."

"I owe you one, Garb." Highbrow snatched a slice of apple, popped it in his mouth while the soldier glared at him. "Good apple." He hurried out of the room before the corporal changed his mind.

A Jeep pulled up as Highbrow mounted his four-wheeler. The Captain sat in back, sunglasses resting on his nose. A hard-looking soldier named Achilles sat in the passenger seat brandishing an M16, disregarding Highbrow. Everyone in the Jeep looked focused, ready for battle. Highbrow heard the Captain call his name and he hurried to salute his commander.

"That's not necessary, Highbrow."

"Sir, I'm glad to see you. Garble sent me to find you. I have news."

"Well, I'm lucky to find you too. I need someone I can rely on to track down Sarge and give him a message. I can't reach him on radio. Scavengers are advancing on the Peak. We need to prepare for confrontation." The Captain leaned forward and handed an envelope to Highbrow. "Sarge is about a mile west, near the main generators. It's a shame we have to rely on you kids to do all of the hard work. Wish I could commission all of you as soldiers. I could sure use more reliable muscle."

"You can rely on me, sir. And the Tigers."

"I know. Cadence and her entire team is one of the best we have."

Highbrow saluted, and the Captain saluted back. Highbrow wasn't military, so the salute was overkill. Like most teenagers at the Peak, though, he wanted to be a soldier. Showing respect for leadership was a good step in that direction. He tucked the envelope into his pocket, and turned to depart. The Captain stopped him before he took another step.

"What did you want to tell me, Highbrow?"

"You probably already know about the jet that blew up over the Garden, sir. The pilot fried on the fence, but he had a backpack that we retrieved. Inside was a black box that Sarge sent to the Professor to examine." Highbrow noticed the commander didn't look surprised. "We also found a zombie kid in Manitou Springs. Cadence wanted it reported immediately, but remained to search for more. She sent me, and I'm anxious to get back to help the team."

"Of course you are. Where there is one zombie, there are usually more," said the Captain, repeating the words Cadence spoke to him earlier. "I'll send backup to the Garden tonight. Hurry and you should be able to report to Sarge and get back to your team before nightfall. Get going son, and be careful out there."

Highbrow quick-paced to his ATV, pleased the Captain thought enough of him to let him deliver a message to Sarge, but concerned about how late he'd get back to Manitou Springs. Cadence and the rest of the team would begin to worry. As much as he wanted to join the Tigers, disobeying the Captain's direct order was out of the question. He sped west, toward the main generators.

Chapter Four

The sun was low by the time the Fighting Tigers finished checking houses and scanned the littered main street of Manitou Springs again. Dark shadows lengthened over lonely sidewalks, making the vacant stores and buildings even creepier. An hour of daylight remained, and Cadence considered another sweep to make sure no more zombies were stalking them. Memories of what it was like before the Captain restored law and order filled her mind. Images of torn, bloody faces and entrail-eating creatures with maggot-infested sores replaced her happy life before the Scourge.

"Seen enough?" asked Dodger, sounding more frightened than he realized. "I don't want to be here when the sun sets. This place is clear. I'm sure the Garden is safe, too, so let's skip riding the trails and set up camp."

"Probably a good idea, but we won't burn a fire tonight. We'll camp topside, in the rocks," said Cadence. The others nodded. It was their usual hiding place.

Rumbling from behind forced her to turn and look over her shoulder. She spotted an Army transport filled with armed soldiers. It had to be Sarge's patrol going to dig up the pilot's body. Whisper slowed his four-wheeler, pulling to the side of the road to watch the transport pass. Cadence scoured the group of soldiers, hoping to see Rafe with them. There were at least fifteen soldiers in the back, but Rafe was not among them.

Cadence remembered when they met, almost a year ago when she first arrived at camp. She saw Rafe in the bed of an Army truck, laughing with his friends. A moment flashed and he noticed her too. When their eyes met, she felt as though an arrow pierced her heart. She stopped what she was doing and gawked at him. Rafe was a vision, and one she didn't want to end. He felt something too. He pushed the guys back, and with a stupid grin lifted his hand to wave as his truck rolled past her. Cadence waved back, feeling foolish when his friends laughed and jeered Rafe. When he returned from patrol, he looked for her and introduced himself. One kiss later, she fell for him.

Feeling like that kiss was a lifetime ago, Cadence pushed Rafe from her thoughts as she and her team followed the truck. The soldiers didn't turn into the Garden of the Gods as she expected, but instead remained toward Colorado Springs. The Captain was taking every precaution, she thought. The scavengers were up north, but might try to sneak in somewhere else. Pike's Peak hosted a mere company of soldiers in total. Their numbers seemed strong, but she worried the scavengers outnumbered them this time. If all the soldiers were on patrol, including the teenage scout troops, she wondered if the Captain was spreading the Army too thin. Who would be left at the Peak?

Cadence looked away from the lights of the transport as her team turned, leading into the Garden. They paused at the place where they buried the pilot. Covered well, she doubted the soldiers could find it, while the plane wreckage lay scattered over half a mile.

"Rest in peace, Lieutenant Joe Strong," said Cadence.

"Rest, Joe Strong," Whisper echoed.

They drove on and parked their vehicles, covering them with green tarps before walking the path forty feet above. The path led to a platform that was no more than ten feet around and situated between tall, thin rocky fingers jutting from the ground. Gaps in the rocks provided a surreal view of the mountains and what was once Colorado Springs. In the distance, Cadence watched the lights of the transport vanish around a bend in the road. She hoped Rafe was back at camp, safe and sound.

"Home again," said Blaze, as she lit up a cigarette.

Freeborn separated herself from the group and smoothed out the braid in her hair. It was as much stress-relief as it was ritual. Cadence continued staring off in the distance, deep in thought.

Dodger was quick to offer light banter to break up the mood, then turned to reassure Cadence. "Highbrow is going to be okay. You've got that look on your face again. Stop worrying. He'll be here before you know it." He caught Smack in a headlock and she was quick to squirm free.

"You're right," said Cadence. "Highbrow can take care of himself."

"Since I've known Highbrow, he's always done well. He made good grades and when he didn't, his dad donated a little extra to the school fund. Never seemed to get into trouble like me. He was a goody-two-shoes even then."

"Cut that out. It's no good talking negative about each other. It hurts morale. We all carry baggage we'd rather keep secret. I suppose that's why the Captain doesn't like us talking about where we came from and what we did before the world turned upside down. What matters now is what we do here."

"That's BS," said Blaze, exhaling a cloud of smoke. "Highbrow's dad was a criminal. Dodger had a dozen misdemeanors. Smack's folks were potheads. Freeborn's family abandoned her. But none of that matters to you. Only what we do now. What do you think of me? Hmm?"

Blaze ran a hand through her color-tipped hair. Sufficiently pierced and tattooed, Blaze was unapologetic about standing out in a crowd. There were certain tattoos she only revealed for trade. She did a lot of things for trade.

"Everybody thinks I'm a slut," said Blaze. "We all know it. Doesn't that bother you, even a little?"

Cadence shook her head. "I know what you do, Blaze, and I hold no judgment. I may not always agree with your choices, but those are your choices. It's you I care about. As long as you don't get knocked up, no, you don't bother me. I know it's been hard on you. Growing up in the city without your dad around, and having to carry a heavy load with your mom and brother was tough. I also understand it was hard when your brother died on the road trying to get you here from Kansas City. All any of us want is a little kindness. I'm not judging what you do on your own time."

"I think you're hot!" teased Dodger.

"Shut up!" Blaze snapped.

Cadence continued. "Look, it's been hard on all of us. Personally, I think the Tigers are the best patrol at the Peak. Together we have the necessary skills, and we work well together. We need each other. We are family now."

"Family," said Whisper.

"What were you before all this, Whisper?" Blaze said, without tact. "Seriously, why don't you ever talk? You're so cryptic. You must have gone through some hell. Tell us."

"He doesn't have to," Smack said, yawning. "You don't have to say anything, Whisper. But if you want to, we'll listen."

Whisper pulled his orange beret from his head and stashed it in a pocket. He zipped up his coat and leaned back against a rock. If he had been anyone else, Cadence would have expected it to simply be a storyteller's way of getting comfortable before spinning a tale. Instead, Whisper got comfortable, crossed his arms over his chest, and closed his eyes.

"Killjoy," said Blaze. "Whisper never talks about anything."

"And you talk too much." Cadence intended her comment to be a shut off valve.

"What about you, Cadence?" Smack snuggled up against Dodger. "You never lose your cool in battle. You always know what to do. How come you never talk about yourself? What are you hiding?"

Cadence shrugged. "I'm from a small town in Kansas. I grew up riding horses and drove a truck to school each day. I was on the swim team and played the saxophone. My dad was a lawyer and my mother a schoolteacher. I had two sisters and a dog named Samson. It was an ordinary life."

"But you're not ordinary." Freeborn relocated to sit in front of the group on a frayed rug she rolled out. "Not once have I seen you run from a fight or leave someone behind. You have to be the coolest chick at the Peak and yet you come off so humble. I had seven brothers and our fun was hunting on the reservation. When things turned to crap, not one of them thought about checking on me. I came home to find an empty house and hitchhiked to get here." She pointed to her shotgun. "My father gave me that gun when I was ten. When I arrived here, it's all I had left of my family."

It wasn't quite the story Cadence expected to hear. She felt sorry for Freeborn, and for all of them. Apparently the Tigers wanted her to share something extraordinary that turned her into a leader and gave her the courage to face zombies without running.

"I know about your past," said Blaze. She tossed the butt of her cigarette over the edge and lit another. "You came here with a bunch of kids from your school on a field trip to raft the Colorado River. They say when the virus hit you were still on the river and that you didn't know about it until it was time to go home. Nobody came to pick you up, so you headed for town, but you're the only one who made it to the Peak."

Cadence shivered with the memory. It was not something she wanted talk about, nor was it anything she cared to remember, but the others grew silent and she felt pressed.

"We had few rations, no radio, and no cell phones. It took three days to reach the main road. Cars drove by one after another, but only one stopped to give us a ride. A man and his wife."

Cadence paused, exhaling.

"They told us what happened and offered to take us to their cabin in the mountains. Some decided to wait for another car, determined to get back home, but I convinced the rest to go and wait things out at the cabin. I didn't know the husband was infected."

She closed her eyes. Flashbacks of the truck slamming into a tree outside of the log cabin raged in her mind. She witnessed the man pull his head from the shattered windshield, turn, and take a bite out of his wife's face. Instincts saved her, and she had been the one to take care of the mess.

"We stayed in the cabin for a week until one of the guys wanted to go to town," continued Cadence. "Everyone listened to him but me, and they left the next morning. Days later one of them came back." She grimaced as she relived the scratching at the door, the piteous moaning, and how she mustered the courage to walk outside with an axe to take care of the problem.

"He came back a zombie, didn't he?" said Smack, her eyes wide with excitement. "What about the others? Did they come back for you too?"

Cadence nodded.

"Leave her alone, people," Freeborn said. "You know what happened. It happened to all of us, one way or another."

The sun set fast behind Pike's Peak, outlining a glowing row of purplish clouds.

"I'm enjoying this," said Dodger. "Highbrow never lets us talk about our past. I know it's the rules and all, but it makes me feel better."

Smack frowned. "He should be here by now."

"Something must have happened back at HQ to delay him. Maybe that's why the soldiers kept going," Dodger reasoned.

"I'd rather be here than anywhere else," Smack said in a soft voice.

Cadence stared back at the Peak. "A lot of things could have happened. All we can do now is sit and wait. He'll get here when he can.

He knows where we are." She sensed Dodger was right. Something had happened and Highbrow was not coming. She felt sick to her stomach.

They spent the next hour sharing rations, and a liter of water.

"Get some sleep, guys." Cadence stretched her arms wide, then reached down to touch the grip of the .44 at her side. "I'll keep watch for the next few hours. Whisper you'll be next, then Freeborn, then Blaze."

She watched the others unzip their sleeping bags and settle in for the night. It was cold and uncomfortable, but no one complained. Dodger and Smack bundled close together. Blaze lay beside Freeborn, embracing her new rifle like a lover. Whisper kept his eyes open and on Cadence.

"You don't need to stay awake, Whisper. I said I'll take the first watch."

"Take a whiff." He stood up and joined Cadence, pointing toward town. He sniffed at the wind like a dog, grimacing when he caught scent of something unpleasant. "Smell it?"

Cadence inhaled deep and gagged. Zombies. The smell carried far when there were enough of them. "It's pretty ripe. I wonder if the soldiers are aware we have company. Maybe I should fire off a shot and warn them?"

Whisper shook his head. "Don't."

Sudden heavy gunfire and violent explosions echoed through the Garden. The rocks shook in protest. Cadence felt a body press up against her. Smack clung to Cadence, terrified as the battle picked up in intensity. Another explosion brought every Tiger to attention.

"Think its zombies, or scavengers?" asked Dodger, nervous.

Blaze held her rifle. "Don't matter," she said. "The soldiers are pounding the hell out of them. Should we send up a flare and get the attention of Base Camp?"

The Tigers all looked at Cadence, waiting for her orders. She knew her first responsibility was keeping her team alive. A night assault was too dangerous.

"Look, I know you want to fight," said Cadence. "The scavengers are miles away and it's our job to watch for them. If the troops can't hold the zombies, it'll be up to us to keep them from reaching camp. That means we sit tight and wait until light."

"Whatever you say," Blaze said, disappointed. "You're the leader."

Fifteen minutes passed and the fighting stopped. Cadence choked back emotion when all was still except for the single cry of a wounded soldier calling out in the dark. His cry was cut short.

"What do we do?" asked Smack. "Shouldn't we go help him?"

"No way." Dodger shivered. "I'm not going. Screw him."

"What if it's Highbrow?" Blaze was furious.

"It's not Highbrow. We can't climb down these rocks in the dark, so forget it," Cadence said, dropping her arm from around Smack's slender shoulders. "I don't want to hear another thing said about it. I made my decision. Now get some rest."

"Zombies don't rest," said Freeborn.

The direction of the wind changed. Cadence smelled only pine trees, but she knew the soldiers lost the battle.

"God help us," said Whisper.

Cadence looked at each member of her team. "I know you're scared, but there's nothing we can do until morning. It's going to be okay. We're together and we're safe."

Out of character, Blaze threw her arms around Cadence and kissed her on the cheek. Suddenly, the entire team pressed in together for a group hug. When it ended, everyone but Cadence and Whisper sat down on Freeborn's blanket, getting comfortable once more. Whisper used his own blanket to spread over the girls. He sat with his back to a rock, rifle on his lap, and pulled the hood of his parka over his head.

Cadence stared into the darkness for a long time, her thoughts drifting from Highbrow to Rafe. Highbrow was cautious, and didn't take risks. That meant he would not arrive until morning. It was too risky to ride alone into the Garden at night. But Rafe was the opposite and went on missions most people would not dare. Part of Rafe's charm was his foolish bravery, and it didn't hurt that he was handsome. Rafe was also the only boy Cadence had ever completely fell for, and now he might be one of the living dead.

A star shot across the sky. Cadence made a wish that both Rafe and Highbrow were safe, wherever they were. Come morning, her first priority was to find them both. She hoped they survived the night.

Chapter Five

O n a barren hill two miles into his westward sprint, Highbrow located parked military vehicles and several soldiers repairing a hole in the fence. They ignored him as he drove around looking for Sarge. The sun was setting and clouds shadowed the Peak. A few soldiers were standing beside the generator shack, while two more sat in the grass studying the horizon with their binoculars. Highbrow found Sarge with two officers standing behind a beat up Jeep. Highbrow parked his four-wheeler and walked to where the officers stood.

Sarge was propped on the hood, smoking a cigar. Two scavengers knelt by the Jeep with their hands tied behind their backs. One was a man in his fifties with a graying, thick beard, decked in leather riding gear. A pretty, red-haired girl leaned against the biker. Her dress was torn, revealing toned legs and too much skin. Both prisoners were bleeding from cuts on their faces and bruises were swelling fast.

Highbrow recognized a tall man as Lieutenant Habit, and the stocky frame of Lieutenant Destry. He nodded at Sarge and saluted the officers when they looked his way. Sarge was in the middle of a war story, and Highbrow knew better than to interrupt. He learned some things the hard way.

". . . and that's how I knew the Iraqis slipped into our camp. These two did the same damn thing, working their way along the fence until they found a section where the electricity was out and cut the wire. I expect more scavengers are already on our side of the fence, hiding somewhere in Cascade." Sarge turned on the prisoners. "You two picked the wrong place to cross. Didn't notice my men hiding in the grass, did you?"

Lieutenant Habit let out a heavy sigh. He was middle-aged and sported a thick moustache that made him proud. "If we can't get that electricity back up and running, Sarge, we will have serious problems. We've been notified a horde of zombies is headed this way from Denver. I suspect they're following the scavengers."

"Sectors 22, 23, and 24 should be back up soon," said Sarge. "Captain has a bunch of kiddy patrols out walking the fence by the highway. He doesn't think the scavengers will get through the Garden, but I still say we've spread our forces too thin." He tapped his cigar and dropped ash on the girl's head, laughing when she flinched. "I suppose you and your biker friend thought you could sneak in under our surveillance and rip us off. Not going to happen." He put his foot on the male prisoner's back and shoved him forward. "What do you want to do, Lieutenant? Take 'em or shoot 'em?"

Highbrow cleared his throat. It was time to interrupt. "I'm reporting, Sarge. The Captain sent me."

"I say we shoot them," said Sarge, not recognizing the Captain's messenger. "We don't have resources for prisoners." He put his hand on the girl's head and she sobbed. "This one is pretty."

"You sure you want to be touching her?" asked Destry. "They both might be infected. I'd be glad to help you search her for bite marks, Sarge. A thorough search is necessary." He snickered. "Why don't we take her over yonder and have a little look? How 'bout it, Lieutenant?"

"No." Habit smoothed his moustache. "I can see it's a good thing I dropped by to check on your progress. Neither of you are to touch that girl." He stuck a cigar between his teeth, but didn't light it, as was his habit. "I want the main generator working and the electricity back on in those three sectors before you leave, Sarge. That is your only objective. Destry, when you're through here, I want you up north. Go join the patrols walking the fence."

Destry walked around Habit and stopped beside Highbrow, giving him a shove. "What are you doing here, Boy Senator? You said the Captain sent you. Well, what did he have to say?"

"I have a message for Sarge." Highbrow kept at attention, his eyes fixed ahead of him. "The Captain was clear that I give Sarge the message personally."

Sarge stormed to stand in front of Highbrow, knocking the girl to the side. Highbrow flinched when the brutish soldier blew cigar smoke in his face. The smell of the bittersweet cigar reeked with the scent of a mistreated liver. Highbrow held back a gag.

"When did you have time to see the Captain? I gave you and the Tigers orders to return to the Garden over an hour ago, boy. Are you trying to earn brownie points by kissing the Captain's butt? It's not going to get you into the Freedom Army any faster." He stuck his finger in Highbrow's chest. "When I give an order, I expect it to be followed."

"Back off," Habit warned. "Give Sarge the message, Highbrow."

"Yes, sir," said Highbrow. He removed the envelope from his coat and handed it to Sarge. "If that's all, gentlemen, I need to return to the Tigers."

"Hold your horses, kid."

Sarge took the envelope and ripped it open with his stained, crooked teeth. Lieutenant Habit produced a flashlight for Sarge to read the note.

"Says here the Captain wants all prisoners brought to HQ. Alive. He wants to question them himself," said Sarge. He crumpled the paper and tossed it to the ground. "When did he go soft? The scavengers cut through our fence. The rules are clear. I say we shoot them both and toss them back over the fence."

Lieutenant Habit bent and picked up the message. He read it and let it fall to the ground again. Despite their difference in ranks, Habit and Sarge both served in the military for years. Swaying an old bulldog like Sarge would take force.

"It's a direct order," said Habit. "These two are coming with me to HQ, and that's final. Highbrow can ride back with me. Send all prisoners to Base Camp. If we can make contact with their leader and avoid a battle, that's what we need to do."

Lieutenant Habit looked at the girl. Highbrow knew Sarge and Destry would rape her if she was left behind, and her friend would be tortured. Sarge would take matters into his own hands if given the chance. No direct order would prevent him for handling things the way he wanted. Habit, at least, had the foresight to save those he could.

"I can take these prisoners in later," said Sarge. "Highbrow has patrol duty and I'm sure you have important things to do, Lieutenant."

Highbrow felt the tension rippling between the older men. He grew nervous when the Lieutenant put his hand on his revolver and eased his fingers around the grip.

"We can't spare you to grunt work, Sarge," growled Habit. "You're too damn important. After you get the electricity on again, join Lieutenant Destry and walk the north fence but be careful. There's no telling how many are trying to break in, and it's not just scavengers out there."

Sarge's eyes narrowed to slits. He blew smoke in Lieutenant Habit's direction and smiled when the officer coughed. "Anything else you need, sir? A drink, perhaps?"

Habit looked away. Highbrow cringed when Sarge glared at him.

"Take Highbrow with you. I don't care." Sarge seethed a wide grin. "As far as I'm concerned you're no better than your old man. I wonder if the Senator is still in his cell, gnawing on his own fingers by now."

"Aw, you hit a nerve Sarge," said Destry, kicking dirt at Highbrow. "Was your daddy a criminal, Highbrow? Did he steal money from the government and get caught? How did your mommy take the news? Bet she was lonely at night without him."

Highbrow was ready to share his mind on the subject, but remained silent. If he let his angry words fly now, he'd never make it to the brig. Sarge and Destry would love to beat him to death, and he knew Lieutenant Habit could not to stop them both. Fortunately, Hawker, the personal driver for Lieutenant Habit joined them. He was a thick and powerful soldier, with a hard jaw and buzz cut to complete the portrait. Hawker was one man Sarge and Destry feared and dared not cross.

"Chief," said Hawker, nodding at Lieutenant Habit. "Time to roll."

"Highbrow, take the prisoners and walk ahead of us a bit." said Habit. "I need a word in private with Sarge and the Lieutenant. We'll pick you up shortly. Walk it off, son. It'll be okay."

Hawker helped the girl to her feet, and then pulled the biker up by his arm. No one said a word until the three had walked beyond earshot. It was Hawker, not Lieutenant Habit, that tore into Sarge and Destry. It took all the discipline Highbrow could muster to keep from turning around.

"You did good, son," said the prisoner.

They walked ahead, enjoying the sunset like they were old friends. He turned his head and took a good look at the biker. The man rivaled Hawker in size and was probably the toughest badass on the road in his heyday. His leather jacket was old, beat up, and torn, as were his skull-printed T-shirt and heavy black boots. But it was the kindness in his deep-set eyes that caught Highbrow's interest.

"Thanks," said Highbrow. "I wanted to say something. My dad was a criminal and I don't care about him, but they had no right to talk about my mom like that."

Highbrow ignored the soldiers at the generator shack who were watching as he walked past with the prisoners. The moon was rising over the mountains, casting a silver light among the pines. Though it wouldn't be difficult, he felt the scavengers would not try to escape.

"Did you come in with Logan? Are you his scouts?"

"I guess you could call us that," said the man. "We got separated when my bike got a flat tire. The two of us walked a few miles before we reached the fence. Zombies were trailing us, so I took a chance and tested the fence. The electricity was out, so we cut through. Your Sarge was waiting for us on the other side."

"I'm sorry for how they treated you," said Highbrow. "Lieutenant Habit is a good officer. If he'd been there when you were captured, he wouldn't have let them hurt you."

The biker studied Highbrow. The girl was shy and terrified, keeping her eyes to the ground.

"I don't think your Sarge is dealing with a full deck. No matter what your father did, he had no right to say what those things. Some of us appreciated what your father did. He saved two national forests and I lost count of how many endangered species he protected."

"My dad was an okay guy, I guess," said Highbrow. "He had me going to private schools my whole life until I got a scholarship to the Academy. A month later, he was in jail. After the Scourge broke out, I never heard from him again." He paused. "We're not all like the Sarge and Destry. Habit's a good man."

"But weak," said the biker. "Booze has that effect on the best of men."

Highbrow smiled when the girl moved closer to him, then he noticed her shivering. Thinking himself an idiot for not realizing the obvious sooner, Highbrow removed his coat and put it around her shoulders.

"It's cold," said Highbrow. "You should be wearing pants and boots, not a dress and sandals. There's poison ivy everywhere. We'll find you something warmer at Base Camp."

"Thank you. By the way, I'm Savannah and this is Nomad." The call of an owl demanded silence in the dark, if only for a moment. When she spoke again, Savannah's voice quivered. "There aren't many nice people left in the world. I hoped we would find a home here, but I was wrong."

"No crying," said Nomad, his signature gruff tone mixed with compassion. "You're hurting, dear, and we're both hungry and cold, but you can't put Highbrow in the middle of our problems. Tears aren't going to do you any good here."

"He gave me his coat." Savannah held back a sob. "That was nice."

Highbrow held the girl's arm as they walked. "Look, I'm not all that nice. I'm just doing my job. I want to help though. Earlier today, I heard two people on the radio. Logan and Marge. I'm sure you know them. They're here, and Hank is stuck on the highway. Denver is a bad place to be. No one goes there."

"There're around two hundred of us," said Savannah. "It was twice that number when we joined Logan. It's hard on the road. I sometimes think it's easier when you travel in smaller groups. It was simpler when it was just me, Nomad, Sturgis, and their bike gang."

"It wasn't a gang," said Nomad. "We just ride together."

"Logan needs to get in contact with the Captain," said Highbrow. "We have strict rules here. That many people showing up at once is dangerous, and we've had trouble in the past. Not everyone who tries to reach the Peak has good intentions. You're lucky Sarge didn't shoot you on sight."

"We're not the enemy, son. We're just trying to survive."

Not knowing where to wait for the lieutenant, Highbrow kept walking until they came to the bottom of the hill, reaching the highway. A patrol vehicle was parked across the street, with two soldiers engaged in a casual smoke beside it. Highbrow had his .44, but he wished the soldiers were paying attention. If zombies or scavengers ambushed them, they wouldn't stand a chance.

"You guys doing okay?" Highbrow called out. "Seen anything, or anyone?"

"Nothing you need worry about, kid," shouted one soldier. He tossed his cigarette and pointed his rifle at Nomad. "Where are you going with those prisoners? You plan on walking to the Peak?"

"Lieutenant Habit is picking us up here. He told me to walk the prisoners and wait for him." Highbrow pulled the girl closer to him.

Nomad chuckled.

"Quiet," he hushed. "I don't want any trouble here."

Nomad fell silent.

"You stay put until your ride gets here." The other soldier trained his gun on the prisoners. "Why are you walking around without a weapon? You want one, boy?" He held his out. "Come get one."

"You need it more than I do," said Highbrow, as he scanned the road.

A walker straggled toward them in the middle of the street and four more zombies stumbled from the tree line, sniffing like hounds. Catching the odor of the living, the zombies advanced toward their position.

"We have company," shouted Highbrow. "Are you going to shoot them or just stand there?"

The soldiers looked both ways, but didn't fire.

"Untie me and give me a rock, son," Nomad insisted. "I'll do it."

Highbrow tensed as his hand dropped to his gun. "I'm armed. I don't want them to know it. Teenagers aren't supposed to carry weapons."

"That's a dumb rule." Nomad rolled his eyes.

When the zombies were close, the soldiers shot and dropped the lot of them with only a few rounds. Nomad gave a husky laugh. Highbrow put his arm around Savannah and held her close. He embraced her until he heard a Jeep speeding in their direction, and turned to watch it navigate the rocky road toward them.

When Habit's Jeep came to a halt, Highbrow helped Savannah into the passenger seat. Hawker wore his beret low over his eyes and watched in silence as the senator's son adjusted his coat over the girl's shoulders. Highbrow opened the door and helped Nomad into the back. Cramped, he knelt on the floor between the two men. As the driver pulled out onto the main road, the girl turned and smiled at

Highbrow. Her smile faded when the soldiers fired extra rounds into the lifeless zombies for fun.

"I'm glad to see you armed, Highbrow," noted Lieutenant Habit. "If anyone asks, you tell them I approved it. That's an order." He removed his beret to rub his bald head. "If we get through the next few days alive, I will recommend to the Captain that he enlists you in the Freedom Army. You're a year shy, but you handled yourself well this evening. Your prisoners didn't attempt to escape. They felt safe with you and that speaks to your character. You're reliable and honest."

"Thank you, sir."

"I'm sorry about what Sarge and Destry said about you and your parents."

"We took care of things." Hawker laughed to himself.

Nomad coughed. "Sorry to interrupt, but we didn't come alone. There're about two hundred of us, and we're not a problem. Look, all we want is safe place to stay for a while. It sounds like you could use our help. We can help you defend this place."

"We can handle it, but I appreciate the information," said Habit. "Our force is well armed, but it might help if you talked to the Captain. Can you speak for your people?"

"Not officially, but I know Logan. He's a good guy. Folks have been talking about coming to the Peak for months. It's the only safe place left in this region of the country. I don't want anyone else to get hurt. If it would help, I'd be glad to talk to your Captain and explain things."

"Good," said Habit. "I'll see if we can work something out when we reach the Peak."

"Diplomacy isn't something your Sarge is familiar with." Nomad rubbed his sore jaw. "He packs quite a punch, and I wasn't the only one he knocked around."

The Jeep turned a sharp corner and started up another wooded hill. Houses, silent and ruinous, were visible from the road. They would arrive at the Peak in minutes.

"The Captain has to let them stay, Lieutenant Habit," said Highbrow. "Savannah and Nomad aren't our enemies. They are fighting for survival like the rest of us. People on the outside don't know they can get shot for trespassing on our land. It's not like there are warning signs posted."

"I said I'll see what I can do. The Captain will be fair. You know that." Habit looked over at Nomad. "Let's hope you can persuade your friends to cooperate."

"News flash, folks. The enemy is the undead," Nomad said, speaking up. "There are millions of them by now. The world is overrun with rotten flesh-eaters. Fighting each other doesn't make sense. I'm not telling you how to run your camp lieutenant, but like I said earlier, we could help."

"Living dead," Savannah chimed, turning to face Nomad. "Get it right, Nomad. Undead are vampires like Dracula. Zombies are the living dead. Don't you know anything by now?"

Her laughter was contagious like the cool night breeze. One by one, they laughed a little before falling silent. Highbrow put his hand on the back of Savannah's seat as the Jeep bounced. He caught hold of the girl's shoulder and tried to steady her. Sympathy swelled in his chest.

"Where'd you two come from?" Highbrow asked.

"Fort Yates, North Dakota. Nomad was in a bike gang, so I joined them. There were more of us at the start. Someone told us about a safe place at the Peak. We met up with a large caravan and headed this way, which seemed like a good idea at the time. We kept away from the cities, but somewhere along the way we got the attention of a large group of zombies. They've been following us for days." She lifted her tied hands and wiped her eyes. "I'm worried the others won't make it."

"Savannah." Nomad sighed. "It will be okay. Marge will get through."

"You're safe here," said Highbrow. "I won't let anything happen to you."

"Enough, Highbrow." The lieutenant tapped him on the shoulder. The girl looked away as Highbrow crooked his head to meet the officer's eyes. "Don't make promises."

The vehicle rounded a dark stretch of road and came to a break that forked in two directions, the right leading to their camp. Torches burned beside a Hummer and an Army transport that were pulled off to the side. The truck lights flashed as the Jeep rolled by. A soldier saluted and Lieutenant Habit returned the gesture.

"This is a weird night," said Habit. "Feels like we should be going home to watch a football game and eat fried chicken. I used to love fried chicken."

"Cherry pie." Nomad laughed. "I'd give my soul for a piece of hot cherry pie. Zombies don't know what they're missing anymore."

"With a scoop of ice cream," said Highbrow.

A walker stumbled in front of the vehicle and faced them, freezing like a deer in headlights. They hit the zombie square, jarring everyone in the Jeep. The impact sent the rotting corpse flying up and over, hitting the ground behind them with a splat.

Hawker offered his apologies. "Won't happen again, sir."

"Like I said, it's a weird night."

The lights at Base Camp came into view. Crystal Lake was stunning with its surrounding trees and clear, blue water. Several log cabins and dozens of tents dotted the grounds.

"We're home," said Highbrow, giddy. "Safe and sound."

Habit grunted. "Yeah, kid. We're home."

Highbrow escorted the prisoners into the main cabin, with the lieutenant and his driver walking ahead of them. Savannah stayed close to Highbrow. Lieutenant Nightshadow was on duty and seated behind a desk flanked by two armed soldiers. Nightshadow was as dark as his name indicated, and a man of mystery.

Habit stepped forward. "This man is Nomad. He's a scout for the scavengers," he said, pointing at the biker. "Tell the Captain he'd like to speak with him on behalf of his friends. Their main group is holed up in Denver, and he says thousands of zombies are headed this way. You might try to get his leader, Logan, on the line while we wait for the Captain."

"Is that a good idea, Lieutenant Habit?" asked Nightshadow, suspicious of the newcomers.

Furious at being challenged, Habit took hold of Nomad by the arm and walked around the desk toward the radio. The soldiers took aim while Nightshadow leaned back, grinning.

"Move aside, Garble. I want Nomad on the radio. Get your radio, contact the Captain, and tell him to get down here."

Garble was terrified. "Okay, okay. What do I do first? Contact the Captain or hail Logan on the radio?"

"Neither," Nightshadow said. "Sorry lieutenant, but I've got to follow protocol. The Captain isn't at the Peak. He's at the Garden checking out that plane crash. Radios can't reach him out there and we're to maintain silence over the air, unless we hear from him first. If you want to talk to the Captain you will have to drive out there, but you can't take the prisoners with you."

"Because it's against the rules," said Habit, dripping with sarcasm. "Hell, Nightshadow, look at the radar. If it's tracking like it's supposed to, those green dots coming this way are zombies, not planes. They're all over the damn screen. The Captain needs to get back here."

Nightshadow threw his hands into the air. "That's what I'm saying, lieutenant. Would you be a prince and go tell him what's going on? I can't leave my post."

"Hawker, let's go," said Habit. His driver headed for the door. "I'm sorry, Highbrow, but I'm going to have to ask you to be responsible for the prisoners. I'll drive to the Garden and get things settled with the

Captain, but you'll need to check them in with Nightshadow, fill out a report, and take them to the Peak."

"You're a decent man, Lieutenant Habit," said Nomad. "No hard feelings."

"None," Habit said. The two men shook hands. Habit nodded at Highbrow and was on his way.

Nightshadow picked up a clipboard and asked for the prisoners' names. "Lieutenant Habit would let every survivor in here if he was in command. He has a soft heart, but I see every scavenger as a potential threat. They should be placed in quarantine for a week before being cleared to enter camp. The Captain is a bit vague on that point, though. He didn't say I couldn't give them a camp name and send these two up to the Peak with you."

"They have more than a hundred in their group, perhaps two," said Highbrow. "You heard Lieutenant Habit. Thousands of zombies are headed this way. There isn't time to follow standard protocol and we could use their help. With that many zombies at the fence, they'll push it over and we'll be overrun."

"Lieutenant Habit is handling things with the Captain, so do what you're told. Take Mr. Motorcycle and Little Bo Peep to Doc for an examination and keep them in the hospital until the Doc clears them. That's all I can do for you, Highbrow."

Nomad stepped forward with respect. "No disrespect, sir, but if Logan contacts you, tell him Nomad is here and I said he's to abide by your rules. He'll want to negotiate terms, of course."

Nightshadow nodded. "I understand, Mr. Motorcycle. Sarge was a little rough on both of you, and I'm sorry for that. Scavengers have come through here before and brought trouble. If your people are looking for a home, that's different. I'm sure the Captain will do his best to accommodate your needs and do what he thinks is best to protect the Peak."

"We don't like being called scavengers either. We're survivors, same as you," said Savannah in a low voice.

Under the scrutiny of Nightshadow, she slipped Highbrow's coat on and zipped it up before crossing her arms over her chest. It was a small act of defiance, but the girl was not as weak as Highbrow first thought. She had spark. He took her by the arm, feeling protective. Nightshadow grinned.

"I'll take them both to see Doc, sir," said Highbrow. "After that, I'd like to come back and speak with you."

Nightshadow walked them to the door. "If this is about your team leader, I can spare you the trip and fill you in now."

"Is Cadence okay? Have you heard from the Tigers? I was supposed to join up with them hours ago."

"Jesus, kid. Take a breath!"

"I just wanted to know—"

"Yeah, I know what you want Highbrow. They're fine. All of them."

Nomad puffed out his chest. With his leather coat and steel-tipped boots, he looked as tough as any soldier in their camouflage jackets and berets.

"Hell's bells," said Nomad. "What's wrong with you people? Don't you care about one another?" He pressed a hand to his side. "All we want is a safe place to hole up until things get back to normal."

"Normal?" Nightshadow shared a cold laugh. "Nomad, is it? Nomad, things are never going to be normal again, not until we kill every last zombie." His dark eyes turned to Highbrow who lifted his chin to stand taller under the officer's scrutiny. "The Little Leaguers and Badgers never made it back from picking berries in Cascade. Corporal Jade reported in a little while ago. A group of elderly folk, including my father, were killed by zombies. They got through a hole in the fence. Seems holes are popping open all around the perimeter."

"I'm sorry," said Highbrow. "I didn't know. No wonder the Captain doesn't want to negotiate with any newcomers."

"I never said he didn't want to negotiate." Nightshadow's face twisted with emotions and his voice sounded shaky when he spoke. "Go on, kid. Take these two to see Doc. I'd send you back to the Tigers, but you seem to like these folks. I should lock them up and you know it, but I'm giving them a chance to get through the night. My father would have wanted me to help them."

"Thank you, sir. Again, I'm sorry about your dad."

Nightshadow nodded and motioned Highbrow out the door. Rules were rules. Every few months, scavengers showed up. Some were allowed in, some weren't. It was the way of things. Now that he was assigned to guard the new arrivals, Highbrow wanted to do right by them. Cadence would be worried and he knew his younger teammates would be anxious without him. It was his first night away from the Tigers, and they would have to make do without him.

Please let Cadence be alive.

Highbrow almost changed his mind, but Savannah squeezed his hand and pointed to the North Star. When Highbrow gazed upward, to his surprise, the girl kissed him on the cheek. The gruff biker rumbled with laughter behind them.

This night was only getting weirder.

Chapter Six

*T*he stench of burning flesh would make the strongest person gag, but Rafe was not about to give away his position. He hid under a tarp in the bed of the transport.

Countless zombies appeared from the dark on all sides. The battle was fierce. Rafe stayed in the truck when his buddies jumped out to fight the wanderers that surprised them. He fired into the throng of living dead, dropping too many to count, but they kept coming. His friends fell, one by one, and when Rafe ran out of ammo he tucked deep into the truck bed and waited out the hell that burned around him.

Rafe watched one soldier escape the fray and flee. Moments later, a cry pierced the darkness. The wounded soldier made too much noise, and the monsters gave chase. The zombies were drawn away from the truck by the man's cries, but Rafe's heart agonized at what he heard and was thankful when the soldier fell silent. He sat for what seemed an eternity and tried not to breathe.

Rafe felt like a coward, but he didn't want to die. Not that way.

He remained hidden through the night, shivering with fear and the cold. His bladder screamed, but he feared discovery. Acquiesced, he pissed in his pants. It was humiliating, but at this point he didn't give a damn. Pride served no purpose here. Rafe remained still and silent, the smell of his own urine mixed with the increasing stench of burning gore was suffocating. He risked coming out when he heard the engines of incoming four-wheelers. It had to be a rescue team.

Rafe slid the tarp back and stood. What he saw around him forced bile to lurch from his stomach. His patrol was destroyed without prejudice. Guts and limbs littered the ground. He choked back emotions when he spotted Cadence jump off her vehicle and rush the truck. She wasn't coming to say hello. Zombies appeared in the brush, staggering toward the Fighting Tigers. She leveled several zombies and held back others as her team joined the fight. Zombies encroached from every direction.

"Head's up," shouted Cadence. "We've got a soldier boy on my six."

Rafe focused on Cadence as the team faced different directions, firing at the incoming horde. A former corporal stumbled from the cover of trees, leading a pack of flesh eaters. Oblivious that his stomach was torn out, the soldier dragged a thread of entrails behind him and rambled straight for Cadence and her team. Rafe caught the sight of a determined teen raise his M24 and place a round in the center of the former soldier's forehead. The body sagged and dropped to the ground.

Zombies multiplied from a jumble of pine trees. Rafe recognized a few, and it made him sick to know these zombies by name. As his former comrades rose from the ground and joined those advancing on the patrol, his stomach challenged his dignity once more. He wanted to scream, to run, but was forced to watch as his former friends crawled and lumbered toward them. Rafe thought zombies the perfect weapon. They are tireless, always advancing and destroying, ever increasing in number.

"Look out," Rafe cried, unable to contain his terror at the growing danger surrounding his girlfriend. "They're coming right for you, Cadence! Get out of there! There's too damn many of them!"

Cadence was too busy shooting zombies to notice her team was outnumbered. *Click, click, click.* She kept pulling the trigger, out of ammo. In a flash, she unsheathed her sword. Rafe was transfixed as

Cadence shifted and swirled, decapitating zombie after hideous zombie. It was like watching a dance, with her teammates orchestrating fierce skill in battle by her side. Rafe was mesmerized by what he could only describe as seasoned veterans moving as a cohesive team. By most perceptions, these were a bunch of kids who didn't know any better. Their actions in battle shattered perceptions, and Rafe considered it a privilege to witness this team in action.

Rafe considered joining in the fight. He wanted to help, but felt helpless. Cadence continued to hold her ground, removing a steady stream of zombie heads with her katana without falter. Seeing her calm and cool in the heat of battle, Rafe realized he loved her more than anything else in the world. He needed to join her, to fight beside her.

Why can't I help them? Why can't I move? His mind and body were at war with shock and exhaustion. Rafe wanted to avenge his squad, but his limbs were locked and sickness consumed him. He was a soldier, trained to fight, and yet these untrained Fighting Tigers showed more zeal and skill than most in the Freedom Army. He thought it was silly how these young patrols gave their teams monikers like the *Panthers*, *Bulldogs*, or *Blue Devils*. There were some teens that acted like gang members, taking advantage of the system, but then there were the Fighting Tigers. This team, however silly Rafe thought their name was, put their lives on the line for everyone else. Any one of them was a better human, a better soldier, than Rafe, and he knew it.

"Kill them," shouted Rafe. "Kill them all!"

He grabbed an abandoned rifle from the back of the truck and fired into a group of lumbering corpses. He felt himself returning. It felt good to engage the enemy. His confidence grew with each kill. Standing in the warm sun, Rafe felt unstoppable. He shot and screamed until there nothing else moved.

"Rafe! Hey! Rafe!"

Hearing Cadence call his name brought Rafe back to his senses. His mind was furious with the vision of his friend and fellow soldier,

Boomer, being eaten alive when the violence started. Pushing the image to the back of his mind, Rafe plugged one more round into the nearest zombie and let his rifle drop. His heart was pounding and his breathing labored as his reluctant eyes settled on Cadence.

"Cadence? I'm so sorry."

"Don't be. What in the bloody hell happened here?"

Cadence sounded like his lieutenant when he was alive and shouting orders. Her temperament aggravated Rafe. His emotions flared as she marched toward him. That assertive, confronting tempo is what gained her the nickname *Cadence*.

"We were camped in the Garden last night and could hear the battle. It was too far and too dangerous to help, but we came here first thing this morning. We've already faced our share of zombies in the Garden this morning." She glanced at the ragged hole in the fence. "I wondered how they got in. We need to plug up that hole. Whisper? Ideas?"

"Truck," said Whisper.

"Right. We can use it as a block. Flatten the tires, and pack logs and debris under it."

"We need to siphon the gas," said Blaze. "The ATVs are on empty. Oh hell, I'll do it. I'll get 'em filled up. Have Smack gather the guns and ammo. We need to burn the bodies. God, they smell!"

"What about the berets?" asked Dodger.

Rafe had seen him around, always playing cards and telling crazy stories to impress people.

"Good thinking, Dodger," said Cadence, "and get their tags. Every soldier has a set." Cadence motioned for her team to get busy.

"Rafe, what happened last night?" Cadence gazed up at him from beside the truck. He felt little next to her. Rafe didn't climb down. "What's wrong with you? Come down here. I was worried about you. Are you hurt?"

"No," said Rafe. He looked at the dead bodies scattered everywhere. "There's a lot, isn't there?"

"Sixty or more, but who's counting? Are you okay or not?"

Rafe started to speak, but fell silent when Whisper jumped in the cab of the truck. He fired up the vehicle and rolled it in front of the hole in the fence. The sniper threw the truck into park, got out, and shot the tires, lowering it several inches. Others dragged logs, rocks, and shrubs and filled in the gap underneath.

"Why are you still in the truck? Get down," said Cadence. Her eyes studied Rafe. Then she asked the one question he wanted to avoid. "Did you fight, or were you in the truck all night?"

"No. Yes. Kind of . . ." Rafe stuttered, trying to form a self-preserving answer. He failed and winced. His pride swelled and Rafe let his anger boil.

"If you aren't bitten, get out of the truck. We have bodies to burn, and we need your help." Cadence scanned the battlefield. "These were your friends. You can do the honors and pick up their berets. Rafe! Can you manage that?"

Rafe swung his legs over the side and jumped to the ground. He fumed to where Cadence was standing, wanting to punch her for embarrassing him. No matter what happened last night, he wanted their respect. He deserved that, at least. His anger began to spill over.

"It was a hard-pressed battle. You weren't here, so you have no right . . ." sputtered Rafe. "It would have been helpful if you had joined us last night. As you can see, we needed reinforcements." He tried to intimidate her.

Her sharp, green eyes cut into his soul. He felt worse. *Coward.* She didn't say it, but she didn't need to.

"Those monsters were on us before we knew what was happening. They were already on our side of the fence. We thought they were scavengers, and then it was too late."

"Where were you during the fighting?" Cadence asked, sounding disappointed. "Your boots are clean, not one drop of zombie juice." She brushed some dried blood away from his face, the only evidence that he had been in the battle. "There's hardly a spot of dirt on you. Explain that."

"I was at the machine gun. I killed as many as I could before I ran out of ammo. They just kept coming. They were everywhere. I had no choice but to hide. That's how it was. Over and done, fast." Rafe wiped his nose. "Why are you looking at me like that?"

"Sorry," said Cadence, bending to pick up a rifle. She examined it and found the magazine empty. "I didn't expect to find you here, and I certainly didn't anticipate finding zombies on our side of the fence."

Cadence continued retrieving weapons and packing them in saddlebags on the ATVs. Blaze and Whisper filled the gap beneath the truck while Dodger and Smack piled the human remains into one big pile.

Rafe watched, doubling over when a horrible pain stabbed his stomach. The pain was intense, wrecking his thoughts and making the situation worse than it should have been. He shuffled to where Cadence was loading the four-wheelers.

"Have things changed between us that much?" asked Rafe in a moment of desperation.

Cadence said nothing, but her eyes dug into his thoughts. He felt like she was reading his mind and his anger surfaced again

"I know what you're thinking, Cadence, but it's not like that! I fought with the rest of them. I ran out of ammo. It wouldn't have mattered what I did. There were too many of them."

"I'm not judging you, Rafe." She sounded condescending. "If you don't mind, I need to help my team. We have a lot of work to do before we can go home." She put her hands on her hips. "I'm really not judging you. If you can't help, go sit down out of everyone's way."

"Shell shock," Whisper called out, overhearing their conversation. "Give him a break." Whisper went back to digging through pockets, not minding the gore spreading up to his elbows. He filled a duffle bag with dog tags, cigarette lighters, wallets, and other keepsakes.

Rafe reached for Cadence's arm as she walked by. "I'm sorry," he said, following after her. "You know how I feel about you."

"Are you trying to drive me crazy right now?" Cadence scolded. "Now is not the time to talk about how we feel. Seriously, I just want to finish and go take a bath. We can talk about this later." Her voice became soft. "Any one of us might have done the same thing. No one is going to say a thing about it any of this. It's in the past."

"It won't happen again." Bile rose in Rafe's throat as he watched two girls stacking corpses. "I promise."

"I believe you, now stop acting so weird. You know I care about you. But this isn't the time or place to be talking about us. You had a rough night, and I'm sorry about Boomer and all the other soldiers. I really am."

Rafe glared at Cadence, his ego sagging. "It doesn't make me a coward, you know." His anger was bubbling again. "It's not like I hid the entire time. I was scared, but I fought back. I was here. Where were you? It's not like I was hiding in the Garden with my little friends, watching the show from a distance. I was in the moment."

"It's my job to keep my team safe. Plus, you and I both know the results had we shown up."

"Just promise me that you and your patrol buddies won't tell any-one what happened. No one has to know I was here. I can say I was patrolling on the north fence. I won't be able to deal if people start talking about me."

Cadence stared at him a long time; he was becoming a stranger to her. "Is that what you're worried about?" Rafe had always been the brave soldier. Something wasn't right. "Then I promise. None of us will talk about what you did, or didn't do, last night," she affirmed. Unsure what to do, she patted him on the arm. "Buck up. It's going to be okay, Rafe. Give me a few minutes and we'll get out of here. We have to burn the bodies first."

Rafe felt another surge of rage. The sharpness in his stomach was worse. *Why doesn't anyone understand how I feel,* he wondered. Cadence put everyone else before him. Stack the bodies. Burn the bodies. She didn't care if he was an emotional wreck and needed her attention and a little compassion. She was heartless and it was beginning to show. Cadence helped drag bodies to the pile. Rafe took every step at her side. It was clear she wanted nothing to do with him. His stomach turned and his anger stoked.

"You always follow protocol," Rafe whispered harshly. "You always do the right thing. You act like you believe me, but I know you think I'm a coward." In his haze, he lifted his hand to strike her, and then noticed her staring at his crotch. He forgot about pissing himself. Breathing a groan, he dropped his hand. "Why do you have to scrutinize everything? I swear if you tell anyone about this, you'll be sorry."

"I have no intentions to embarrass my boyfriend," Cadence snapped. "Stop taking everything so personal. This isn't about you. Believe it or not, there's more at stake here than your precious reputation. You want to push me, to lose me? Is that where you're going with this? Okay with me. It's not like you were faithful, but I never said anything about that either. Until now. It's over, Rafe. Now back off and leave me alone."

He stood motionless, shocked. She knew and never called him out. He wanted to apologize, but couldn't. There was no defense. It was over. Shame consumed him as he watched Cadence walk to stand by her team. The group gathered close as Cadence whispered something to them. The tension was palpable. The Tigers glanced in his direction, and then turned back to their leader. They were buying whatever it was she was feeding them.

Rafe turned and stared at the pile of corpses, trying to regain composure. It did no good. Boomer lay somewhere in the mix. He couldn't stay and watch his friends burn, nor could he stand being around his girlfriend—ex-girlfriend now—while he was in so much pain.

He had to leave. The Tigers didn't need him and Cadence wanted nothing to do with him. Thinking of himself alone, Rafe jumped on the closest four-wheeler, and peeled out. He could hear Cadence shouting behind him.

Cadence came to a halt. Chasing Rafe wasn't worth it. She placed her hands on her knees and hung her head in disappointment as the sound of the engine trailed thin in the distance.

Chapter Seven

*I*t was noon before Cadence and her team finished piling the bodies and setting them ablaze. The fire roared, setting black smoke against the blue sky. The odor was foul, making it difficult to breath.

"Wrap it up people," called Cadence. She wiped her brow and stepped back from the fire.

Whisper tossed a severed limb into the fire and gave her a nod, indicating the task was complete. Cadence took a moment to reload her weapon and take a brief survey of the team. Blaze loaded a collection of berets and dog tags, while Smack collapsed exhausted after lugging a large bag of weapons onto Whisper's vehicle.

"Fourteen berets," Blaze reported. "We're one short, in my opinion. Rafe doesn't deserve his. That loser should be booted out of the Freedom Army."

Blaze was right, but Cadence remained silent. Rafe did not deserve to hold rank in the Freedom Army. He was a coward. She was glad he was alive, but she was disappointed by his cowardice, and angry for how he had overreacted. Their relationship was over, that much was certain.

"You know, when I was a kid I never thought I'd end up pickpocketing the dead." Dodger expressed his disgust as he walked by Cadence. "It's not that I mind stealing things I want, but you have to admit that what we do for a living is pretty much grave robbing. It's just gross, boss."

Everyone was dirty, tired, and discouraged. "I want to go home," said Smack. She looked up from where she sat on the ground, her face smudged with soot from the fire. "I miss my parents."

Dodger knelt beside her. "Sure you do, kiddo." He punched her in the arm. "Come on. Smile for me. You were great today. You handled that gun like a pro."

Smack looked proud. "I did, didn't I?"

"You did, and your parents would have been proud of you. I am," Dodger said, holding up a necklace with a curious medallion. He slipped it over her head. "I think it's Wiccan. Something I know you like. Wish it was diamonds, though."

Cadence turned and watched the bodies burn. The fire crackled and smacked its jaws. They had killed so many zombies and survived the onslaught today. Beyond that, they worked as a team to clean the area, secure weapons and block the hole in the fence. Above all, she felt by collecting the berets they honored the fallen soldiers in some small way. She felt good, and lucky. The Tigers were a unit. They were family.

"Good work, team." Cadence patted Whisper on the back. "A lot of credit goes to you, Whisper. I don't want to give you a big head, but nobody is a better shot than you. I mean that."

Smack let out a whistle, while Blaze and Dodger applauded. Freeborn saluted from where she stood. Whisper pulled the hood of his parka over his head. His dark, mysterious eyes peered from the shadow.

"Thanks, Cadence," said Whisper "I was worried there for a second, until you charged and laid down the law. You fight like a real-life ninja. Dragon taught you well."

Cadence was shocked. Whisper had spoken. Whatever Whisper experienced during the Scourge, he kept to himself, along with his voice. It was rare to hear him express himself. She tried to think of a witty comeback when the roar of motorcycles forced her attention to what approached behind her.

The Vikings rode in from the main street, led by Thor. His second-in-command and girlfriend, Raven, rode behind him. Thor was seventeen and full of bravado. He was big, handsome, and arrogant. The real brain of the Vikings, however, was Raven. She was a year younger, Latino, and drop-dead gorgeous. Her biggest problem was keeping her temper in check. Raven had few friends and was always fighting with some other girl, mainly about Thor.

"First one off his bike gets shot in the head," Cadence said.

Cadence aimed at Thor, with full intention. Heimdall, a strapping, tall Viking, reached for his rifle. Loki, Baldor, and the squinty-eyed Odin froze on their bikes. Raven disregarded the threat and slid off her bike. She sauntered over to Cadence. Painted lips, leather-clad visage, and her signature rattlesnake tattoo, complete with a red rose between its fangs, communicated boldness and an '*I don't care what you do*' attitude.

"Did you not hear what I just said?" asked Cadence. "This is our kill. You don't get any credit for it, Raven, and you're not taking anything from us. Not this time. Try it and I'll shoot Thor." She heard the leader of the Vikings swear softly at the threat.

"Pay up, Cadence," said Raven. "You know the score. You fetch, and we take."

Raven gave a smug look and Cadence wanted to deck her. Her voice was tense. "I'm serious, Raven. I'm in a real bad mood, so I suggest you get back on your bike and get moving. This isn't like last time. You're not cheating us again." She pointed her gun at Raven. "I mean it. Back off."

Raven yelled a few expletives in Spanish and glanced back to her boyfriend, motioning for Thor to stay on his bike. He was furious. So were the rest of the Vikings. Hatred emanated toward Cadence.

"Fine," said Raven. "We'll go, but give me a beret for my collection."

"No. You didn't earn it, as usual," said Cadence. Wasting no more time, she shouted, "Mount up, Tigers. Let's get out of here."

Cadence holstered her gun, pushed Raven aside, and marched to Whisper's four-wheeler. With one less vehicle, he was her ride back to camp. Raven returned to Thor and whispered something in his ear.

Cadence pointed at the blonde giant. "Try anything and I'll wipe that smile off your face. Try to call my bluff and you'll see I'm not kidding."

Raven fumed at the threat. Thor lifted his head a notch, remaining silent.

"Me either," said Smack.

"That makes six of us," Dodger called out. He waved a handgun in the air. "See you later, punks. Better luck next time."

"If they have a next time," said Blaze, laughing.

The Tigers lined up next to each other, each one aiming at Thor. The leader of the Vikings acted like it was a conspiracy and hung his head. Raven pointed her finger at Blaze, and then slid it across her throat.

"Like to see you try!" said Blaze.

Cadence felt the tension building and feared Thor would react and start shooting. She did not want any trouble, and she couldn't afford to lose any of her team over something like this. However, the Vikings were not leaving and she needed a change of plans to avoid bloodshed. Cadence pointed toward the truck that was blocking the breach in the fence.

Cadence lowered her weapon. "Look. Some of the zombies got through the fence. I don't know how many. I don't like it, but I think we should ride back together. We're safer with more numbers."

Raven looked around, nervous. "Maybe you're right. It's safer in a pack." She pointed at the guns on the back of a four-wheeler. "There are more than enough guns to give us each one. Give us all a rifle and we'll ride with you."

"I don't trust you," said Cadence. "Past experiences with your team haven't won you any points with the Tigers. If we give your team weapons you'll shoot us or our gas tanks and steal everything. I'm tired of your team getting the credit that belongs to us."

"Man, you're so uptight. Let's make it official, okay? I'll give you my blood oath." Raven spit in her hand and offered it to Cadence. "If we trick you, you have the right to cut the oath giver. That's me. It's the Viking way."

Thor revved his motorcycle. "Yeah, we promise not to screw you this time Cadence. If we get attacked, it would be better if we're all armed. The Captain will take all the weapons the moment you get back to the camp, so what's the big deal?" He glanced over his shoulder. "Raven gave a blood oath. If anyone on my team betrays her and she gets cut, I'll personally kick their ass."

Blaze counseled her leader. "Don't trust them."

"Screw the Vikings," Dodger and Smack said at the same time.

Whisper shook his head at Cadence, making it clear how he felt. Freeborn engaged her shotgun for emphasis. Cadence hesitated. She knew how her team felt, but she was worried about making it home in one piece. Raven sensed she was about to get her way and stuck out her hand.

"How about it, Cadence?" Raven spread her lips into a smile. "Pretty please."

"Done, but on my terms. The Vikings ride back with us all the way to camp. No leaving us if we run into zombies in Manitou Springs, and you take no credit for any of our kills. In fact, no one talks about what happened here. Let me handle this with Sarge. Agreed?"

"Deal," said Raven. They shook hands. "Now give us the guns. Make mine a Smith & Wesson."

"You'll get what we give you."

Cadence passed by the Tigers on her way to the weapons bag. She selected two rifles and two revolvers and gave them to Raven. Raven let out a yelp of delight and hurried over to distribute the weapons. Cadence motioned for the Tigers to break formation, feeling like she had let them down. That was confirmed by the look Whisper gave her.

"Where's Highbrow?" asked Thor with a smirk and sliding his new rifle over his shoulder. Raven slipped a revolver into the front of her pants, and kissed her man before climbing on her bike.

"He's back at camp on some secret mission," she said, being evasive. "If you're done asking questions, then I suggest we get moving. You take the lead, Thor." She pointed directly at him. "If we run into any zombies, I'm counting on you to fight with us. Got it?"

"Hey, I get the drill. Raven gave her blood oath." Thor patted Raven on the thigh, showing his big horse teeth. "I'm not about to let my girl down. You can count on the Vikings, at least this time." His smile faded. "I guess I owe you one."

"Don't forget it either."

Cadence lifted her gun and circled it in the air. At that signal every engine started. The Vikings pulled out in single-file, spinning tires and revealing their immaturity, waving at the Tigers as they rumbled down the street.

"Get moving, Whisper," said Cadence. She might not like the Vikings, but she wanted to ride with as many people as possible to the Peak. There was no way to know how many zombies made it through. Raven was a user and a liar, but she was good in a fight. Cadence wished she could say the same about Rafe. At the moment, all she wanted was to be at a higher altitude and find out what happened to Highbrow.

A raised fist from Thor brought the two patrols to a crawl as they entered Manitou Springs. Signs that read *LOOTERS WILL BE SHOT ON SIGHT* and *THEFT—PUNISHABLE BY DEATH* were posted in store windows, placed there by the Freedom Army. Nobody had ever been shot for stealing, but a few had been placed in the stockades overnight to think about their actions. Cadence and Whisper pulled up next to Thor and stopped. Thor pointed to a store that was intact with a good stock of merchandise inside.

"There's no rush to get back to camp," said Thor. "Why don't we take some time and scout around. We can fill up on whatever we need. I could use a few pairs of socks and a new flannel shirt. I know what the signs say, but the soldiers are patrolling the fence. We own the town today, so why not have some fun. What do you say? You and your team can wash up in the creek. You need it."

"Fun?" Cadence thought it the strangest suggestion yet. "We're needed at camp. There isn't time to fool around, Thor. We're Code 4. If we're caught looting, as patrol leaders we could be shot."

"Oh, come on, you big sissy," Raven purred. "Take your team and go that way and we'll go the other way. Highbrow isn't here to tell you what to do. We're teenagers and could use a little fun. I'm tired of rules and officers bossing us around."

Thor kept his eyes on Cadence. "If we're caught, we can say zombies got through the fence and we're hunting them. They'll believe us. In the meantime, there's free merch everywhere. Get yourself a new coat or sweater, or something." He motioned to the Tigers. "When's the last time you let any of your Tigers go shopping? We don't need money. Take what you need. If you find any food, we can meet back here and have lunch. One hour, what do you say leader?"

"A picnic!" exclaimed Raven in delight. She slid off the motorcycle and gestured for her team to follow, not waiting for Thor. She waltzed into a nearby store, gun in hand. The Vikings followed behind her.

Thor climbed off of his motorcycle but held back, waiting for Cadence to make the call. His show of respect surprised her.

"We haven't had a day off in weeks. Maybe it is a good idea," Cadence said. Her team cheered. Thor gave her thumbs-up and left to meet Raven. Cadence found herself surrounded by the Tigers. "I don't want anyone going off alone. This is dangerous, so we hang together. That zombie kid we found yesterday was only a block away. There might be more. There always are."

"We'll be careful," said Blaze. "I need some makeup and undies. I'll be sure to get enough for Star and the other girls. If you want, I'll help make them a little gift package."

Cadence smiled. "Yeah, that would be nice."

Whisper stayed on his four-wheeler and gestured for Cadence to go on without him. The girls and Dodger crossed the street to a clothing store. The place reeked of death.

Blaze went for anything black and started trading her old clothes for new ones. Smack and Dodger both found jeans and changed, telling each other how good they looked in their new threads.

Cadence took her time looking through the dusty racks of clothes until she came upon a light-blue silk shirt. She dropped her coat and fleece jacket, shed her long sleeve t-shirt and slipped into the new shirt.

Dodger walked up to her eating a piece of licorice and clutching an ugly, fluffy green sweater under his arm. "It's for Whisper," said Dodger. "His favorite color is green. I have a pair of socks for him, and I found some boxers, too." He kept his scruffy brown leather coat and boots, but everything else was brand new.

Cadence tugged at a blue t-shirt hanging on the rack. "Maybe I should pick something for Highbrow?"

"And let him know we broke the rules? No way. He thinks this is scavenging. He might not report us, but he won't be happy about it."

Sweeping off her orange beret, Cadence gave her hair a shake and let it fall around her shoulders. "He'll see we have on new clothes and know what we did, Dodger. Go find him a sweater. His favorite color is blue. He likes flannels, too."

"Fine, I'll shoplift for him too."

By mid-afternoon, the two teams sat in the park near the hot springs the town was once known for. Some found snack foods, while others found some drinks. Everyone was sporting new clothes and looked much cleaner than they did an hour earlier. Even Whisper donned his new green sweater and seemed happy to be munching on chips.

"Thanks." Thor lifted his drink, toasting Cadence. "I know this isn't your style, but we all needed a break today. You're a nice person when you aren't threatening to kill people." He laughed and tossed a bag of chips to Raven.

"You're not so bad either." Cadence exchanged a smile with Thor. She noticed Whisper pointing and looked to see a squirrel gathering some nuts someone had tossed its way. Gazing upward, she thought of the pilot and wondered about the black box. "This has been a good day. It started out pretty bad, but got better. Good idea, Thor."

Everyone grew quiet.

"What?" Cadence looked around at everyone. One by one, they started laughing. No one had to explain. It was the first time she had ever said anything nice to Thor. She had to chuckle. "Just keep those ideas coming, Thor. You might have a brilliant one someday."

"Not likely," said Whisper.

Everyone laughed a little louder.

Chapter Eight

Rafe sat with a group of soldiers who were fresh out of action. He stared at his scrambled eggs, three strips of bacon, and buttered toast. A glass of milk sat untouched in front of him. His buddy Wizard lit up a smoke next to him. Rafe was starving, but felt too sick to eat.

He took the pack of cigarettes from the table and slipped one out. Smiling, Wizard leaned forward and offered a light. Rafe stuck the tip into the flame and drew the smoke into his lungs, coughing.

"What's up, Rafe?" asked Wizard, whose nose had been broken so many times it lay flat against his face. "Not hungry? You normally eat the scraps off everyone's plate."

Rafe shoved his plate toward Wizard. "I'll trade you my food for another cigarette. In fact, give me a pack and you can have my milk too. I don't like powdered milk anyway." All he could think about was getting out of the mess hall. Wizard pushed the pack toward Rafe.

"You sure you're okay? Up to a game of Warfare? Garble has the computers up and running good." After a moment, Wizard slid a book of matches into Rafe's front pocket. "Go see Doc. You look sick."

Rafe felt horrible. He noticed something was wrong since the battle. Zombies hadn't gotten close enough for a bite, but what he was feeling wasn't normal. His guts rumbled. He stood uneven, knocking over the glass of milk. Rafe reached for a towel to clean up the mess, but Wizard was already wiping off the table with napkins. Rafe's stomach lurched and he bolted from the mess hall and made it outside just before vomiting.

Wiping his mouth across his sleeve, he heard someone yelling across the street. "Get out of my way! I'm going to see Doc. I've got friends waiting for me in there." It was Highbrow. "I said move! I mean it!"

Rafe looked down to see a spot of blood on his hand. He looked back up to see Highbrow faced off against three soldiers without a chance. Rafe gave a whistle and crossed the road to where the group was standing and threw his arm around Highbrow. He glared at the soldiers. "We don't want any trouble, boys," said Rafe. "This here is Highbrow, the late senator's son. Show him a little respect and get the hell out of the way."

"Sure, Rafe," said one of the soldiers.

"Whatever you say," another replied.

Rafe's stomach beckoned again. This time he held it in. It was bitter and tasted like blood. "You say you have friends at the hospital," asked Rafe, "well, let's go see Doc together. I need some Pepto or something. My stomach is killing me. I've felt like crap all day."

"You hear anything from Cadence? I haven't seen her since yesterday."

"I saw her this morning in Manitou Springs. I was on patrol last night and things got messy." Rafe failed to elaborate. "She's probably still there cleaning things up. I would have stayed, but I feel horrible. Don't worry, she'll report in soon enough. You care about her, don't you?"

Highbrow pushed Rafe's arm away. "Yes. Sometimes I think I care for her more than you do. I wouldn't have left her to clean up my mess." He studied Rafe and looked troubled. "Your face is pale. Maybe you're coming down with the flu." He reached for Rafe's forehead and was batted away. "Hey! I'm a medic. I'm only trying to help."

"I feel fine," barked Rafe. "You're not my mother."

Rafe walked ahead of Highbrow. In the distance he heard the large generator turning its gears, providing an ambient soundtrack for their walk. He glanced back and saw Highbrow trudging along. An image of Cadence entered his mind and for a moment Rafe felt love for her, and then it was gone. His care for her was replaced by hunger. He wanted her. All of her. Cadence belonged to him: heart, body, and soul.

Highbrow watched as Rafe wrapped his arms around his stomach, turned away from the hospital door, and ran. Highbrow paused at the nurse's station to report Rafe's strange behavior before walking into the clean, white room. Nearby a child was immobilized with a broken leg and arm. He spotted Savannah and Nomad sitting on beds at the far end of the room. Two kids were seated next to Nomad talking about baseball. Nomad was patient and taking time to help the kids figure out which baseball cards to trade.

"Highbrow!"

Savannah waved at him. Highbrow smiled.

"We've been waiting all night for the doctor. Apparently there is an outbreak of the flu." Savannah gave a nod toward Nomad. "And we got to eat! Guess they served everyone at the hospital last. Did you sleep well?"

"Not much. People snore too much in the barracks."

"Well, well, well," said a familiar voice. "It's Highbrow." Doc, a fit man in his fifties, walked into the room from a side door.

The sound of clicking nails followed as a German Shepherd pup trotted behind him.

A nurse approached Doc and whispered in his ear. He looked at the two newcomers, gave a nod, and walked to where Highbrow was standing. "You seem to have made quite an impression on these folks."

Highbrow grinned. "Do they check out, Doc? Are you going to give them a good report? I would hate it if they were turned away."

Doc picked up a clipboard hanging at the end of Savannah's bed and reviewed it. "Seems we have Little Bo Peep and Mr. Motorcycle. Ouch! Those are horrible names. Nightshadow must have been in a bad mood, but no matter." He smiled at Savannah. "Not all of us have lost our sense of humor, young lady. If you don't mind a piece of advice, watch out for the ones wearing blue berets. Bunch of Neanderthals, if you ask me."

"I agree with you there," said Nomad with a chuckle.

"Truth is, Doc, this is Nomad." Highbrow held his hand out toward the girl. "And this is Savannah. I don't like their nicknames either, and I don't intend on using them. It's a stupid tradition anyway." Glancing at the girl, he said softly, "I think my name sucks."

"It's okay," said Savannah, offering a timid smile.

"You're a good guy, Highbrow. You care about everyone, even strays," said Doc, with a nod of approval. "I have you to thank for Ursula."

Highbrow grinned at the pup and gave him a pat on the head. "Dogs deserve a chance too, Doc."

Not long ago, he brought Ursula to the doctor after finding it alone and hungry. Now a few months older and trained, Ursula sat on the floor chewing a rawhide.

"It was love at first sight. You fell hard, I'd say." Highbrow laughed.

"Ursula is a fine dog and she is, indeed, my true love." Doc smiled wide and held his hand out to Nomad.

The biker raised an eyebrow at his rubber gloves.

"It's a habit from the old days," explained Doc. "It's not like it will protect you from the disease since it's now transferred from bites, but old habits are hard to break."

The two men shook hands.

"Heard it was airborne when it first arrived," said Nomad. "I was on the road when I caught the news. Damn shame no one found a cure before the dead got up and started fighting back."

"It was never airborne. If it had been, everyone would have caught it. It was spread initially by mucous from sneezing and coughing. The smart ones wore rubber gloves and a mask. I was one of the smart ones who didn't contract the disease, even when exposed to it. I guess God had a purpose for me."

"I'm not a church going man myself, but I have said quite a few prayers since it happened."

"Me too. I have treated a lot of infected people, and I'm sorry to say I never considered whether zombies have souls. I leave the killing to the soldiers and let God sort it out. Not my place." Doc whistled at the pup. She lifted her head, wagged her tail, and went back to chewing on her bone. "I'll take care of you two the best I can with our limited supplies."

Nomad shrugged. "We're fine, Doc. I hope we don't have to stay in here a week. You'll find we are accommodating in every way. Poke me. Take my blood. Do whatever you medical guys do, but just get it over with."

"Sorry. We don't have lollipops for big boys."

The biker belted hearty laugh. He knelt, lifted his pant leg, and reached into his boot retrieving a silver flask. "This is real Kentucky bourbon, Doc. I always keep a little on hand. Why don't we get this examination behind us and finish this conversation over a game of chess? A smart guy like you plays chess, right?"

"I'm considered one of the best on this mountain. Be warned."

The two men walked toward the door to a side room. Highbrow put his hand on Savannah's shoulder and sat beside her. He relaxed when he noticed her smiling. It pleased him to see she had been given jeans, a sweater, and a pair of boots. They suited her.

"I'll hang out here if you want." said Highbrow. "I need to get back to the Tigers, but I know it can be boring waiting to get cleared."

"I would like that. I don't play chess, but I can play cards."

Joining the Tigers became the last thing on his mind. Savannah was the nicest girl he had met in a long time. Being with her was precisely where he wanted to be. He smiled at her, and she blushed. He felt like a superhuman.

Base Camp was crowded with more vehicles than Cadence had seen at one time. Scouting patrols were not being allowed up the mountain road or to the main camp at the Peak. Only the youngest teams, with kids twelve and under, were taken to Top Camp.

The Fighting Tigers and Vikings arrived at camp together, fueled up, and went back out to check the northern fence line. They ran into the Green Hornets and helped them block another gap in the fence with a large boulder.

When the Tigers returned to camp in late afternoon, campfires were burning and people sat around chatting, goofing off, and acting like everything was normal. There were sixteen teams in total, but not all had yet returned.

"I heard a kid got bit by a zombie yesterday," said Dodger, sitting down with Cadence outside their tent. He brought a supply of chips, drinks, and hot dogs. "We're lucky we found Rafe and patched up that hole in the fence. How many zombies do you think got through?"

"No telling," Cadence said.

"The Vikings aren't so bad. I had fun today."

She nodded. "I did too. I don't think any zombies got through the second hole we found, but scavengers may have cut through. I heard Sarge was up there. It's no surprise he didn't walk the entire fence."

Cadence watched Dodger distribute food around the campfire. She heard plenty of rumors since reporting to the officer on duty. There was an ambush by zombies in Cascade against many elderly and young children. Kids were saying Sarge killed the stray zombies, with no injuries to their own forces. She took a cold drink from Dodger. "Hey, that's contraband," said Cadence, as he gave her a hotdog. "Only soldiers get the good food." She devoured half of it in one bite. It was a welcome treat. With a mouthful, she asked, "Did we get regular rations as well?"

"Yep. In my backpack." Dodger shuffled next to Blaze and Whisper and dropped his backpack to the ground. Kneeling, he unzipped the bag and dug inside. "While the soldiers were stuffing themselves, I walked into the office and helped myself to extra rations. Nobody even noticed." He lifted a pack of frozen dry beef. "Got eleven of these little babies. Not much of a selection though. I'll do better next time."

Cadence let out a sigh. "You are the artful Dodger and the best horse thief in the land."

"I do my best, chief."

"I am so hungry," said Blaze.

Dodger grinned at Cadence. "If you're wondering where Highbrow is, I think he's up at Top Camp. I heard he came in last night with a couple of prisoners. Stop worrying. I'm sure he's fine."

Sitting beside the Tigers at the fireside, Cadence looked around at the other tents. "Actually, I was looking for Star. I haven't seen China Six return to camp. I saw Luna and got the skinny from her. No one knows about the battle, and Raven and Thor aren't talking about what happened. No one has heard a thing about Rafe, either. I wonder if he made it back," she studied the ground, the toe of her shoe circling the dirt.

"Who cares? He's a coward." Dodger popped a drink open. He took a quick sip and continued. "Anyway, I heard the Freedom Army brought in a bunch more scavengers this morning. They were just brought to HQ and a medic is coming down from the Peak to check them out. Garble swears they're infected, but I didn't stick around to find out."

Cadence took off her beret, and shook out her hair. It was chilly as the sun set behind the mountains. She zipped up her coat and asked for another hotdog.

"What about the kid that got bit?" asked Blaze. "Did they kill him?"

"Yes," Dodger answered with his mouth full. "Kid was a Little Leaguer. They got ambushed in Cascade picking berries. Heard lots more got killed, too. They won't say who or how many. That's why all the little kids are being sent up to the top. Guess they'll be in their own beds tonight."

"I guess." Cadence didn't share the rumors. They would only upset her team. She crossed her legs, sucking the salt off a chip before eating it. "Sarge said we got lucky yesterday, but what's luck anyway? The odds are against us every time we go on patrol. Sure, picking berries beats picking dog tags off a corpse, but we're always in danger. Little kids shouldn't leave Top Camp. I don't care how many adults escort them."

"Bet the Captain is pissed," Blaze said.

A sudden, thunderous roar filled the air. The China Six patrol barreled into camp on ATVs with their petite leader, China Star, riding point. Their vehicles were painted bright yellow with a red *6* on both sides of the gas tank. Cadence jumped and ran toward the self-proclaimed ninja team.

China Six was named by Star. Chinese by heritage, she was a high school champion in gymnastics and fencing. Dragon was her second-in-command, who was responsible for the intensive training that gave them their reputation as modern-day ninja. He also trained Cadence, the Amazons, and the Head Hunters in the art of sword fighting and other bladed weapons. Four other girls of mixed Asian descent rounded out the team. They were smart and athletic, with a theatrical mystique about them.

The patrols all worked well together. The Amazons and Head Hunters were the only two all-girl teams at camp. They were tough and loved fighting with swords. The Vikings were the rough types with sketchy histories, intimidating to their peers. Cadence's Fighting Tigers were a band of misfits, an unlikely group that became more like family each day.

Star pulled up outside their yellow tent with the rest of her team. Dressed head-to-toe in leather, she carried two crossed katana on her back and sheathed a long dagger in her boot.

"Hey, Star!" Cadence hurried toward her friend. China 6 silently moved into formation surrounding their small leader, wearing serious expressions. It never got old watching them perform. Star laughed and broke rank.

"Where have you been?" Cadence threw her arms around Star. Her best friend smelled like gasoline and a flowery perfume. "I am so glad to see you."

"Me too, girlfriend," said Star, in a merry voice.

They hugged a little longer before walking back toward the Tiger's campsite. China Six trailed behind their leader, never breaking formation.

"I hoped I'd find you at Base Camp," said Star. "When I heard there was a Code 4, I knew you'd be in the middle of the action. We've been riding mountain trails all day and spent last night in a cave. Didn't see a thing. The Head Hunters and Amazons joined us. Can you imagine Dragon's delight getting to spend the night with all those girls?" She giggled. "It was great fun. We roasted marshmallows and told ghost stories around the campfire. What about you? What have you been doing?"

"Spent the night in the Garden. We actually spent the majority of the day with the Vikings." Cadence knew Star was seeing Dragon, but she still had a crush on Thor. Her friend looked envious. "We had a picnic in Manitou Springs and that's pretty much it."

Star sighed. "Lucky girl. I wish I'd been there. One day I might get enough courage to tell Thor how I feel. It's not serious with Dragon, and I actually think he's a little sweet on Freeborn but won't admit it. You know how guarded he is."

"I'm sure if you told Dragon how you felt he'd understand. He's a deep thinker." Cadence looked over her shoulder at Dragon standing in the middle of the four ninja girls. "I like Dragon. Most of us wouldn't be alive if he hadn't trained us how to fight. He may be too young to be a soldier, but he's a better fighter than anyone in camp. If the Captain had any brains, he'd make Dragon an officer."

Star waved at Blaze, Dodger, and Whisper as they neared the

campfire. The Tigers liked China Six and motioned at their team to join them. Cadence picked out a good sized log for a seat and pulled Star down beside her. Dodger sprung up and tossed a bag of chips to Dragon. Dragon caught the chips and passed them on to Star. The rest of the girls plopped down around Dodger's backpack, pulling out and devouring the newly acquired rations.

Dragon declined food, but downed a bottle of water. His long, black hair hung in his face as he sat across the fire from Cadence and Star. He removed a cloth and polished his katana, while the others traded stories about their day. Dragon was young, but he was a fierce warrior and held a deep respect for tradition.

Dragon leaned forward. "A little birdie told me the Tigers saw action today?"

"Is that true?" Star asked Cadence, eyes growing wide. "I thought you said you had a picnic with the Vikings?" China Six muttered whispers among themselves.

"Well, sort of," Cadence said with a smirk.

Star glared at her friend. "You can't keep a story like that quiet for long. I want to hear it. And Dodger, please, let Cadence do the talking."

"Fine. If you can't handle the details, I'll shut up," replied Dodger.

Cadence picked up a stick and tossed it into the fire. "I'll give you the short version. Zombies got through the east fence and we had to take care of things. The Vikings turned up later. Of course they didn't help, but Thor did suggest we take a break in town. We needed to change clothes anyway. Too much zombie goo. It was pretty disgusting."

"But you're all okay?" asked Star. "No one was hurt?"

"We're all fine. But an entire Freedom Army patrol was slaughtered last night. We heard the fighting from the Garden. The Tigers wanted to help, but I made them wait until morning. When we arrived, we found a large group of zombies waiting. Everyone fought great. You should have seen them. That reminds me . . ." She reached into her pocket and handed Star a small gift bag.

Star opened the bag and her eyes lit up. "Eyeliner! Foundation! This is incredible. Thanks!" She grinned at Blaze. "I'm sure you picked this out for me. Cadence doesn't know a thing about makeup."

"I might have," said Blaze. "Who's been talking about the fight?"

"Some of the Green Hornets," said Dragon. "I don't think they're telling anyone else, but you know it won't take long for news to spread. They were pretty shaken up by the zombies inside the fence."

"We've got more to worry about than zombies." Cadence reached out to warm her hands. "There's a large group of scavengers coming this way. Their scouts are already here. We heard it on the radio yesterday. If they made it out of Denver, they should be rolling in tonight. That's why there's a Code 4 and all of the patrols are camping here. This is pretty serious, Star."

"Sounds like it. But I'm sure the Captain has a plan. He always does, so I'm not that worried about scavengers," said Star. "You guys are lucky you made it back. I heard Rafe was with that patrol, but he was riding in this morning as we were leaving. Guess he didn't stick around to help. That was pretty crappy of him."

"Tell her the truth." Blaze said as Cadence avoided Whisper's stern look. "Go on. Tell Star where we found Rafe. Oh, I will. He was hiding in the back of the truck. I don't even think he fought last night. He was too scared. Then, to make it worse, he ran out on us."

"Rafe did what he could, which sadly didn't amount to much," Cadence explained, keeping her voice low. "I don't know what to think. Rafe was acting really strange. I can't say I blame him for bugging out on us. All of his buddies were slaughtered, including Boomer. I said some really mean things to him. I regret it now, but at the time I wanted to hurt him. I felt like he let us all down."

"Rafe is a coward," said Blaze. "A yellow-bellied-coward."

"The guy is a loser," Dodger said. "Cadence dumped him, too."

Star waved everyone quiet. "Okay. I get the picture. Rafe was the only survivor. You got there, found him hiding and lost your temper. I understand. The question is just how many zombies were on our side of the fence?"

Blaze held out her hands, fingers spread, and opened and closed her fists a half-dozen times.

"Are you serious? That many?" Star glanced over at Dragon. "This isn't good. They could be coming here. No one sleeps tonight."

"They didn't get through," Dodger said. "We also had to kill the soldiers. A second time. Rafe was the only one not bitten. He left after we finished his crew off. Blaze is right, he's a coward. You shouldn't feel sorry for him, Star. Be glad Cadence broke up with him. I am. We all are. He's bad news."

"I don't feel sorry for the jerk. I'm mad at him, too," Star said. "Honestly, I've always disliked Rafe. He's conceited, unreliable, and a cheater. I'm sorry, Cadence, but it's true. You never wanted to believe it, though I tried to warn you many times. All Rafe has going for him is good looks. Highbrow is far more your style. Where is he anyway? He wasn't with you today?"

"No," said Cadence. "He had a secret mission. Must have been important or he'd have joined us. Then again, maybe it's a good thing he wasn't there. Highbrow goes by the book. He wouldn't have let us have that picnic, and you wouldn't have any new makeup." She lowered her voice. "Blaze got you a new bra. It's on my four-wheeler in the saddle bag. I'll get it for you later. Luna gets one, too. Pink."

Star was delighted. "Way to go, Blaze. I appreciate you thinking of me. I'm going to have to do something nice for you, too. Is there a boy in camp you'd like to go out with? Someone special?" She eyed Whisper. Blaze frantically shook her head. "I'll think of something appropriate, but if you need a messenger, I'd be glad to deliver one to the right guy."

Blaze was quick to change the subject. "We should find out what's going on with the scavengers. Dodger said they have a bunch of prisoners in the office. I saw Destry go in there a few minutes ago with a medic. Let's go ask him what's going on?"

"I'd rather not. I don't like Destry," said Cadence. "Anyway, I know they've been picking up scavengers all day, but I'm concerned there's only a handful being kept in the office. Where are the others?"

"If Sarge found them, he probably shot them on sight," Blaze said. "You know Sarge doesn't like to take prisoners. They should have made contact with the Captain and asked for clearance so they could come into the camp. If they get shot, I don't feel sorry for them. A lot of people could get killed if this thing blows up. We need to know what's going on."

Cadence frowned. "People got killed last night, Blaze. I'll check it out later. Let me relax for a few minutes. I'm worn out."

"Don't worry so much, you two," said Star. "You know we don't have to stick around here. I've told you before, this place sucks. There is supposed to be a safe zone up in Canada. We should go there take anyone who wants to come with us. I don't trust Destry, Habit, or Sarge, and I still can't believe Rafe left you behind. When I see him again, I'm going to kick him. Very, very hard."

"Forget Rafe," said Cadence. "As for Canada, I don't think Highbrow would leave the Peak. He's always hoped his dad will show up one day. I know he can take care of himself, but I could never leave him. Highbrow is my balance. I feel like half a person when he's not around. It doesn't mean I'm in love or anything, so don't get silly on me. He's a Tiger, we're family, and we work well together."

"Highbrow is reliable," Star said, rising to her feet. "He's also cute, and it's okay if you like him. He's always been there for you and the Tigers. It's not such a bad thing that he's a senator's son. If things ever get back to normal, he might be a politician. His old man was rich. You could be in a good position one day if you two get married."

Cadence didn't know if she should laugh or cringe. "Knock it off and let's go look for Luna," she said, changing the subject. "Anyone else want to come with us?" No one replied. "We'll swing back by later, Blaze, in case you want to go with us to talk to Garble. I know you're worried about Highbrow, too."

"Not as much are you are," Blaze sang out. "Besides, I have everything I need right here." She leaned against Whisper and stretched out her arms. "Don't worry about me. I've a starry sky, a warm campfire, and the company of some very cute boys. Well, not you, Dodger. Later, girls."

Cadence had to hand it to Blaze. She certainly made flirting with boys look easy.

Chapter Nine

Under the darkness of night, Rafe crouched behind a dumpster. Dumpsters smelled, but for some reason he found the odor irresistible and wrestled with the urge to look inside. He didn't know where the day had gone, nor did he care. In the main courtyard, a crowd of adults were fussing over a couple of youngsters sitting on a bench. He watched Mother Superior walk out of the Captain's headquarters with several nurses. All of the younger children were taken to their bunk house, but the two kids on the bench were infected and needed to be dealt with.

Mother Superior was in charge of the Peak. The Captain was rumored to be her ex-husband. Whenever together, they were usually whispering and standing close to one another. To most people, they looked like a normal couple.

Rafe liked the Captain. He was a good man. Mother Superior, however, was a stern woman. Rafe found her nagging a bother, though he did like the way she smelled at that moment.

"Hey, Rafe!" Wizard came out of the shadows. He wore his Army jacket zipped up to the neck with gloves and a stocking cap.

Was it cold? Rafe hadn't noticed. The night air felt the same as the sunlight. Wizard put his hand on Rafe's shoulder.

"Where have you been all day? I looked around for you earlier, but couldn't find you. Are you doing okay? Feel any better?"

"Been busy," Rafe answered, unsure of what he had been doing.

"Did you hear about the attack in Cascade? Zombies attacked Corporal Jade's berry picking patrol. I heard a lot of old people were killed and one kid was bitten. They've got two Little Leaguers over there that may or may not be infected. When they brought the kids in, they were drenched with zombie juice. One of them has parents and they're trying to convince Mother Superior to quarantine them for now. She ordered the bitten kid to be terminated, so you know she'll do the same to these two."

Rafe became excited. "Did they swallow it? Did it get in their eyes? How does she know they're infected if they weren't bitten?"

"Hey, slow down a minute pal." Wizard grabbed Rafe by the arm to keep him from running off. "Don't get involved. You can't help either kid. You need to get some rest. You look like hell."

"I have a cold, that's all."

"Maybe a hot shower would make you feel better. I've got to report to the Captain on the front lines. Scavengers have been sighted close to camp. The teen patrols will guard Base Camp, and I heard they've handed out guns already. What a mistake."

"I forgot about the scavengers," said Rafe. His friend's scrutiny made him nervous. "Tell you what, I'll go shower then meet you at the truck. We can ride together. I won't be long."

Wizard nodded. "Well, hurry up. I'll try to find out what's going on."

Relieved his friend was out of the way, Rafe walked toward the community showers. Most people bathed during the day when the water was heated by solar energy. Night baths were cold. He was already numb from head to toe. What was a little cold water?

Avoiding the security lights positioned on every building corner, Rafe made it to the showers without incident. Rafe stripped and tossed his clothes on a bench then caught his reflection in a mirror. What he saw took his breath.

Rafe was pale and dark circles hung under his eyes like half moons.

His eyes had a strange film that made them look dead. He pinched his neck hard and was surprised it didn't hurt. He flexed his muscles, letting out a sigh.

"Playing with yourself again, Rafe?"

A soldier nicknamed Feather came into the shower and tossed her jacket aside. He ignored her and slipped behind a shower curtain, turning on the water.

"I could join you," said Feather. "We could soap each other's backs. You game, Rafe? Or are you still with Cadence?"

"Leave me alone," snarled Rafe. "What are you doing here anyway? We're all supposed to report in for duty. We're going to the front lines."

Rafe stepped under the steaming hot water, but feeling nothing as it hit him in the face. He could smell Feather and knew she was naked. Her odor reminded him of barbecue.

"I have a cold, so I don't have to go. Anyway, since everyone is with the Captain at the front that means the water is hot tonight. No one is using the showers." Feather's voice was enticing. "I could use some help washing my hair. It's all tangled." She let out a loud sneeze. "Sorry. If you catch my cold, it won't kill you."

Rafe filled with a sudden and irrational sense of rage, mixed with lust. He stormed out of his shower and forced the curtain open to reveal Feather. Her back was to him as she massaged shampoo into her long black hair. Needing no further invitation, Rafe came up behind Feather and slid his arms around her. As he kissed her neck, she let out a sigh and wiggled against him. Then she screamed.

"What the hell? You bit me!"

Rafe felt an explosion of pain worse than any migraine explode in his head. He pushed her into the wall, thinking nothing when she fell to the floor. She looked up at him in rapid blinks as the water hit her face. A trickle of blood ran down her neck from two clean puncture wounds. He fought the urge to bite her again.

"Sorry about that. It was meant to be a hickey. You taste good."

"Get the hell out of here, Rafe. I'm going to report you. You had no right to bite me." She sat up, wincing. "With the way the infection spreads, you know it's dangerous to . . ." She fell silent, a look of horror spread across her face as he moved closer.

Feather didn't finish her sentence before Rafe's fist connected with her jaw. Her head snapped and hit the wall. As she sank to the floor, he looked away.

"You liked it," Rafe said, cold and without feeling. He licked blood from his knuckles before stepping under the water to rinse. When he was clean, he turned off the water in the showers, dried off, and got dressed. He felt better, only now he was hungrier than before.

Glancing in the mirror one more time, Rafe knew he was infected. He looked terrifying. He opened a bag Feather brought with her and used her makeup to cover the dark circles and color his cheeks.

The moment he walked out of the shower, Rafe saw soldiers carrying the two children away from the hospital. They weren't going to be given a chance, but a bullet, right between the eyes. He glanced toward the trucks, thought about Wizard, and wondered if he should go meet his friend.

One of the children let out a whimper and something snapped inside of Rafe. He lost his rifle, but couldn't remember where. He wanted a weapon as he trailed behind the soldiers with their victims. Rafe paused to pick up a rock and imagined hitting each soldier in the head. The idea was sound. He followed, making no sound. The soldiers didn't notice Rafe until it was too late. The first went down in a heap. The child dropped on the ground and stared at Rafe, frightened. The second soldier spun around and Rafe slammed the rock into the man's nose. Before the man hit the ground, Rafe struck him once more, killing him. He caught the little girl before she hit the ground.

"Are you going to kill us, mister?" asked the boy.

Even in the dark Rafe could see the boy was pale and had dark circles under his eyes. His nose was bleeding, and there were drops of blood in the corners of the girl's eyes. It was clear they were both infected. He grasped the boy by his hand and pulled him to his feet.

"Does that mean you're not going to kill us?"

"I don't think so," said Rafe. "That wasn't my intention. I knew they were going to shoot you, so I saved you. Didn't your parents want to save you?" he asked the boy.

The child nodded.

"Well, it's not safe for me to take you to them. You're infected like her. Like me."

The boy's eyes grew wide. The girl threw her arms around Rafe's neck and pressed her cheek to his face.

"We need to stay together for now," said Rafe. "I'll find a place to hide and we'll figure something out in the morning."

"I'm hungry," said the boy.

Rafe released the boy's hand and like a savage he ripped open the jacket of a soldier and buried his teeth into the exposed stomach. The girl wiggled out of Rafe's arms and joined the boy in the gory feast. He let them eat their fill. After a few moments, Rafe reached down, picked up both children and walked off into the night.

Highbrow was taking a much needed nap when a thump on his head gave him a rude awakening. He scowled, only to find the Professor standing over him. One of a few teachers on the Peak, the Professor was in his sixties and looked the part of a scholar with his tweed jacket, bow tie, and horned-rimmed glasses. His bald head and plump belly went a long way to help that image. Highbrow had fallen asleep in a hammock hanging on the porch of the Professor's two-story cabin, which served as a classroom as well as his living quarters. Highbrow wiped the sleep out of his eyes.

"What do you want?" said Highbrow. "Let me sleep a few more minutes, Professor."

"Why don't you come inside? It's cold out here. I don't know how you slept through the commotion. I was about to settle down to a cup of tea when I heard the trucks pull out. I thought you were at the hospital with that young girl. All the soldiers have been sent to the front lines. I'm sure the teen patrols are at Base Camp. You probably should get down there."

"Crap!" Highbrow reached into the pocket of his coat and pulled out his radio. "I wonder if I can reach Cadence. I'm sure she's worried sick about me. Have you heard anything from the Tigers? They should have been back at the Peak hours ago."

"Did you hear anything I said? I said the patrols are at Base Camp. You might check with Mother Superior. She might have details, but I'm sure she'll send you down the mountain."

The Professor removed his glasses and rubbed his brow. Highbrow respected the teacher. They had grown as friends and spent many hours talking about life. The teacher was probably the only man on the planet who could have persuaded Highbrow to read Shakespeare. What the Professor lacked in physical stature, he made up for with intellect and class. He had a deep, rich voice that was fun and soothing to listen to, no matter the topic.

"Look, son, I know it's none of my business," said the Professor, "but at some point you need to realize there is more to life than chasing after a girl who doesn't want to be caught."

Highbrow felt torn. Yesterday morning, he thought the sun rose and set with Cadence. But now there was Savannah.

Savannah was soft and kind. He could imagine himself reading Shakespeare with Savannah under the stars, holding hands and sharing long kisses. She wouldn't laugh at him. Chasing Cadence was far from his thinking today.

The Professor patted Highbrow on the arm. "You're not the only one who has ever felt this way," he said, grinning. "I had a crush on a girl once myself. I know what you're thinking. Looking at me now,

I hardly seem cut for romance. It was a different story in my younger years. I had more hair then." He chuckled. "Her name was Amanda. I kept chasing her and she kept running until, eventually, I was exhausted with it all and stopped chasing. That's when I met the love of my life, my late wife Sarah. The whole time I was chasing Amanda, Sarah was patiently waiting for her turn to chase me."

Highbrow frowned. "This is good advice, Professor, but I'd rather not talk about girls tonight, Cadence least of all. You know how I feel about her. Or felt. I'm done chasing. I think I've found my Sarah."

"Very well," the Professor shrugged. "On another note, I've been reading some interesting material. If you want to check on Savannah and Nomad, we can talk about what I found in the black box later."

Highbrow stood up and straightened his jacket. "Savannah can wait. I want to know what you found. Can you tell me?"

The Professor smiled, missing half of a front tooth. One of the professions they lacked at the Peak was dentistry.

"It took a bit of tinkering, but I managed to get the box open." The Professor tapped his bald head. "Thinking men use mallets."

Highbrow lifted his wrist and looked at his watch.

"Midnight. It's later than I thought."

"This won't take long," said the Professor. "Actually, I'm glad I found you out here. It's a relief to be able to tell someone I trust about what is in that box. I believe we've come into the possession of some highly classified information from our government."

"Like what?"

"What I'm about to say doesn't go beyond you and me. Promise?"

"I promise." Highbrow leaned in.

"You remember the first soldier who returned from Afghanistan, the one infected with a strain of the swine flu? The virus at that time was transferred through a sneeze or a cough. It spread fast. Asthmatics were first to fall ill, then the elderly, the obese and children. Hospitals filled up quickly, but the usual drugs simply did not work. After a week, people started to die. More than fifty million people fell ill that first week."

The Professor looked up as a soldier walked by with a girl on his arm. He waited until they were out of earshot before he continued.

"Then the disease mutated and the dead sat up and began to feed on the living. The new strain was called H1N1z. I won't bore you with the details. In any case, merely getting a drop of their blood in your mouth or eyes, or an open wound, would cause infection. Now, according to this report, the virus continues to mutate."

"We all know if you get zombie juice in your mouth, you'll turn into one of those freaks," said Highbrow. "But you said the virus is mutating. Do you mean we could turn into something else? Something worse?" He shivered when the professor nodded. "I can't imagine anything worse than turning into one of those things. Who's the report from? The CDC? Who? Tell me."

The Professor sighed. "I really don't know what this new strain of the virus does and the report isn't clear," he said. "Thing is, while you may have been told that our government has fallen, it's not true at all. This report was meant for the President. I don't know where he's hiding, but I do know your pilot came from Cape Canaveral, which is supposedly where the last of our scientists are working on a cure. Only there isn't a cure, Highbrow. Your father thinks the virus will go on mutating, spiraling out of control, until the human race is obliterated."

Highbrow felt his mouth grow dry. "Wait. My father?"

"Son, your father isn't dead and he never went to prison. Senator Powers wrote the report. I know it's hard to believe, but your father was working for the C.I.A." The Professor put his hand on Highbrow's shoulder, trying to calm him. "All that hype about his embezzling money and being sent to prison was a cover. From what I gather, your dad was working for the Agency a long time. He's leading a think tank at the Cape, trying to discover a cure. It's a shame that pilot died. I have a million questions begging for answers."

Highbrow's mind spun, and he buried his face in his hands. "All this time! All this time I thought my dad was a creep. I had no idea." He looked up. "This is crazy, Professor. Are you sure it was written by my dad?"

"The report was signed by him. I know it's been hard on you. Your father wasn't there for you or your mother when the Scourge broke out. I've heard how the other kids in camp tease you. I'm sure the scandal was hard on your family. You're a good kid and you have nothing to be ashamed of, but no one can know what I told you."

Highbrow crossed his arms, feeling frustrated. "My dad left us when we needed him. I tried to take care of my mother, but one of those things, when it broke into our house . . . I couldn't save her, Professor. I couldn't even kill her. I left my mom in the house and came to the Peak with friends. All this time I've tried to believe my dad was coming here to save us. Now you tell me he wrote the report and he's in Florida, a thousand miles away. He doesn't even know I'm alive."

"Don't give up hope yet, son. A few minutes ago you thought your father was dead. Somehow his report landed in your lap. I don't know about you, but I don't believe in coincidence. Would you like to come inside and take a look?"

Highbrow wiped his face. He had to be tough. His father was alive and trying to sort things out. It seemed a miracle the box had landed in his possession.

"I don't know if I want to see it," said Highbrow. "It kind of freaks me out. Freeborn is always talking about fate and how we're destined to fight at the Peak, but I always thought she was full of it. Now I don't know. You think the pilot really meant for me to have this report? Do you think it's fate, Professor, or just dumb luck?"

"Son, your dad is alive and he's trying to get the word out about this virus. Does it matter which it is?"

"Professor, you should burn that report and forget you ever read it. If the soldiers knew, they'd start killing anyone with a hiccup. They won't know who to trust, and this place is crazy enough without those jerks getting trigger-happy."

Highbrow was unsure of what to do and stuck out his hand. The Professor looked at him, amused, and shook his hand.

"Why don't you go check on your new friends? You can come back and chat with me later. I won't burn the report quite yet."

"Thanks for telling me," said Highbrow. "I know you could be in big trouble for doing it, but I'll keep it secret. I'm just blown away by what you told me. I need to sort things out in my head. I'll be back later."

"I'll have a cup of tea and conversation waiting when you do."

"I'd like that. See you, Professor."

Highbrow pushed the collar of his coat up and walked toward the hospital. He resisted the urge to contact Cadence and tell her the news. Instead, he went inside and looked for Savannah. Her smiling face was all he wanted to see in that moment.

Chapter Ten

C adence and Star went searching for Luna.

The two all-girl patrols had a large fire roaring between their tents and sat around talking and eating. At the approach of Cadence and Star, they nodded and pointed to Luna's tent. Cadence heard muffled voices inside, and realized Luna was not alone. Star grinned and unzipped the tent, intent on catching Luna in the middle of something wicked. They both looked inside to find two girls wiggling together under a sleeping bag.

"Greetings," said Star, trying hard not to laugh.

The first head out of the sleeping bag was Luna's, with her platinum-blonde ringlets, heavy blue-frost eye shadow, and thick, black eyeliner. The Head Hunters were gruesome in appearance, and in battle Luna was as blood-thirsty as the rest of her team, but she was beautiful as any Hollywood starlet.

Her accomplice was none other than Raven. Before anyone could reply, Cadence tossed a light blue beret at Raven who caught it mid-air, laughing in delight.

"Thanks! I thought you'd forgotten," said Raven.

"I did or I would have given it to you at lunch," said Cadence. "Mind if we come in? We want to talk about the Code 4."

Without waiting for a reply, Cadence entered the tent and Star followed. Luna struggled into a pair of tight, designer jeans. She grinned at Raven as the Viking got dressed.

"What the heck are you guys doing here?" asked Luna. "I thought my team was standing guard? I'll need to chat with them about privacy. No one was to come in here." She pulled a sweater over her head. "But if you're interested, we're going to the Panthers tent. They found bottles of scotch and vodka. It's going to be a fun party."

"You do know there's a Code 4 in effect, right? We could be called into action any second," Cadence said, reaching into her coat. "I have something for you."

Cadence produced the care package for Luna and tossed it to her. Luna let out a joyful cry upon seeing the makeup and pink lipstick. Raven wasn't in the least bit interested in more lipstick, but the pink bra Luna pulled out of the bag was another matter. Both girls liked fancy lingerie.

"Keep it down, goof balls," hushed Cadence. "I don't want to draw attention to the fact we're all in here."

Luna perked up. "Secrets. I love secrets. Tell us what's really going on."

"The Freedom Army brought in some prisoners. Destry showed up a little while ago with a medic, and I thought you might want to come with us to find out details. The scavengers from Denver have to be here by now. Soldiers have been scouring the road all evening, so it looks like something big is happening."

"Who cares?" Raven said. She had finished dressing and was lacing her boots. "It's not our business what they do to prisoners. We're gophers, nothing more. Stop acting like you're a real soldier, Cadence. Give it a rest."

"Show a little respect," said Luna, exasperated, now dressed in a light green sweater, jeans tucked into fur trimmed boots, and a black, down-filled jacket. Pink lipstick was in her hand and ready to apply.

"Freeborn dropped by earlier," said Raven. "I already told Luna about the fight your team had with the zombies." She glanced at Cadence as she dabbed on lipstick. "I think your guard is going around camp telling everyone what happened."

"It's true," said Luna. "Freeborn said you blocked a huge hole in the fence, but apparently zombies still got through. I really don't think that's the kind of secret people need to know about, especially during a Code 4. The Bull Dogs will be looking to shoot anyone who looks suspicious. Freeborn needs to be careful what she brags about."

"And she's drunk," added Raven. "You need to get her under control."

Cadence let out a soft curse. "She knows that kind of talk can land us in trouble, especially me. No one was supposed to know we all had guns. If they find out we took extra weapons, I'm the one who will pay for it."

"Can't blame the Vikings this time," Raven said with a smirk. "We didn't take credit for your kills and we didn't talk about it. Nor did we turn in our guns. I was true to my blood oath. I told Freeborn to keep quiet, but you know how she gets. That girl is trouble."

"Loose lips sink ships," said Luna, smacking her newly painted lips.

"I'll deal with her my own way. If you two are ready, let's go do a little damage control."

Cadence was pleased when Luna gave a nod. She started out of the tent and stopped when she heard a garbled sound coming from Star's leather jacket. Star reached inside and pulled out a radio. Cadence let out a growl and tried to grab it, but Star evaded her.

"Give it to me. That's got to be Highbrow!"

"Hush. You don't know that." Star motioned for the girls to be quiet. She fiddled with the dials and heard someone speaking softly. "It's on a classified channel. I don't think it's Highbrow."

"Turn it up," hissed Raven. "I want to hear."

Star turned the volume up and held the radio so they could listen.

"*. . . sir, we found two soldiers half-eaten up here.*" The voice belonged to Nightshadow. *"Found another body in the shower. She was rising to feed, so we took her out."*

The Captain answered. *"Nightshadow, you're in charge of the Peak right now, so you deal with it."* The sound of gunfire peppered the background. *"I'm busy right now. We're fighting scavengers at the north fence. I've got reports that zombies broke through at Cascade. They have us surrounded. Send all the reinforcements you can muster from Base Camp and do it now!"*

"What about the civilians?" said Nightshadow. *"The virus might spread, sir. With all these kids up here, I don't know who has it and who doesn't. Rafe was reported as acting sick earlier. Apparently he's missing, and so are two infected Little Leaguers. Mother Superior gave orders to shoot them on sight."*

The handheld filled with static.

Raven let out a whistle. "So that was his boggle. Rafe is infected. He's a zombie!"

"You need to find Freeborn," said Star, grabbing hold of Cadence and shaking her from her thoughts. "Things are heating up fast. We should gather our teams and meet at the Tiger tent in ten minutes. We can go to HQ together for more info."

"Agreed." Cadence could not say more without getting emotional. Rafe was a zombie. It was not what she expected. She crawled out of the tent and gazed up at the Peak, drying her eyes. For all his faults she still cared about Rafe, and now he was to be shot on sight. Why hadn't she been more understanding when she last saw him? Why had she been so mean to him? He was infected and she hadn't noticed.

Trying hard to keep it together, Cadence felt both relief and rage when she spotted Freeborn stumbling around and drinking. Cadence charged the girl and Freeborn froze in her tracks. Cadence knocked the beer can from her hand and punched her in the jaw. Freeborn hit the ground, laughing.

"Why did you have to blab your mouth? Why did you tell people what happened today?" Cadence wanted to strike her again. "You're so damn stupid sometimes. This is no time to be drunk. Get up. We have work to do."

Cadence reached down for Freeborn. The girl slapped her hand away and staggered to her feet.

"So I bragged a little," grumbled Freeborn. "People should know zombies are on the loose. They need to know the Freedom Army is a joke. This isn't the U.S. Army. It's not like these idiots know what they're doing. Let's just stop pretending, okay?"

Everything important to Cadence was suddenly reduced to insignificance by her friend. The Freedom Army was not perfect, but they tried. They survived for a year, and that was something. Without rules and respect, there would be only chaos. She could not believe that's what Freeborn wanted, but when she was drunk not even she knew what she wanted.

"I should kick you out of the Tigers for this," Cadence said in anger. "The only reason I'm not is because the Captain is in a battle and surrounded right now. We've been called in to help. That means you need to sober up, and do it fast. I know the Army means nothing to you but you need to realize that if any officer learns what we did today, I'll be the one who is punished"

"I seriously doubt any officer is going to give a damn if the Tigers have a few extra guns," Freeborn said. She reached into her coat pocket for another beer, but tossed it in the grass. "If you don't want me around, kick me out of your unit. The War Gods are looking for a replacement. One of their members vanished. Just took off yesterday."

"You are my guard," said Cadence, grabbing Freeborn by the arm. "I'll be damned if I let you join those show offs. You're better than any War God, and you're better than this. I don't know why you drink, but as of today it's over. You're going to pull yourself together and get back to the Tigers. That's an order."

"Screw you!"

Cadence narrowed her eyes. Freeborn backed down and lowered her head. Cadence was the dominant one between them and the reason was simple. When Freeborn first arrived at camp, she was confused, hurt, and angry. She had been unapproachable and everyone avoided her. No one liked her or wanted her on their patrol. Her drinking had been worse then, but Cadence saw something in the proud Cherokee that no one else noticed. The girl had heart. Nightshadow gave her the name because she was wild and free, and born to kick ass. Cadence was not about to lose the toughest girl in camp over a can of beer and gossip. She extended her hand once more and this time Freeborn shook it firm.

"Okay, chief. I'll go to the tent and get the team ready." Freeborn turned to go, and then stopped. "I'm glad I told everyone what we did. We never get any credit. No one ever hears about what we do to keep this place safe. Well, now everyone will say we are heroes." She pulled her braid around and brushed her hand along the eagle feather in her hair. "I want my people to be proud of me, and of the Tigers."

"I'm sure they are," said Cadence. For Freeborn, her people were still alive. The spirit world was as real and tangible as the physical world, and meant a great deal to her. "I am too, Freeborn."

Cadence grabbed Freeborn's arm and they marched toward the Tiger's tent. They arrived to find Thor and Whisper staring at a dying fire.

"I see Crazy Horse is at the liquor again," said Thor. He patted the ground next to him and held out the edge of the plaid blanket he was wrapped in. Neither of them realized they were about to be thrown into the middle of a fight. The other teams hadn't shown up yet. Cadence noticed a flurry of activity among the soldiers camped nearby. They were loading up and getting ready to leave. The Captain's order was swift in its reach. Cadence knelt beside Thor and Whisper.

"Listen up. We just heard the Captain on Star's radio. He is surrounded by zombies and scavengers at the north fence. The fence is compromised and all soldiers have been mobilized. Look," she pointed toward the military units. "They're already on the move. Put out this fire and get ready to roll. Our teams are meeting here."

Thor jumped to his feet. Whisper was slower to rise, but he was up.

"There's more," said Cadence, catching hold of Thor's arm. "There's been an outbreak at the Peak. Nightshadow is there with only a handful of soldiers. Apparently Rafe brought the virus back with him. He's turned and is to be shot on sight."

"Rafe? Infected?" Thor was shocked. "I thought you said he was fine when you saw him last? Why didn't you strip him down and check him? You know the rules. Why didn't you follow him?"

"He was clean, except . . ." Cadence remembered the blood on Rafe's face, eyes widening.

"You should have known something was wrong when he bugged out on you the way he did. That's not like Rafe and you know it."

"It doesn't matter," said Cadence. "We're in for a fight. Stay here. I need to go to HQ and find out what's going on. I still haven't heard from Highbrow. He might be at the Peak and I intend to go get him."

"I'll go get the Vikings," said the hulking blonde, and hurried off.

"Our savior," said Whisper, shaking his head.

Smack, Blaze, Dodger, and Freeborn appeared from their tent, weapons loaded and at the ready. Whisper reached inside and dragged out three saddlebags filled with more weapons. He located his favored M24 and made sure it was loaded.

"Anyone need a bigger gun?" asked Whisper.

In the next few minutes, the camp bustled with activity. Soldiers were loading into trucks and pulling out. Others from base headquarters dashed out, climbing onto their motorcycles. A mass of teenagers gathered in the parking lot. There were not many vehicles left. Less than two dozen four-wheelers, a motorcycle and a large Army transport with a smashed windshield remained.

Cadence took a fast head count. There were more than a hundred teenagers standing around, looking confused and asking questions.

Not one officer or soldier was left in the camp. They had all deployed to join the Captain at the north fence.

"Are we going to the Captain?" Blaze asked with a cigarette clenched between her teeth. "Or are we going to the Peak? You think Highbrow is up there?"

"I do," said Cadence.

Thor walked to the Tiger tent accompanied by the Vikings. Raven stood beside him wearing her blue beret. The Head Hunters arrived following Luna with their customary war paint, and dressed for a fight in metal-studded leather and chain mail. Barbarella, a large, square-jawed girl carrying a double-edged axe, marched behind Luna, leading the Amazons. They were adorned with all manner of armor and carried a range of weapons, from swords to axes to crossbows.

Star and China Six rolled up on their ATVs. More teams filed in and joined the Fighting Tigers.

"We're all here," said Thor. "I see you have plenty of weapons. Everyone should take a gun, even if you have a sword. That's my suggestion, of course."

Everyone was staring at Cadence. By an unspoken, unanimous vote, she'd been given charge of this ragtag army. Cadence gave a nod to Whisper, and he began distributing weapons to those he knew could fight, regardless of their age, patrol, or position. Those receiving weapons did not shout in excitement or revel in being armed, but fell in line like the soldiers they were being asked to become.

"Okay folks, listen up," shouted Cadence. "We know we've been on Code 4, but I just heard the Captain is up north in a fight against scavengers and zombies. Zombies are coming here from Cascade and there are infected people at the Peak. All available soldiers have been sent to join the Captain, which means we just moved up to a Code 5. Since we have no officer here to give orders, this is what we're going to do—"

Interrupting her instructions, Corporal Garble ran out of the building screaming and holding his bleeding face between his hands. Whisper and Thor pointed their weapons at the hysterical officer as he ran toward the group. The situation went from tense to insane as Garble's scream intensified.

"The scavengers! They're infected. One of them bit my face."

Without hesitation, Thor dropped Garble with a shot to the head. He spun his revolver and slid it back into its holster, turning to Cadence with a sad look. "He was already dead."

Dragon glanced at Freeborn, and together they walked to HQ to take defensive positions at the door.

"What are your orders, Cadence?" asked Star. "Scavengers are at our doorstep and we have zombies on the Peak. Do we fight here, go to the north fence or to the Peak and make our stand there?"

Everyone waited for Cadence to answer. Her team stepped back, giving her space to be seen and heard by all. The scene was surreal to Cadence, but she was confident.

"We make our stand here," shouted Cadence. "Vikings and Green Hornets take up position at the front entrance. Amazons and Head Hunters take flanking positions at HQ. Panthers and Buccaneers, watch the mountain road. The Blue Devils can patrol the parking lot with the Bull Dogs. Team leaders assign someone from your patrol to check the soldiers' tents for supplies. If you don't have a weapon, find one or make one. No one is to be empty-handed. Leaders outfit your teams now!"

Cadence marched straight toward headquarters. Smack ran up and handed Cadence her katana and a rifle. Cadence slung the rifle over her shoulder and readied her sword. Luna, Star, and Raven waited for Cadence and together they approached HQ. Freeborn and Dragon stood on either side of the open door, while Cadence held at the entrance and listened. Growls, snarls, and sloppy feasting came from inside.

"It's going to get messy," said Freeborn. "Highbrow isn't around. Guess you get the honor of going in first, Commander Cadence." The tall girl smiled at the title. "We've got your back."

"On me," Cadence said, her sword held out before her.

One good thing came to mind as Cadence entered the cabin. At least the lights were still on.

Chapter Eleven

*A*lone, uninfected scavenger cowered in the corner. His hands were bound and he attempted to inch his way outside. Three of the remaining seven in the room were being eaten by the others who were infected. Three unarmed soldiers were bitten and attempting to fight as long as they could.

Star, Luna, and Raven stayed with Cadence as she entered the cabin. The girls opened fire on two zombies shuffling toward them. Cadence severed the head of a soldier with glazed eyes, before dispatching a zombie still hunched over a body on the floor.

The fight was over in seconds.

Cadence did a quick scan of the room. Luna and Raven held the surviving scavenger by his arms, checking for bites and signs of infection while he babbled a story nobody listened to.

"Star, see if you can find any more radios," Cadence instructed, "and try to reach Highbrow. Raven, go through every drawer for weapons. Luna, take the ones from the soldiers and get them in people's hands, and Freeborn, get in here and shoot anything that twitches."

Freeborn, Dragon, and Dodger walked in and took hold of the captive. He babbled his story again to them, while Cadence fiddled with the radio. She found a channel being used, but heard only gunfire and screams.

"What do we do with this guy?" Dodger asked, pulling his captive forward by the front of his shirt. When he needed to be, Dodger was all alpha.

"Is he infected?" Cadence asked.

"He didn't try to eat me, but I still don't trust him."

The scruffy scavenger wore a Harley jacket and torn jeans. He didn't look sick, but was thin. Dragon kept a tight grip on his arm.

"I'm Sturgis. I came with Nomad and Savannah," said the scruffy-looking biker. "They were taken to the Peak by some guy called Highbrow. I'm not infected."

"Where are Destry and the medic?" asked Cadence, turning toward Dodger and Dragon. "Are they among the dead?"

"They took off when the Captain called for backup," said Sturgis. He shrugged when Dragon gave him a stern look. "Sorry, but she asked."

Whisper stepped inside and held up a radio. "Highbrow."

Cadence holstered her revolver, slid her sword in the sheath strapped to her back, and grabbed the radio from Whisper. "Highbrow? Is that you?" Her voice trembled, and she strained to hear him. "Everyone out. It's too loud in here."

"Move it, people," said Star, herding them out the door. She walked up to Sturgis. "This guy is splattered with blood and gore. He stays here, and don't untie him yet. Dragon, have the teams take up a defensive position outside the cabin. Use the cars to create a barricade and light a fire at the front gate. Fire is our friend. Freeborn can stay here with Cadence."

Raven grinned. "You got it, China Star." She ducked out the door.

"I'm coming, too," said Luna, hurtling toward the door.

Star left with the rest of the group. Dodger tied the scavenger to a table leg, then closed and locked the windows before exiting. Freeborn took guard at the open door, emotions rippling across her face as she stared into the darkness.

"Cadence, can you hear me?" said Highbrow. "It's bad up here."

Cadence heard shooting, both on the radio and in the distance.
"What's your position?"

"I'm at the Professor's," said Highbrow, his voice crackling in and
out. "I was at Doc's when all hell broke loose. Don't come. It's too
dangerous."

"I'm coming to get you whether you like it or not."

She could hear his sigh, but he didn't argue. "Two of the scavengers
are with me, but they checked out. Not infected. You okay?"

"Yeah, but the Captain is under attack at the north fence. The Freedom Army pulled out, so only the teen patrols are here. Stay put and
I'll be there as soon as I can."

Highbrow's voice faded and the connection was lost. Cadence put
away the radio as a large figure pushed past Freeborn and entered the
cabin.

"Sorry to interrupt," said Thor. "We need a plan of action. There
are a number of boats at the lake. If I load them with shooters, we can
go out on the water, light up the main gate, and shoot anything that
comes through."

When Thor had an idea, it was like a grenade going off in his head.
One big, brilliant explosion of an idea. From the lake, he would have
a circular view of the entire area, and the water provided perfect protection from any incoming zombie threat. Zombies were full of nasty
gasses in their rotting guts, which meant they floated.

"Make it happen," Cadence said.

Freeborn pointed at the man tied to the table. "Old man, you need
to get your poker face on. You can't be crying in a dog fight."

"I don't want to die," said Sturgis. "You heard what that boy said.
It's hell! Put me on one of those boats. Floating in the middle of the
lake sounds good."

"Leave him tied up," said Cadence. "Freeborn, have a team come
in here. This will be our command post. Have the War Gods get up on
the roof, then find me a truck. The Tigers are going to the Peak."

"Right." Freeborn dashed out the door.

Cadence went outside and was surprised to find the teams organized and ready. A barricade constructed from remaining vehicles was being set up around the cabin. Enough logs and trash had been dragged to the front gate and set on fire that it could be seen for miles. Snipers were positioned on the roofs of all three buildings and the Panthers hurried past her, entering the cabin and taking position at the windows.

Wrench and his mechanics were at the garage setting up their own barricade of empty oil drums and wooden crates. The Valkyries jumped in to help them. Razorbacks, Bandits, Buccaneers, and Green Hornets were busy lining up the barricade around the cabin. At the lake, the Vikings positioned boats, shining lights on the gate and as far up the mountain road possible. The Fighting Tigers waited beside the last military truck in the parking lot. Blaze stepped forward as Cadence drew near.

"Going to the Peak is a suicide mission," Blaze said. "I care about Highbrow too, Cadence, but you should stay here and defend Base Camp. Everyone is looking to you as commander."

"Raven will command the ground troops. She has Luna, Star, and Barbarella to help her. We're going, Blaze, and that's all there is to it."

Not waiting for a rebuttal, Cadence opened the door and confirmed the keys were in the ignition. Raven was nearby, giving instructions to a group of teenagers.

"Hold down the fort, Raven," Cadence called out. "I'll be back."

"Will do," Raven replied.

The Tigers mounted up as Star and Dragon approached. They were carrying a large, heavy bag. Cadence had not asked them to go and couldn't imagine what they were carrying. Dragon threw the bag into the passenger side and climbed in. The end of an M16 pointed out of his window. Star jumped behind the wheel and Cadence joined her team in the back. She pounded on the roof of the truck and they were soon making their way toward the Peak.

"They're outside," said Highbrow, peering behind the curtain.

He stared at the growing number of zombies, holding a rifle the Professor gave him. With the lights off throughout the cabin, Nomad watched a front window armed with an axe, while the Professor guarded the back door with a chainsaw and a myriad of kitchen knives. All other doors were closed, locked, and barricaded as much as possible. Savannah crouched behind a couch, holding a frying pan and a butcher knife.

Nomad let out a soft growl. "Man, they stink."

"*Shhh*," hushed Highbrow. He turned off his radio when the tattered and bloody victims started gathering outside the cabin. Most of the zombies were so mangled and ravaged it wasn't surprising they had turned so quickly. Usually it took several hours for someone with a bite to turn, but what he was seeing was more than a few bites and it was ghastly.

A young zombie with no arms staggered to the front door. She pounded the door with her head. *Thud, thud, thud.* Silence. *Thud, thud.*

Heavy groans and the sounds of snapping teeth followed, like dogs fighting over a bone, then another *thud.* Highbrow stayed cool and silent.

Rapid gunfire and a close-by explosion rattled the frame of the cabin. Highbrow thought it came from the hospital. Doc, the nurses, and patients retreated inside, but Highbrow convinced Nomad and Savannah to come with him to the Professor's cabin when things turned ugly. He felt bad that he hadn't convinced Doc and his staff to join him as well.

Glass shattered in the kitchen and the Professor shouted. Highbrow, Nomad, and Savannah ran to his aid. The windows surrounding the back door had been broken and torn, bloody faces pushed through the shards. Highbrow pushed the Professor aside and fired into one window, and then the next. Nomad buried his axe into a creature's head that was crawling through, and then went for the fridge. Using brute strength, the biker toppled the refrigerator and pushed it against the door. Highbrow wedged a chair into a broken window, while the Professor and Savannah used the kitchen table to block the other window.

"That won't keep them out," said Nomad. "If you have an attic, that's where we need to go."

The Professor nodded. "To my bedroom. Come on."

The Professor's bedroom was humble hosting a twin bed, a table stacked with books, and a small wardrobe. There were no windows in his room. He pulled a cord hanging from the ceiling and lowered a flight of narrow, wooden stairs.

"Shall I go first?" said the Professor, hesitating. "I hope nothing is up there."

"Get moving, Professor. I'm right behind you." Nomad brought his axe and a few knives from the kitchen.

Highbrow waited for the men to climb up, with Savannah at his side looking frightened. He found her beauty stunning, even in this heightened state of danger. Highbrow reached for Savannah, pulled her against his body, and planted a passionate kiss on her lips.

"Just in case I don't get a chance later," said Highbrow as he set her back. "Watch your step, Little Bo Peep."

With an unexpected giggle, Savannah darted up the stairs. Highbrow heard another window crash in the living room, and the sounds of clumsy bodies hitting the floor followed. The insufferable groaning grew louder as they closed in on the Professor's room. Highbrow followed Savannah up and pulled the stairs closed. Nomad pulled a large wardrobe over the trap door for added safety.

The attic was vaulted and filled with boxes of books, and facing the front of the house was a balcony. The Professor stood at the veranda doors that opened to a starry night, and overlooked the town filling with clouds of smoke and fire. Highbrow walked out and looked down to see bodies scattering the ground. Some still twitching, he didn't see anything human left fighting in the courtyard. Somewhere, a child was crying.

It was dark at the hospital and the front door was smashed in. The bodies of soldiers littered the entryway. Glancing toward the road, he saw no sign of Cadence or the transport and stepped back inside with the others. Zombies beneath the balcony saw Highbrow and started making strange sounds, as more monsters lumbered toward the cabin.

"I might as well tell you, Highbrow," said the Professor. "I burned the report. I wish now that I had waited. But I did save your father's signature for you." He pulled a small piece of paper from his pocket and handed it to Highbrow.

Highbrow opened it up, revealing his father's handwriting. "Thanks." He tucked it into his jeans pocket. "Doesn't really matter now, does it? Mother Superior and The Captain are out there with the zombies."

Nomad took a step onto the porch. "How safe is this balcony?"

"There's not much to see," said Highbrow. "The camp is lost."

"*Sh*," hushed Savannah. "I hear an engine."

The sound of a truck rumbled like thunder in the night air. Cadence and the Fighting Tigers were firing on zombies from the back of an Army transport. As they pulled into camp, bodies were hitting the ground and being crushed under the wheels.

"Over here!" Savannah shouted. She joined Nomad on the balcony.

Highbrow propped himself on the wooden railing, positioned his rifle, and took aim. He shot at zombies on the road as the truck pulled up below the balcony. The Tigers were laying waste to zombies advancing on the truck from every direction. Highbrow was punched with guilt as Doc and the hospital staff, covered in blood, limped toward the truck. Whisper relieved Doc with a single shot.

"Lower the girl down first," shouted Cadence, "then the men." She looked back at her team, "Be ready to catch the girl."

"Your buddy is crazy," said Nomad. "I'm being rescued by a girl. This is priceless." He picked Savannah up and dropped her toward the bed of the truck. "You're next, Professor."

"I'm too fat," said the Professor in protest. He was given no option, being ushered onto the railing by Nomad, and then lowered into the truck bed. Several Tigers tried to catch him, but he landed on his backside.

"You're next, Mr. Motorcycle," said Highbrow. He nudged Nomad forward. "Hurry up and get going. We're still the main attraction."

The balcony creaked beneath them. Nomad looked worried as he climbed over and jumped into the truck, twisting his ankle.

"I'm okay, I'm okay," he called out.

"Great. My turn," Highbrow sighed. He hated heights.

Cadence heard the balcony giving way and watched as Highbrow leaned forward, flying off the balcony as it crashed to the ground. He fell hard into the bed of the truck, knocking Smack down with him. Savannah helped Highbrow to his feet as the two shared an affectionate look. *Was this redhead why Highbrow hadn't returned to the team?* The question burned inside Cadence, but she had no time to consider it further. The thought hurt as she pushed it from her mind and continued firing on people she had once known and cared for.

Star drove out of camp, putting some distance between them and an approaching mob of zombies and then stopped. Dragon climbed out of the cab, dropped to a knee, and shouldered a bazooka. Taking aim at the mob, he fired. He followed with two more rounds that took out a building and hastened the spread of the fire. Whisper continued sniping zombies as Star called for everyone to load back in. The hospital erupted in flames, along with HQ, and the train. The fire spread, engulfing the zombies and reaching the fuel depot. Star sped away as explosions rocked the camp, raining down violence on the remaining zombies.

"Stay sharp," Cadence shouted. "Be sure you have the shot before you take it. I don't want any of our people shot by accident."

"The difference is the walk," said Dodger, demonstrating an exaggerated zombie limp.

Everyone laughed, but soon came to silence once more as Whisper fired on straggling zombies following them. The team sat back and held on for the bumpy ride.

"Thanks," said Highbrow, shifting toward Cadence. "You risked the team by coming to get us, but I'm glad you did."

"No problem."

Cadence felt her eyes moisten, and she held back her tears. The life they had built for the past year had just been ripped away by savage greed. Not everyone seemed upset. Much less than they should be. The red-haired girl looked frightened, but her biker friend seemed calm. Smack was excited and blowing bubbles, while Dodger joked and teased with Blaze. They grew quiet as the transport approached the midway camp.

Cadence remained in the truck with Freeborn as Highbrow led the team, joined by Dragon. Zombie soldiers stumbled around outside of the cabin. Whisper and Freeborn dropped them one by one as Dragon kicked down the door and entered the small shack. The lights were on as Highbrow and Dodger pushed through the door, Blaze and Smack providing support outside. Heavy gunfire erupted inside and a front window shattered as a body crashed through, mangled and hanging over the frame.

Dodger rushed out, leading a group of children screaming and running for the truck. Smack and Star helped the kids pile into the cab, bunched in tight. Three soldiers ran out of the cabin followed by Dragon and Highbrow. Blaze turned and ran toward the truck with them, reaching the team as the shack exploded and flames billowed through a spew of fire.

The group packed together in the back of the truck, and Cadence was surprised to see Corporal Sterling among the survivors. A dark, broad-shouldered man of stoic repute, she watched tears roll down his face, which he made no attempt to hide.

"When the fighting broke out at the Peak," Sterling began, "I managed to lead the children out of the school. Wizard and Dill met us coming down the mountain. Hiding in the cabin seemed like the right thing to do. I know the children come first, but I'm ashamed."

"For hiding?" Cadence asked.

Sterling turned away, saying nothing further.

"You should have seen what was going on inside that cabin," said Highbrow, reporting to Cadence. "They were locked in the bathroom with the kids. That door wouldn't have held much longer. Mother Superior was crazed and vicious. Dragon killed her, and there wasn't anything else to do but burn it down. There was a propane tank out in the open and leaking."

"Calloway lit the match," said Sterling. "Not much was left of him, but he had sense enough to light it once we were out. I shouldn't have left him. He was my friend."

"You saved who you could." Eyes narrowed, Cadence pounded on the back window. "We've got to get moving! More of them are probably headed toward camp and will outflank the patrols."

Star caught her eyes in the rearview and she picked up speed. A few kids turned around and stared at Cadence with shock and horror, but when she smiled a couple smiled back. She knew they would be okay.

The road was rough and narrow. Cadence had to kneel like everyone else to avoid being knocked around. The Tigers distributed fresh ammo to everyone for reloading. Cadence tensed when Highbrow put his hand on her shoulder. His grip was firm.

"We're doing okay," he said. Reaching into his coat pocket, he pulled out a handheld radio and gave it to her. "Told you I'd get you one."

Cadence slid it into her pocket.

"Thanks for saving us." Highbrow smiled. "I might not show it, but I'm a nervous wreck. You seem to be handling it all in stride. Big step up in responsibility, but it suits you. You're a natural leader, Cadence."

"Thanks," said Cadence, grinning. She wanted to tell Highbrow how much she had missed him, but it seemed a moot point after seeing how he looked at Savannah. She had waited too long to admit her feelings for him and now there was someone else.

"Our escape was nothing less than miraculous, Cadence," said the Professor. He held onto the side of the truck, groaning every time they rounded a curve. "This is Nomad and Savannah. They were a big help. I don't think I would have survived without them and Highbrow. Of course, all the credit goes to you and the Fighting Tigers. You saved our lives."

"It's going to be ugly down at Base Camp," said Cadence. "Every soldier has been called to the front. We'll drive straight to the barricade and let everyone off. Corporal Sterling, I'm putting you in charge of the civilians. Get them inside HQ and stay with them."

"Who did you leave in command?" asked Highbrow.

"Raven." Cadence tensed when he looked surprised. "She's in charge of the barricade and Thor has a flotilla on the lake. The fire at the front gate should keep the zombies back, but if they got through we're going to be outnumbered big time."

"I'm sure you deployed your troops well, commander. It's not like we're all that stands between civilization and the end of the world."

Highbrow looked out at the dark. "The Captain is out there fighting, too. We'll do our best to make him proud."

"We'll follow you, Commander Cadence," said Wizard, handing her a blue beret.

Cadence placed the coveted cap on her head. Enthusiastic cheers from the team lifted her spirits. The group fell silent as they were met with explosions and the *rat tat tat* of gunfire around the next turn. Cadence presented a brave face, praying she wouldn't let anyone down.

"Let's give these monsters a one-way ticket to Hell!" shouted Cadence.

Her people answered with a roar.

Chapter Twelve

*T*he cave was dark, or at least it should have been.

Rafe didn't understand why he could see so well in the dark, or how he had walked this far carrying two bloodthirsty children without getting tired. The children seemed weightless to him. If he had attempted this a few days ago, he wouldn't have made it. He set them down at the mouth of the cave and they ran inside laughing and chatting like normal children, but this was far from normal.

Rafe heard the scream of a mountain cat in turmoil. The injured animal dashed by him and vanished. Inside, he found the children kneeling and devouring a small fawn. It was the cat's meal. After a few swallows, the boy turned his head and vomited and the girl stopped eating. She held her stomach and began to cry.

"Now don't start that," said Rafe, picking the girl up. Holding her close, he wiped her bloody tears and kissed her on the nose. "You two injured that mountain lion and chased it off. That means you can take care of yourselves, so there's nothing to be scared of. Plus, I'm here to look after you."

"But I'm hungry." The boy wiped a hand across his mouth. "The fawn tasted bad. It didn't taste good like the man."

"I couldn't hold it down," said the girl. "I'm sorry." She shared a shy smile as Rafe sat down with her on his lap. "You're so nice. I miss my daddy. Will you be our daddy?"

"That's a job I'm not really cut out for, but I'll do my best."

Rafe leaned against the wall of the cave and stretched his legs. The girl kept her arms around his neck and her little face pressed against his. Rafe was filled with strange ideas and feelings. The only thing keeping him calm were the two children cuddled next to him.

"I'm Billy," said the boy. "Billy Goat Gruff. It's a stupid name. Nightshadow gave it to me but I'd rather be Dracula. Doc was reading the book to us. I liked the vampire."

"Seems appropriate," said Rafe, smiling, "but a little overused. If you want a cool name, I'll give you one. I'll give you both new names."

He held the girl at arm's length and gazed at her with his newfound vision. She remained pale, with dark circles under her glowing eyes. She looked healthy, and not at all in the process of zombie rot.

"What about Cinder, short for Cinderella? That sounds like a cool name. Do you like Cinder?"

"Funny," the girl said. "My real name was Cindy. Everyone called me Mouse at camp because I'm quiet, little, and I liked cheese. I like Cinder."

The boy hit Rafe hard in the shoulder. Rafe dropped to his side and almost dropped Cinder. The boy laughed and started dancing until a *'click, click'* from the girl halted him. The boy stuck his hands in his jeans pockets and hung his head.

"I'm so hungry," the boy said. "I know it's wrong, but I want more soldiers."

He showed off his new fangs, long and wicked. Rafe glanced at the girl and saw that she, too, had grown fangs. He felt his own teeth, puncturing his finger with a sharp point. Cinder grabbed his finger and sucked with bloodlust, and he didn't stop her.

"I don't know what's happening to us," said Rafe, "but we aren't human and we certainly aren't zombies. They don't talk like this."

"What's Billy's new name?" Cinder said, with an air of authority that caused the boy to kneel before them. She noticed how he quivered, waiting for a new name. The control she commanded excited her. "You will always be Rafe, our protector. But he needs a scary name. Something that will make bullies think twice about bothering us anymore."

"They won't bother us," whispered the boy. "They're dead now."

"Cerberus," said Rafe.

The beast from Greek mythology was the first name he thought of. A bit of classic storytelling wouldn't hurt them. The boy looked to be about eight, and the girl younger. All kids loved stories.

"Cerberus was a three-headed dog that guarded the gates of the Underworld. In ancient Greece, the gods lived in a place in the clouds called Mt. Olympus. Zeus was their leader, Poseidon was god of the sea, and Hades was god of the Underworld. Cerberus protected Hades' home, and he was frightening."

"And he will protect me," said Cinder, content in their strange new life. She took the boy by the hand, drawing him close. The boy gazed at her with adoration. "Cer . . . ber . . . us. Guardian of the Underworld. It suits you."

Rafe squinted at the children, listening to their words mature and their demeanors change before his eyes. It was eerie. Come to think of it, he never had much interest in mythology. They weren't the only ones changing.

"I like it," the boy said. "But what are we to eat? I'm still hungry."

He had no idea what to feed the children. He was shocked when they attacked and overpowered him, but he didn't resist. Cinder sank into his neck and Cerberus into his wrist. When he felt the life draining from his body they stopped, drawing away and reaching for each other's hand. They both gazed out of the cave, and then back to Rafe.

"We have drained you," said Cinder, concerned. "Now it's our turn to find you something to eat. We'll be back. Stay here."

Rafe was weak and had no intention of moving. He watched the two little demons walk out of the cave. These were fearless, powerful creatures.

He just hoped they would return with something large enough to satisfy his own aching hunger. If the gruesome duo wanted to hunt, there was no reason to stop them. It was with relief and a strange satisfaction that he was left to rest while the children took care of him.

Cadence felt like they dropped into pandemonium. Hundreds of zombies were streaming through what remained of the fire, advancing toward the barricade. Many of them had caught fire, posing an even greater danger. Shooters on rooftops fired at stragglers coming in the gate. The main group positioned behind the barricade held back the advance, but a few crates had toppled creating a hole filled with rotting corpses trying to push through. A hundred or more zombies gathered around Lake Crystal. The teams under Thor's command shined their spotlights on the road and picked their targets with care. Scores of zombies floated in the water, twitching, while creatures on fire waded into the water and floundered near the shore, easy pickings for shooters in the boats.

Cadence watched as the Amazons, Head Hunters, and Green Hornets fought the creatures with swords and axes. The battle was medieval. Flamethrowers and modern weaponry mixed in to define chaos in a whole new way. Raven was statuesque in the back of a broken truck behind the barricade outfitted with an automatic rifle, mowing zombies as they crawled over the fallen. The teen patrols were outnumbered and ammunition was precious. The tide of battle could shift in the blink of an eye.

Cadence pounded the roof of the cab and the truck stopped. She climbed to the top of the cab, motioning Corporal Sterling to get the civilians behind the barricade. Dragon and the Tigers opened fire. The children were tossed over the barricade by Sterling into the waiting arms of the teenagers. The Professor, Savannah, and Nomad followed along with Sterling. Wizard and Dill stood with the Fighting Tigers, firing at zombies that swarmed the truck.

Bright lights swung across the truck and into the parking lot, focusing on the Bandits who were caught in the open. The team circled their four-wheelers in the center of the parking lot, and began firing in every direction. Cadence heard a scream and saw a teen being pulled across an ATV. Whisper shot the offending monster in the head. The teen scrambled and ran toward the barricade, but was caught and dragged to the ground.

Without thinking twice, Cadence jumped from the truck and charged the circled Bandits. She wasn't sure who followed before seeing Freeborn, Dragon, and Highbrow running beside her. Cadence thrust and stabbed her way through the horde of zombies, and Dragon's swords flew like a choreographed masterpiece of lethal grace. A blast from Freeborn's shotgun cut through a zombie's skull giving Cadence time to join the Bandits in the shelter of the circle.

"Get to our truck with the Tigers," shouted Cadence. "We'll keep them off you."

The Bandits led the others toward the truck as Star drove their way, making an effort to massacre every monster in her path. Whisper remained mounted in in back making every shot count. Cadence, Dragon, Highbrow, and Freeborn made their run to the truck, jumping over bodies flattered by Star. The truck rolled up and blocked the gap in the wall and a loud cheer went up from the rooftops.

Cadence was caught behind the barricade when the opening collapsed with decaying bodies. She tried to run around a zombie, but it saw her and opened its maw exposing raw flesh hanging from its blackened teeth. Now behind the barricade and alone, she was surrounded and felt hope slipping away.

She kept fighting, until two small children appeared at her side. Glowing eyes and corpse-pale dimples smiled at Cadence. In the moment of distraction, a large zombie fell on her. Cadence felt its grasp and caught scent of its fetid breath, then thrust her blade into its stomach. The creature staggered backward, swinging its arm and knocking Cadence off her feet.

"Help her," said the girl.

Cadence watched a boy fly through the air and land on the back of her attacker. His small hands closed around the neck of the zombie, shredding its head from its shoulders. The girl circled Cadence with inhuman speed, striking zombies lifeless with effortless force. Both children were swift and lethal. Zombies piled around her, and Cadence felt like she was watching a movie in slow motion. The girl stopped her onslaught and reappeared at Cadence's side covered with black goo, leaving the killing to her companion.

"I know who you are," said the girl. "You're Cadence of the Fighting Tigers. I'm Queen Cinder and that glorious vision is Lord Cerberus. We wanted to see how many of these foul beasts we could kill, but it's too easy. I'm bored now."

"You're the Little Leaguers who were infected," said Cadence. "Billy was the lookout for your team, right? And you're Mouse. I recognize you."

"Not anymore. We have evolved."

Cadence felt the girl grip her sword arm. The boy was too busy dispatching zombies to pay them any attention, but Cadence realized Cinder was walking her away from the battle and into the trees. She turned and saw the barricade diminishing in the distance. The boy returned to his queen and bowed, leaving a few zombies for the teen patrols to finish off.

"I killed them," said Cerberus. "Now what? Are we taking her with us?"

Cinder let go of Cadence and she felt a bruise swell from the girl's grip. Cinder motioned for Cerberus, and for a moment Cadence thought he would kill her. He stared at her for a short time, then the eerie light in his eyes dissipated, replaced by warm, natural brown eyes. Fear melted from Cadence, leaving her with a strange desire to hold the boy close. She let out a sigh as Cerberus took a step toward her, unable to look away. Cadence dismissed the sounds of gunfire and shouting from beyond the tree line, and looked deeply into his eyes. She felt an attachment to him, bending down and opening her arms. The boy stepped into her embrace.

"You have no fear," said Cerberus. "I could kill you in an instant, yet you cannot resist your desire to hold me. Interesting." He glanced at Cinder. "Our protector spoke to us of Valkyries, who had the task of claiming the souls of the fallen in battle. Rafe said Cadence is such a warrior. He wants her."

"I think we should find someone else," Cinder said. "This one will never take orders."

Cadence felt her thoughts clear the moment the boy looked away. She lifted her sword, prepared to fight back. Cerberus opened his mouth and exposed long fangs. Cadence was struck with horror and amazement.

"You know what we are," said Cerberus. "Had I not broken contact, I could have made you do anything. I could make you my thrall, if I so desired."

"Good word use, darling," said Cinder. She dispatched a zombie that lumbered too close, snatching its head from its shoulders with one hand.

Thrall, Cadence thought. *Servant. Slave.*

She tried to move her arm to strike down the boy, but she couldn't. The world could end right now and Cadence would feel only love in her heart. It made no sense. Her sword arm dropped and Cinder took the gun from her other hand.

"You want to tell me something, don't you? Something you haven't told anyone else." Cerberus laughed, villainous. "Tell me your thoughts."

"I'm in love with Highbrow," Cadence blurted. "He doesn't know. He thinks I still love Rafe, which I do, but we had a fight. I love you, too. If you bite me, will I become like you?"

"I don't want you turned," said Cinder. "We will let you go. You're a killer, like us. It would be a shame to make you a slave. Let her go Cerberus."

The boy laughed. "This is your lucky night. My queen wants you spared. I'll find another to replace you."

Cadence felt the strange thoughts fade away. She scanned the parking lot and found a lone zombie, a child in bloodied pajamas, shuffling toward them. She was able to lift her sword to strike, cutting the girl's head off and watching it roll across the ground. When she looked up, Cerberus was missing.

"Nicely done," said Cinder. "Be thankful Rafe still loves you. He is one of us. If he didn't, I would not hesitate to rip your throat open and drain you. We will deal with Highbrow later."

Cadence's throat was dry. "Tell Rafe I'm sorry. Tell him I still care and want to talk to him."

"You may regret that offer," said Cinder, and then she, too, vanished.

Shouts from the barricade caught Cadence's attention. She turned toward the battle, but it was over. They'd won. People were jumping, shouting victory cries, and hugging each other. Members of the Head Hunters and China Six walked through the carnage, double checking each kill. Cadence heard her name and looked up to see Star and Luna running toward her. Star carried a sword dripping with black gore. Luna was clean of any blood. She carried a Civil War cavalry sword she purchased on the internet years earlier, and her bright pink lips held a superior smirk. Luna made killing zombies glamorous.

"Wow!" remarked Luna. "I'm impressed."

"How did you kill so many on your own, Cadence?" asked Star, concerned. "We saw you surrounded and then bodies started dropping like flies. Not even Dragon killed as many as you did."

Highbrow joined them, breathing hard from running. He had a worried look on his face. Cadence wanted to slap him and kiss him at the same time. Lacking words, Cadence stabbed her katana into the ground and held out her arms. "Group hug!" Confused, the four embraced.

Standing in the tree line, Cadence saw Cinder and Cerberus holding Savannah by the hands. They chose her over everyone else. Cadence wanted to tell Highbrow, but knew there was no way to fight the children. They waved at Cadence before vanishing into the trees. A pit of worry grew in her stomach. Cadence tried not to think about them as the Fighting Tigers and other patrols surrounded her.

Smack bolted from the pack and threw her arms around Cadence. "I was so worried about you. I'm glad you weren't hurt."

"You were fantastic in battle," said Dragon. He arrived with Freeborn, hands locked. "You fought like a Shaolin priest trained in the old ways."

"Like a Cherokee warrior, a real warrior woman." Freeborn said, laughing. "You are our War Woman."

Cadence felt her cheeks blush. Today was a small victory, but it was not hers to claim. The real heroes were two dangerous vampires.

"Dragon taught me how to fight," said Cadence. "I am honored that you took the time to make a fighter of out me. You're a true master, Dragon. I am your student."

Dragon bowed, and Cadence returned the respect.

"Okay, show's over," shouted Highbrow. "Let's get a head count and start burning these bodies. There's still a few hours before daylight. We need to find out what's happened to the Captain and the Freedom Army." He left Cadence, dispensing instructions and bringing some semblance of order back to the camp.

A steady line of teens flocked to Cadence as she walked toward HQ, thanking her and shaking her hand. She had never been more proud, annoyed, and confused. As she pushed her way inside the cabin, Raven was standing in front of the shortwave radio with Sturgis listening to a battle. Cadence heard sporadic gunfire and shouting. "What's going on?" asked Cadence. "Have you been able to contact the Captain?"

"I'm doing my best," snapped Raven, realizing how she sounded. "Sorry, didn't mean to be gruff. Turns out, Sturgis knows how to operate this dumb radio. Sarge is pinned down in Cascade and someone said the Captain is dead, but most of it is noise."

"You did great. I can take it from here. Go check on your team. Sturgis, keep trying to get a response. If someone could get me water, I'd appreciate it."

Smack handed Cadence a bottle and stood beside Dodger. The Fighting Tigers were all together inside the cabin, and the Professor sat in a corner surrounded by the children. Whisper and Blaze collapsed on the floor beside the kids, while Freeborn and Dragon stood guard at the door. Corporal Sterling and Nomad were missing. Cadence tried to relax for a moment while sipping her water and noticed Highbrow sitting on the edge of the desk. They stole a glance between each other as Sturgis found a clear channel, cutting into a conversation between two scavengers.

"*Damn straight we made it through,*" said a familiar voice. It was Logan. "*Those soldier boys laid a trap for us, but we outsmarted them and double-backed to Manitou Springs. Cascade is overrun with those things. We pulled out in time, but the militia is trapped. A few of their soldiers asked to be taken prisoner. Their sergeant is a blabbermouth. We know all about their operation and the Peak looks ripe. Meet us at their Base Camp when you can get through. Over.*"

"*Should we hold up at Manitou Springs?*" said a woman, sounding nervous. "*We're there now. Where are you located? Over.*"

Cadence heard enough. She grabbed the receiver interrupted their conversation. "Listen here. Harm any prisoners and there will be nowhere safe for you to hide. You can tell Logan that he's public enemy number one. If any of you show up at Base Camp, it'll be the worst mistake you ever made."

There was a pause. "*This is Logan. Who is this?*"

"Cadence, of the Fighting Tigers. I'm in command of the Peak."

The radio shredded into static. Clicks were heard, which further annoyed Cadence.

"People, please. I know Morse code," said Cadence. "There's no back road to the Peak. Try hiking through the trails and we'll find you. We're heavily armed and you are outnumbered. If Cascade is overrun, the Peak is the last place you want to be. Just stay in Manitou Springs. You have until tomorrow to clear out."

"*We need water, food, and shelter,*" said the woman. "*If you're a smart little bitch, you'll let us stay, or Logan will kill your sergeant.*"

Cadence put her hand over the receiver. "Highbrow, we need to step it up. Place more guards on the entrance road and block it off with whatever you can find. The mountain road too. Freeborn, Dragon, go with Highbrow."

The three headed out. Cadence spotted the Professor waving his hand at her, like a kid wanting to ask a question. She ignored him. Nomad had returned, but now he and Sturgis were leaving together. Looking for Savannah, she assumed. Cadence turned back to the radio and removed her hand from the microphone.

"Logan? You still there?"

"*I'm here,*" he said, laughing. "*Over.*"

"Then listen close. You've got until morning to clear out of town. We'll be coming down the mountain and if we find any scavengers, we'll kill every last one of you, that is, if the zombies don't get you first."

Blaze slid her hand across her throat. Cadence waved her off.

"I mean what I say, Logan. But if you've got the balls to show up, bring a white flag and hope I'm in a mood to accept your surrender. You got that?"

"*I do,*" said Logan. "*A white flag.*"

"Cadence out."

Setting the receiver down, Cadence pulled off her cap, rubbed her scalp, and collapsed into her chair. Smack was handing out the last of her bubble gum to the kids. They all looked worn, but not as frightened as earlier. Dodger was entertaining them with magic tricks, and the Professor still had his hand up.

"What do you want, Professor?" asked Cadence.

"Your performance was very convincing, Commander." The Professor didn't sound pleased. "Do you have any idea how scary you are when you're riled up? These children are traumatized. Just what are you hoping to do? The Peak is destroyed and I doubt many tents survived the battle. We can hardly stay here for any length of time."

"Then figure out a new place for us to live, Professor. I'm going to catch some shut-eye."

Chapter Thirteen

*T*he morning brought surprising changes that Rafe had not imagined. In his mind, he played through the old stories about vampires, like Dracula and Nosferatu. He never once considered they might be based on truth. Vlad the Impaler was a real person, the granddaddy of the legends as far as he knew. Rafe never imagined he would become such a thing, or that they even existed. As he hauled the girl's body over his shoulder, he wondered if she was still alive. He had come close to draining her dry.

Rafe followed Cinder and Cerberus into the historical district of Manitou Springs. The two apparently knew where they were going and walked straight to Miramont Castle on Capitol Hill. For whatever reason, the forty-six room mansion with stepped gables and stone battlements was in pristine condition. It was the perfect place for the little queen and her guard dog. Rafe was well fed, but he wasn't sure he wanted to move in with the demon children. They creeped him out more and more as time rolled on. As well, he liked being on his own.

"Take the girl to your new room, Rafe," instructed Cinder.

She sped up the stairs to the front door of the beautiful Gothic mansion. Somewhere along the journey, she found a long leather coat the color of blood and far too big for her small frame. As she ascended the stairs, the coat trailed behind her in regal fashion. She broke the seal on the door and entered. Rafe followed, still carting the human girl. He sniffed the air, but smelled no death in the mansion.

"Shall I stand guard?" asked Cerberus.

"No," Cinder said. "We don't yet know our limitations or strengths. If the stories we have are true, we need to be inside." She pointed toward the sun breaking the horizon in the east. "To be safe from this point forward, we base our behavior on our understanding of vampires. From now on we only feed on uninfected humans. None should become whatever we are unless they are exceptional. It's the way of things now. It's my way. We will rule here as queen and consort. You Rafe, you will be our champion. No one can defy us. We are, after all, unique. Now close the door."

"Yes, my queen," said Cerberus. He closed the door at once and locked it, before joining Cinder in a sitting room with red velvet furniture and matching drapes.

Rafe had not felt the sting of the morning sun, or the weight of the girl he carried. It was tedious, however, having to deal with two small teacups trying to act like titans. He should not have filled their heads with stories of legend. They brought the girl to him. She smelled so good, and he fed on her but hadn't the heart to kill her.

"You may keep the girl," said Cinder, "if you can turn her into a vampire."

Rafe placed the girl on a couch, while the boy stood before a marble fireplace, admiring the ornate fixtures and oil paintings on the walls.

"Why did you bring me this girl?" Rafe asked. "Why not Cadence? You know she's the one I want. I told you both how I feel about her."

"Don't be droll. Leave the girl here and make sure we are safe. I want you to report to me if you should discover something new and interesting regarding our condition. Cerberus and I are going into the cellar to sleep a while. The sun is rising and I say we are tired. I say we are vampires, and I alone give approval for you to make that red-haired witch into one of us. She's to be your playmate, not Cadence. I was at Base Camp and saw everything I needed to see. Cadence is far too dangerous."

Left to his own devices, he explored the mansion. Finding no one hiding or rotting in a forgotten corner, he locked the doors and returned to the girl. He carried her to the third story, where he found a room he liked. The room was large with an impressive bed and heavy curtains at the windows. Rafe laid the girl on the bed and covered her. He closed the drapes, content no sun could breach the room.

Unsure how to turn a human, Rafe tried what he had seen in countless films. He slit his wrist with a knife kept in his boot and put his bleeding wrist to her mouth. It took a few minutes for the girl to stir. When she did he watched, fascinated, as she drank with eyes wide open.

"It's okay," said Rafe. "I don't understand what's happening either. Everyone else is drinking me. You might as well too, sunshine." She glanced at him and continued to lap up his blood. "It doesn't feel that bad. Truth be told, it kind of makes me hot." She responded with a moan of affirmation. "I'm Rafe. Welcome to Hades."

She lowered his arm and licked her lips. A drop remained on her chin.

"Two little monsters run the place. You'll meet them soon enough. Hopefully Cinder will take a liking to you. I don't know her very well. Then there's Cerberus. They're no more than children in body, but in spirit they seem to have aged. You must do what they say, when they say, or they may decide not to keep you alive."

"And you?" The girl's eyes were large and green. She didn't appear afraid.

"I . . ." He hesitated. "I am the queen's protector. I want to live, so I'll do what she commands."

The girl sighed. "I'm Savannah. I'm tired, so let me sleep."

"Sleep away."

A noise at the front door sent Rafe down the stairs and charging into the foyer. The door was open before he arrived and several humans stood in the threshold, armed and road weary. Their guns lifted at Rafe's appearance. A woman and two men stared at him, their eyes wide and wild. He smelled fear cling to their skin like a heady perfume. Rafe lifted his hand to his mouth and felt for fangs, found them receded and smiled. "Are you looking for shelter? This place is taken, as you can see. If there are more of you, we may have a problem."

"There doesn't have to be," said a middle-aged, dark-haired woman who appeared to be in charge. She lowered her gun, laughing as she tapped at one man's rifle, helping him to lower his barrel. "What are you doing here? Did you desert your troops? We ran into a few of your soldier boys last night and took a few prisoners."

"Actually about ten," said a tall, bald man. Draped in a long black leather coat, his left eyebrow was pierced with a silver ring that lifted as he was scrutinized by his adversary.

The man towered over Rafe at six-foot-five and had the hands of a basketball player. Rafe guessed the man to be in his early thirties, and allowed a smirk to accentuate his handsome face. His posture and demeanor suggested he held a previous career, legitimate or otherwise, that demanded a high level of street cred and smarts. Rafe was certain he did not belong among scavengers.

"You leave the wounded behind?" Rafe asked. Bleeding humans might arouse Savannah or the two children. He didn't want a blood bath.

"When you're in a gunfight," said the tall, dark man, "it isn't expedient to worry about the wounded. If you can't keep up, you're left behind. That goes for either side."

"All's fair in love and war," replied Rafe. "I understand."

"Both sides were evenly matched, but we were losing until a herd of walkers arrived. I'm talking hundreds of them. They came in from every direction. Those of us able to get away didn't look back. Your soldier friends decided to come with us. We obliged and took them prisoner. Seemed the only logical thing to do was to head the opposite direction of the zombies and that brought us here, same as you."

Rafe nodded. "Same as me."

"The name is Logan. This is Marge, and Hank, her old man."

Rafe glanced at the others. Hank smelled of disease. Rafe frowned. Was that cancer? Could he smell cancer?

Marge was debating in her own head whether to fight or stay. Noises outside alerted Rafe there were more people waiting to come in. Revealing his best game face, Rafe stepped forward and stretched out his hand. He laughed when Logan grabbed hold for a hard shake.

"I'm Rafe. Consider me the manager of this establishment." He looked toward the door, the odor of living humans ripe in his nostrils. "How many are with you, Logan? The house only has forty-five rooms."

Rafe hoped his act would lower suspicions. If they accepted the hospitality, he wondered if he was really doing them any favors.

"We have a kitchen with running water. No electricity but plenty of candles, beds, blankets, and a fireplace in most rooms. You're welcome to stay as long as you want."

The woman stared at Logan. "You're going to trust this guy just like that? His soldier friends killed most of our people. That leaves a bad taste in my mouth."

Logan shrugged. Rafe regarded the woman with disdain.

"We'll stay as long as we want," she said, posturing. "With or without your permission, soldier boy. There are more of us than there are of you."

"You have no idea who resides here," Rafe said, his voice lowered to a growl. "Don't press your luck, lady. Take what is offered or clear off."

"We need a place to stay, so can it Marge," said Logan, glaring at the woman. "It's a nice place, Rafe. We saw other houses that looked okay, but this place seems the safest. There's about twenty of us, plus the prisoners. Did the rest of your group come here, then?"

"Enough to hold off any army, I assure you. But if you accept my invitation, I expect you to play nice with the children. Do you accept or shall I wake the others?"

"Don't bother," said Logan. "I've had enough bloodshed. We accept."

Rafe nodded. "Just like our camp at the Peak, you have to be invited to enter. So enter."

"We didn't meet your Captain. Some girl named Cadence is in charge now." Marge grunted. She patted the barrel of her gun. "I'd like to say hello to that little girl sometime. She made it clear we're nothing but scum. Maybe we are," she smiled, exposing yellow-stained teeth, "maybe we're worse."

Logan laughed. "Serious Marge, shut up. This guy invited us in and that's all we wanted." He sent the other man to bring in their friends.

"I'm counting on you to keep your friends in line, Logan. Those are the house rules." Rafe moved back. "Marge and her husband can have the master quarters. It's on the second floor. We're on the third, so don't go there, and don't go down into the basement. We have prisoners, too."

Marge was giddy with delight as she scanned the interior and eyed the exquisite design and accessories. Rafe discerned her greed. He knew they would not be allowed to stay long, at least not as humans. Thirty plus people sauntered in carrying weapons and backpacks. The Freedom Army soldiers were tied together and numbered more than a dozen. There were no serious injuries, but Rafe smelled fresh blood as they passed him.

"Got a place for the soldiers?" asked Logan. "They won't mix well with my people, so I need to lock them up. I'll figure out what to do with them later."

"I assumed that," said Rafe, considering options. "If anyone is infected, shoot them in the head and leave them outside. We don't take chances. The wounded can stay in the living room. Have your people tend to them. As for the prisoners, there's a small study in back without windows. Lock them in there for now. Don't go in the basement."

Logan stepped closer and placed his hand on Rafe's shoulder. "I know you don't trust us. We don't trust you either, but no one is going to cause trouble. If they do, I'll shoot them myself. Is that good with you?"

"Perfect. I'll retire now. Have a nice evening."

"I will." Logan sounded sincere. "Thanks again. It's nice of you to let us stay when you don't have to."

Rafe turned to the stairs, eyes narrowing as a woman walked in with her arm in a bloody sling. It took all his will not to make her his next meal. Logan didn't notice the hunger in his eyes and pulled a bottle of bourbon from a pocket.

"Don't run off yet, Rafe," said Logan. "Have a drink with me. There's nothing a glass of bourbon won't cure."

Rafe joined Logan in the living room. A group of biker types filed in smoking and making themselves at home on the couches and over-sized chairs. A familiar scent caught Rafe's attention. He recognized Sarge and Destry as the Freedom Army soldiers were marched to the study. He hoped they wouldn't recognize him, as Logan placed a glass of bourbon in his hand.

"Here's to new friends," said Logan, clinking his glass with Rafe's. He took a sip and turned to observe the room.

Rafe sniffed the liquor, found it repulsive and poured it in the pot of a dead plant. Logan noticed his empty glass and poured him a refill.

"Slow down friend, this is sipping bourbon." Logan plopped on a couch, and waved off the cloud of dust. "You should fire your maid."

"Or just find a new one." Rafe tipped his glass toward Logan.

The sun streamed in through an opening in the heavy drapes and a ray fell across Rafe's hand. He expected his flesh to burn, but nothing happened. The sun had no effect. He was sure it was a fact Cinder would find interesting. It also appeared he passed for human in the company of others.

Logan stretched out his legs. "The former owners had good taste. Figure I'll hang out here a while and then go find a room."

"Very well. I should go check on my girlfriend," said Rafe.

"Whatever," said Logan as he leaned back and closed his eyes.

Rafe handed his glass off to the nearest human and slipped out. He wondered if the children would devour their guests or try and blend in when they woke. Time would tell when darkness fell on Manitou Springs.

Highbrow spent the morning searching around the lake and surrounding woods for Savannah, finding no trace of her.

While searching, he took a mental count of the living and estimated about eighty left from the original scout teams, and that at least three teams had been wiped out. Families on the Peak and the Freedom Army soldiers were dead. The Captain, Habit, Destry, and Sarge were assumed dead or missing, and no other soldiers or scavengers had arrived at the camp. Thor, his Vikings and the Razorbacks spent the early morning hours pulling bodies out of the lake and burning the remains.

"Highbrow, I've been looking for you," said a transformed Cadence.

He was shocked to see she had her hair cut short, decked in a new blue beret. Highbrow mentally compared Cadence and Savannah, though he knew it was wrong. Savannah was soft, with hair like the sunrise. Cadence now seemed even stronger than before, rigid and unreachable. With her promotion to commander, she was advancing to places he wasn't prepared for.

"God, Highbrow. Didn't you get any rest? You look like hell. At least wash the blood off, you look like a ghoul."

"I can't find Savannah. She's not in any of the pits," said Highbrow. "I looked. Nomad looked. Whisper and Freeborn did too. I can't imagine where she could have wandered. The Green Hornets and Panthers have been patrolling the main road. They haven't seen anyone.

No zombies, scavengers, or anyone from our teams who might have run off last night."

"Do we have deserters?" Cadence demanded. Her tone was sharp as she squeezed the grip of her gun. Highbrow stared at his best friend, sorrow and confusion clouding his face. She reached out and put her hand on his shoulder.

"I didn't mean to sound so rough. I'm not going to shoot anyone for deserting. If any of those counted as dead show up, I'll give them a hug and a bowl of soup. We're all that's left, Highbrow. We have to stick together."

A lump grew in his throat. He was thirsty, tired, and longed to be in Mapleton Hills with its elegant trees and spacious houses. He missed home, and he missed Savannah.

"Did Sturgis pick up any more transmissions from the scavengers?" He tried to focus. "What's the plan?"

"China Six checked out Seven Falls," she said. "They say it's good, so I'm moving the camp there today. You should search for Savannah while you can. Take the Bandits and use the ATVs. I'll give you two hours and then we're heading out."

"Why don't we stay here? We can use tents. What does the Professor say? Does he think it's a good idea to leave?"

Cadence looked annoyed. "He thinks we should move on, too. We've burned the bodies, but the lake is polluted and the ground is poisoned. Seven Falls will have fresh water, wildlife, housing, and a means to fortify our position. It won't take us long to build a wall at the canyon entrance."

"That's just great, Cadence. I'm so glad you asked for my input." Highbrow looked off in the distance, trying not to lose his cool. "It doesn't even bother you that we've killed hundreds of people in the last few days. Now we're leaving for some fool's adventure. We're vulnerable outside the fence."

"The fence is down. We're moving and that's not negotiable. Go look for your girlfriend and report back in two hours. If you're going to be the new captain, you need to start acting less like a love-struck boy and more like an officer." Cadence reached into her pocket and shoved a blue beret against his chest. "Put the damn thing on and act like you care. People look up to you. Give them a reason to Highbrow."

Highbrow went through the motions. He cleaned up, got something to eat and drink, cleaned and reloaded his rifle, and donned his new beret. The Bandits waited for him outside the main office. Though he felt it was useless to keep searching for Savannah, he didn't want to give up. A red-eyed Nomad joined the search with them. After an hour of riding the trails, Highbrow led the team into Santa's Workshop. There wasn't much left of the former amusement park.

"We can split up and cover more ground, Highbrow," said Nomad. His voice was gravelly and strained. "I don't think we'll find Savannah here, though."

An hour later, Highbrow stood with Nomad in the center of the park. Some of the Bandits were raiding the stores, returning with sacks full of clothes, toys, and old candy. A few zombies had greeted them and were handled with ease. Nomad had a new black hoodie draped over one shoulder and a bag of fresh clothes.

"I'm surprised your Captain didn't clear out all of the supplies here long ago," remarked Nomad. "I found a few things for the little ones."

"The Captain didn't allow patrols here," said Highbrow. "He didn't let us go into Manitou Springs either. It was against the rules to hangout or rummage. Some did anyway, but if you were caught you'd get lashes. Savannah would have liked it here. None of the rides work anymore, but it still feels like Christmas in the park."

"A dead Christmas," said Nomad. "Savannah's gone, Highbrow. She got spooked during the battle or something else happened and we just don't know yet. I don't know where else to look for her. I'm broke up about this too. She was like a daughter to me, but we can't keep looking for her. Others need us now. Cadence is moving the camp and you need to back her up."

"I get it. We can move on, but I don't believe she's dead."

Nomad handed Highbrow a large candy cane, patted him on the back, and began rounding up the Bandits. Highbrow pulled off the wrapper, took three licks and tossed it.

By the time they returned to Base Camp, vehicles were loaded with people and supplies. Every four-wheeler in working order carried two riders, and many others were hanging on the sides of the Army transport. The Bandits made a U-turn and followed the convoy out of camp. Highbrow and Nomad waited until the last vehicle left and made a final sweep of the former HQ before joining the exodus to Seven Falls.

Chapter Fourteen

adence walked onto the porch of a small tourist cabin located beside the waterfall, which served as the new HQ and her personal quarters. She placed Thor in charge of a team building a barricade at the entrance. Whisper and the Professor worked on restoring the generators in each of the buildings. The cabins were in perfect condition and provided enough housing for everyone. Several members of the Tigers, along with others from various teams, were gathered around a small pond and grilling out. It could have passed for a normal summer day.

Seven Falls was a picturesque setting, cascading into a large pool that fed a stream running along a rock wall. The stream brimmed with trout and a handful of youngsters were fishing under the supervision of Freeborn. An iron staircase on the side of the rock wall led to another stream and hiking trails. The only way out of the canyon was by the front entrance, which was being blocked off, or by climbing the two-hundred twenty-four steps leading to the trails at Midnight Falls. It was a fortified stronghold.

"I proclaim this haven zombie-free," said Dodger, tapping his drink against Smack's.

"Zombie-free, indeed." Smack echoed.

They sat enjoying the evening in their newly acquired fleece jackets from the gift shop, while Blaze and Luna assigned patrols their new cabins and roommates.

Smack smiled. "I like it here, Dodger. This place feels like a home. You'd never guess Colorado Springs is just a half-mile away, filled with zombies. It's so peaceful and quiet."

"And you said you weren't homesick." Dodger leaned in and planted a kiss on her cheek. "It'll be okay. Cadence did good. This is way better than the Peak."

"I think so," said Cadence.

Dodger blushed as she and the Professor joined them. They both grinned at the sight of the couple. Cadence scooted far enough across the bench, giving the Professor room to sit. He produced a book from his coat pocket. "We have been fortunate thus far, but we lost many people. We would be wise not to forget. Raven gave me this book on edible plants in the area. I suppose I'm the one to decide what can and can't be eaten."

"Now you're talking my language," said Freeborn. "I'll help you with that, Professor."

Peering over the railing, Whisper watched the fish swimming below. Cadence observed the group cooking out, breathing in the aroma of saltwater, fire, and grilled food.

"Professor, what do you think our chances really are?" Cadence lifted a hand to the back of her neck. She already missed her long hair, but Smack insisted it would be a nice change. "Highbrow said they've spotted scavengers at Miramont Castle. I considered going back and torching the place, but I've seen enough bloodshed for a while. They wanted a place to stay and now they have it. Hopefully, they won't give us any more trouble."

"I doubt they'll be coming here," said the Professor. "We lucked out getting here first. Being this close to Colorado Springs is both a positive and negative. With the entrance to the canyon secured we should be safe enough against zombies, at least for now. We're also close to stores and pharmacies when we need supplies, and Thor has a few ideas along those lines. I like that young man."

"I'll talk to Thor about it," said Cadence. She looked around for Highbrow. He was the only one missing from her team.

"That all sounds positive. What's the negative?" asked Dodger, injecting himself in the conversation. "I don't know about the rest of you, but in every western I ever saw, anyone making a last stand in a box canyon didn't usually survive. Except maybe John Wayne, but he's not around to help."

"Pity," said Whisper.

The Professor removed his glasses and wiped them on his sleeve. "The only exit is the staircase up to Midnight Falls. That's the one major drawback to this paradise of ours. We'll have to keep a constant eye on that. It might be beautiful and seem peaceful, but we must never let our guard down. Ever." He balanced glasses on his face. "But the positive outweighs the negative. At least I believe so. We have a tunnel that remains comfortable at fifty degrees year-round and an observation point with a view of the entire area. Whisper assures me it will serve our snipers well. The cliffs keep us out of view from the outside and we have fresh water and game. Plus, we're not fourteen thousand feet high where I was in jeopardy of having a massive coronary. I like our odds here much better."

Cadence leaned back and stretched. "I'm not exactly sure how I became the new commander, but it seems everyone has accepted that. I'm good with it and I feel good about this place, Professor."

"Promote those within your own team," said the Professor. "It's always wise to place those you trust in leadership. Assembling an elite fighting team is where I would start. What about scout teams? Are you eliminating those? You don't have the fence to walk, but we still need to know what's going on in the big city."

"I've already asked Thor and Star to set up elite teams, reorganize the patrols, and develop a duty roster. Dragon volunteered to train people in hand-to-hand combat, and Xena is giving private sword lessons." Cadence glanced at her own teammates. "I'd like Blaze and Freeborn to head up security, which leaves Dodger and Smack in charge of supplies."

"So we get to go into town?" asked Dodger, excited. "Cool."

"Real cool," affirmed Smack.

Cadence looked at Whisper. "You're on target practice. Teach everyone how to shoot like you. I need snipers who can hit their marks. Professor, you're head of communications now. There's a nice short-wave radio here and laptops in my cabin you might make use of."

"Cool," said Whisper.

"Would everyone stop saying that?" Cadence begged, her team snickering. "Dodger, you and Smack take inventory of supplies and let me know what we need. It might include a run into town for our team, but I plan to use all of the existing patrols."

"Cool!" The team teased in unison.

"Okay. Say it again and see what happens," responded Cadence.

The Professor chuckled and everyone let out a collective laugh.

The Tigers were pleased with their new assignments. Cadence did not want to run things like the Captain and Mother Superior. She also wanted a proper militia, but she needed a captain to help run things.

"This isn't going to be like the Peak," she explained. "Everyone will remain armed. I'm done with most of those stupid rules and regulations, and that includes the whipping post. Demerits will be given for anyone who steps out of line and it's the brig for the worst offenders. We'll set up a system of discipline that is appropriate."

"That sounds wise," said the Professor.

"What about me?" Highbrow came walking down the wooden deck, followed by Nomad and Sturgis. They befriended quickly. "And do you have jobs for these guys?" He paused, glancing at Blaze. "Nice hair. You look like a grape."

Blaze flipped an offending finger toward Highbrow and joined Freeborn on the bench.

"Nice of you to join us." Cadence refused to let Highbrow's attitude get her down. She knew he was upset about Savannah, but didn't know how to tell him the truth. "I'm commissioning you as captain. I need someone to run the camp and I can't think of anyone better than you, Highbrow. I'll remain in command, and we'll make major decisions together."

The two older men walked to an ice chest and pulled out a few beers. Sturgis leaned against the railing, while Nomad handed a beer to Highbrow. He opened it and drained half the can. Nomad offered one to Cadence, but she refused.

"So, if I'm the new captain," began Highbrow, "I should be responsible for selecting teams to go into town. We need someone to keep people in line, like Blaze. In fact, I think she should be our new Sarge. She likes to boss people around, so she should do it officially."

"I don't want to be the new Sarge, and I don't want to babysit," said Blaze. "But I can give great archery lessons and would love to help Dragon train the people how to fight. Barbarella has done her best training archers, but I can do better. Let Freeborn and Luna handle security."

Highbrow finished his beer and opened another. Cadence had never seen him drink before. He had an angry look in his eyes.

"Why don't you have Nomad and Sturgis be our new mechanics?" asked Freeborn. "Most of the trucks we salvaged from the battle are in bad shape. The ATVs need some work too. Of course, I'm just making suggestions here."

"Those are all excellent ideas," said the Professor. "I think Nomad and Sturgis have both proven themselves."

Nomad grinned. "Why thank you, Professor. I appreciate the vote of confidence. We have been through some pretty tough times. You can count on us, commander." He patted Sturgis on the shoulder, who nodded in agreement. "Whatever you need, just ask."

"What about Wrench?" asked Cadence. "I saw him during the fight, but I haven't seen him since. He should remain in charge of the garage."

The Tigers shared a sad glance. The Professor met Cadence's eyes and explained.

"Wrench's injuries are more serious than we realized, Cadence. He was bitten and he chose to stay at the Peak. I'm sorry you weren't told earlier. Highbrow, were any Freedom Army soldiers found?"

"Just the two we picked up at mid-camp," answered Highbrow with increased tension. "Uther has a few ideas about using the old fence and generators to set up our own perimeter, but it will take time. We'll avoid the Peak for a few days until the zombies clear out."

"From now on there will be no separation between patrols and soldiers," said Cadence. She never took her eyes from Highbrow. "I never liked the age requirements or gun restrictions. Everyone is now in the Freedom Army. If Nomad and Sturgis don't want to be soldiers, they'll maintain civilian status like the Professor. Is that okay with you?"

Highbrow glared at her. "Sounds like you have it covered. I'm surprised you asked me to be captain. After last night, I figured Raven earned the right to be your new right hand."

"Raven has some medical training," Cadence maintained an even voice. "Her father was a doctor, and she was a hospital volunteer. She's overseeing the new infirmary."

"Then it's settled." Highbrow kicked the ice chest hard, wincing. Dodger and Smack chuckled. "Everything we've come to know and love in the last year is now gone. You're in command of the new Freedom Army." He grabbed another beer, opened it, and took a long swig before continuing. "Bet it makes you proud to have us wearing those damn blue berets. Do we get to wear dog tags too?"

"You can have a leash," said Cadence. "Keep it up and I'll put you in a dog house. What is your problem, anyway?"

"He needs a rabies shot," Blaze snorted.

Freeborn stood. "I'm going to find Dragon and look around camp, but we'll be back. The fish on the grill smells good."

With a gesture for Highbrow to follow, Cadence walked to the side of the cabin. He followed her, still chugging his beer and stopped beside a pool of water. Cadence stalled while Highbrow stared up at a waterfall. Dusk was falling and Cadence imagined two monster children standing on a cliff somewhere watching.

"You have an attitude," Cadence began. "Lose it. You're the new captain and my second. I expect you to carry your weight and stop moping. I'm sorry that Savannah is gone. Rafe is gone too. If I knew where they were I'd go get them, but I don't."

Highbrow gave her a strange look. "They're alive? How do you know?"

"Something happened last night that I can't explain. I didn't kill all of those zombies. I couldn't hope to move that fast in my wildest dreams. I took the credit because I didn't want to alarm the others."

"Then who gets credit for all those kills? Bigfoot?" Highbrow finished his beer, crushed the can, and threw it on the ground. "Look, if you're afraid I'm going to be angry, forget it. You saved my life last night. I owe you one."

"I'm not sure what I saw," said Cadence. "Two little kids found me while I was fighting off those zombies. They were Little Leaguers and both were infected, but they weren't zombies. They were something else. The girl told me Rafe is alive, that he's their protector and she's made herself some kind of queen. The boy was Billy, but he now calls himself Lord Cerberus."

"And what about Savannah? How does she fit into this story?"

Cadence felt a tear escape and brushed it away. Tears weren't going to soften the blow. Highbrow would not forgive her.

"A zombie caught me. He was trying to bite me when the boy flew through the air and twisted its head off, and then killed all the other zombies. His strength and speed were unreal. I've never seen anything like it. When he was finished, I saw them both with Savannah. They walked into the forest. She went willingly, Highbrow."

"And you didn't think to raise an alarm?"

Highbrow howled like a mad dog, balled his fist and punched Cadence in the face. She hit the ground and he stood there glaring at her. His face turned blood red. "You knew how I felt about her and you didn't help her! You let those little freaks take her and do God knows what to her, and you're just now telling me about it? That's screwed up, Cadence!"

"They were taking her to Rafe. I'm sure she's alive. They said they selected her."

"Selected for what? Dinner? You knew, Cadence. You knew all this time and you didn't tell me the truth. I hate you so much right now! You're so selfish and conceited. Find yourself another captain. I'm going to find Savannah."

Cadence stood and drew her gun. It seemed crazy to draw a weapon on one of her best friends. "You're not going anywhere, captain." She wiped the blood away from her nose. "What I saw last night wasn't normal. Those kids mutated into something else. They weren't human. I watched that little boy kill more than fifty zombies in less than a minute. There's no way I could have stopped them. You're not going after one girl, Highbrow."

"Savannah's not just a girl to me. She's my friend. You didn't even try to save her," Highbrow said, holding back a sob. "If you want to stop me, you'll have to kill me."

Cadence put her gun away. "This is stupid. I don't want to fight with you. I'm sorry I didn't tell you, but I didn't want you going after her and getting yourself killed. I need you, Highbrow. This camp needs you."

"I told Savannah that I wouldn't let anything happen to her."

Cadence frowned. "It couldn't be helped."

"This is how you wanted it," he shouted. "You wanted her gone and now she is!" He stared at the water, silent. Several moments passed, as did the edge of his anger. "I'm sorry I said I hate you. It's not true.

I don't, but I'm upset, a little drunk, and I'm not handling things very well."

"I don't blame you." Cadence reached out to touch him, flinching when he drew back. "I hate myself right now. This is so messed up. I used to be on the swim team. I used to play the sax. It's another life now. I'm not who I used to be, nor are you."

"I think I'm pretty much the same. The only thing that's changed is my name. I used to be Marc Powers, the math whiz in school, son of the senator-turned-convict. Honest, reliable."

"You still are those things, and more."

"Who did you use to be? I mean, what was your real name?"

"Cadence Sinclair. Nightshadow took one look at me when I arrived and said my name was Cadence. I thought he knew me, but then realized it was a coincidence. It freaked me out at first, but Nightshadow didn't know he gave me my own name. I thought it was fate, so I never said anything."

"You do march to a different beat," said Highbrow, forcing a smile. "I'm sorry. I shouldn't take my frustration out on you. You're doing the best you can, and you're right. I would have gone after her and got myself killed."

Highbrow put his arm around Cadence, but he wouldn't look at her. It felt good being held by him.

He continued. "You were trying to protect me. That's what friends do. I'm going to let you in on a big secret that I've been keeping from you."

"You're in love with me?"

Cadence sounded sarcastic, although it was what she wanted to hear. She put her arm around his waist. He was getting skinnier. When she put her head on his shoulder, he caressed her cheek.

"Well? Why aren't you saying anything?"

Cadence lifted her head and looked into his eyes. He was staring at her, but without any notion of romance. She released him, confused and embarrassed, and stepped back. Highbrow caught her by the arm.

"The Professor found out what was in the black box. It was a classified report written by my father. My dad is alive, Cadence. He's alive!"

"What?" It was the last thing she expected to hear. "He's alive? Where?"

"He's in Florida, in some kind of think tank. That pilot was carrying a report from my father to the President. The Professor thought the pilot might have been trying to deliver it to me, which would mean my dad knows I'm alive. I'd let you read the report, but the Professor burned it. After you told me about those two kids, I knew the report has to be right. It said the virus is mutating. I bet those kids are the next generation of the virus, and if my dad is right, it will keep mutating."

"And is there a cure?"

Highbrow shook his head. "No. My dad said the only cure is death. If they weren't zombies, and aren't human, what are they?"

Cadence's heart was pounding. "What I saw made me think they were superhuman. Your guess is as good as mine, but if they changed into something else, maybe Rafe did too." She paused, remembering the dried blood on Rafe's face, feeling guilty.

"The Professor said those kids got zombie juice in their mouths or eyes. But what's confusing is why this is happening now. Before it was the flu that killed people and turned them into zombies, then it was a bite. Think of how many times we've come home covered in zombie blood. No one got infected that way before. Maybe it was a fluke, but we won't know unless we find Rafe and those kids."

"They moved like lightning and were lethal. They also seemed older than their years and smart. Too smart for kids that age," Cadence recalled. "If Rafe and Savannah are with them, I'd say she's probably been turned as well. I tried to fight back, Highbrow, but the boy had me in some kind of trance. I would have done anything he asked of me, but he let me go and I think it's because of Rafe. Rafe told them he cared about me, so they let me go. But they made threats against you. So again, I think Rafe is behind it."

"I'm glad they didn't take you. I don't know what I'd do without you."

Cadence was startled when Highbrow pulled her into his arms and kissed her. It was not romantic, but more like the kiss of a friend. His warm embrace and soft lips were what she needed. When he pulled back, she knew what needed to be done.

"I want to talk to the Professor about your father's report. We need to tell him about those kids and see if he can figure out what is happening." Cadence put her hand on his shoulder. "I suppose the next thing we need to do is rescue Rafe and Savannah. Maybe they'll want to help us. It could be worth the risk."

"What will you do when you find them?" Highbrow sounded calm. "If their bloodlust is as strong as the zombies, we may have to kill them. The one thing we can be sure of is that the virus is changing. We haven't seen any infected animals, but it could be the next change in the evolution of the virus. Zombie rabbits."

They laughed at the absurdity, realizing nothing was out of the question at this point.

"We'll figure it out as we go along, my captain."

Cadence stole a kiss from Highbrow, adding the passion that lacked in his. She took his arm and led him back to talk to the Professor.

From the corner of her eye, Cadence thought she spotted the flutter of a bee or a dragonfly. She wasn't sure, but she took it as a good sign.

Chapter Fifteen

*M*iramont Castle stirred as night fell.

The scavengers had chosen bedrooms and locked their doors. A few passed out in the living room, and some in the study. Rafe didn't trust the scavengers, and considered them fools to trust their host. He counted forty-nine guests while they slept, including the prisoners. Logan posted guards, but Rafe slipped past unseen. They found sanctuary here and showed no intention to leave.

Rafe waited at the foot of Savannah's bed for her to awaken. "Oh," Savannah sighed. "I must be home in bed. Thank God." She opened her eyes and cried out in alarm. "What am I doing here? Where are Nomad and Highbrow?"

"It's just me. My name is Rafe. You're at Miramont Castle. Your friends left the Peak, and they may be out of state by now. You're here with me, and you're safe."

Rafe moved closer. The girl was lovely. She threw herself into his arms and sobbed. He felt tears chase along his neck. He reached up and cupped her face in his hands, drawing her head back. Her tears were tears of blood. Instead of wiping them away, he raised her lip and exposed her fangs.

"You're one of us now," Rafe said. "There's no going back to the others. Highbrow is no longer safe with you. I think you should look in the mirror and try not to scream."

"Why? What's wrong with me?"

Savannah pushed Rafe aside and flung herself from the bed. She ran to a mirror and stared at her image. In a fit of rage, she knocked everything off a nearby table. Bottles of perfume and animal figurines fell with a crash. Rafe feared the noise would attract the scavengers, or worse, the children. The drapes were closed and the room was dark, and Savannah's eyes began to glow an iridescent shade of blue. She grimaced at her reflection and bared her fangs.

"Am I a vampire?" Savannah pierced her fingertip with a fang and sucked away the blood. "Yum." She drew her finger away from her mouth. "Did I just say yum?"

"We have a problem," said Rafe. "Our queen and lord will be waking up soon. I expect they'll want to sample the new menu. We have about fifty scavengers here under the leadership of a guy named Logan, along with some of my Freedom Army friends. Logan's okay and keeps his people in line, but when they get a look at those two little freaks there'll be trouble."

Savannah started opening drawers and tossing garments, searching for suitable clothes. She found panties and a lace bra, then sped over to an ornate wooden wardrobe and swung the doors wide. Inside were dresses and ball gowns, and a few items of men's clothing. She chose a black silk dress with spaghetti straps.

Rafe watched as she stripped naked and dressed in her new clothes, returning to the mirror to brush her long, red hair until it curled around her shoulders.

He was taken. "You're beautiful," said Rafe with sincerity.

"Change out of that stupid Army getup and put something else on." Savannah turned, admiring her reflection in the mirror. "I thought vampires couldn't see themselves in mirrors?"

"I don't think that's really what we are, but I guess it will do."

Savannah chose a set of clothes for Rafe. He knew nothing of her, but he imagined she had been much nicer as a human. The virus had brought out a petty, nasty side of her personality, like it had with the children. He himself had experienced no fear since his infection.

Savannah tossed a pair of black slacks, a black turtle-neck sweater, and fresh socks onto the bed. She watched as Rafe undressed. When he was standing naked, she moved close and sniffed him.

"I'd rather you not bite me." Rafe felt her lips nibbling at his neck, and then her tongue slide along his collarbone. "And we don't have time for that either."

"You're no fun," whimpered Savannah. "Don't you want to play with me?"

"Not now!" Rafe pushed her away. "There are fifty humans here, and I need to go downstairs before those kids turn this place into a morgue. Something has happened to us I can't explain. I don't know if it was my bite or my blood that turned you into whatever it is we are. If our host and hostess turn homicidal, they'll give birth to their very own vamp family."

"Really? Could I bite someone?" asked Savannah, clapping her hands. "Every inch of my skin is crawling and I'm so hungry. I like you so much better than Highbrow. Are we going to be together now? Will it be forever?"

"I don't know. Stay here and wait for me. I'll bring you something to eat?"

"Like what?" she whined, sliding her hands down her neck. "Let me bite one, Rafe. Come on. I've done much worse than hide when zombies attacked. Back in Deadwood, I threw a kid into the path of those ghouls so I could get away. I felt bad then, but not now. I'm relieved to finally tell someone. I feel incredible. It's like being inside a dream where I have so much strength I can tear anyone apart who tries to hurt me. You can't imagine how incredible it feels to finally be free." Her eyes were wide, enthralled in a morbid power trip.

"Our ideas of being free aren't remotely similar," said Rafe. "For the first time I know what I'm doing and I want to make up for the wrongs I've done. But you . . . you have no remorse or guilt for what you've done or for what you're about to do."

Rafe finished dressing, and walked into the hallway. He heard Savannah behind him and moved aside for her to prance out of the room. A few people had come to the third floor looking for rooms, despite Rafe's warning to Logan. They greeted Savannah, and then turned to follow her.

Gliding down the stairs, Savannah smiled at everyone she passed. Rafe pushed through the crowd, finding Logan standing at the front door, gazing toward the street. Logan turned and caught sight of Savannah and his entire expression changed. The man stepped back into the shadows as another scavenger walked into the room.

"Savannah," the scavenger said with passion. "I'm at your service."

Savannah moved closer, sniffing at the man's neck. The man showed no concern that a predator was ready to seize him. Charm was not a quality Rafe possessed, but Savannah oozed sex appeal on a supernatural level. The humans weren't able to resist her.

"All of your friends are here, so you need to mingle," said Rafe. Savannah flashed her fangs at him, but the man didn't notice. In the shadows, Logan's hand found his gun.

"Be a good girl and leave him alone," Rafe continued. "You and I are in a relationship that's very special. How are you making everyone swoon over you like you're a goddess?"

"It's just my way," said Savannah. "I couldn't do it before. I want everyone to fall at my feet and worship me. Look at them! They're holding on to my every word and gesture." She tapped the scavenger on the nose. "Hey big boy, want to go to my room?"

Rafe's eyes found Logan in a corner. He noticed how he watched Savannah with suspicion as she played the room.

"I know it's late, but dinner's on," shouted Marge from the kitchen. People funneled into the kitchen, sharing lusty looks with Savannah as they passed by. Rafe noticed the cellar door open and two small forms appear in the foyer. Soon they were among the scavengers and all attention was on them. Cinder and Cerberus found costumes straight from Camelot. A long white gown, laced with pearls, adorned the queen, while the little lord strutted about in a blue velvet doublet, tights, and boots. They collected words of praise and admiration from their new fans.

"Did someone say dinner?" Cinder asked, purring. Her fangs extended.

"Let's eat," Savannah said.

The vampires raced into the kitchen. Screams of terror and frantic scuffling told Rafe all he needed to know. It would be a slaughterhouse within minutes. Logan finally drew his gun, a steeled look on his face.

"Whatever you're thinking, don't," Rafe warned. "If you leave I won't stop you, Logan. But if you're going, do it now."

The tall man took too long, something dark in his expression. Rafe sped to the door, opened it, and propelled Logan outside. Logan stumbled hard down the stairs. Rafe left the door open and went back inside. People scattered in all directions, trying to escape the kitchen. Only those who found the front door lived. A young woman limped into the foyer, blood streaming from two puncture holes in her neck.

She ran toward Rafe. It was a mistake.

Overwhelmed by her scent, he caught hold of her, sinking his fangs into her neck. He lost himself as the warmth filled his mouth. Unwilling to stop, he drained every last drop and let her limp body fall. Eyes aglow, Rafe was at another man's side in an instant, mauling his neck like a savage. He let the body slide to the ground when the man was empty.

Disgusted with his own weakness, Rafe stumbled to the living room and sank into a couch. Several humans were hiding behind the furniture. Pretending they weren't there seemed the best solution, but his indifference didn't last.

"For God's sake," said Rafe. "Open the window and slip into the night, you stupid scavengers. Take your car and leave. You have three seconds. They're coming."

A mad scramble sent them running for the window. One threw a chair through the window and leapt without looking. The other two disappeared through the broken glass an instant before Savannah burst into the room, carrying a woman in her arms. Placing the listless human on the carpet in front of Rafe, Savannah bit into her own wrist and placed the wound against the woman's mouth. She didn't respond. Savannah rubbed her wrist across the slack mouth, growing angry when there was no reaction.

"What are you doing?" asked Rafe. "Is she dead?"

"This is Daisy. I always thought she was attractive, but she never noticed me. Why don't you turn a few? Let's give her your blood and see if that works."

The queen and lord appeared in the doorway, red with gore. The children stared at Rafe as if they were to be punished. Rafe walked into the foyer, seeing bodies and blood everywhere and suppressed the urge to wring their little necks.

"Did you bite everyone?" inquired Rafe. "Are they all dead?"

"Not all." Cerberus leaned into the foyer and beckoned Rafe. "You better get in here. Something is wrong with Daisy. Savannah can't get her to wake up."

Groans and snarls emerging from the living room and kitchen announced their new family had not been turned into vampires. Rafe found a sword hanging on the wall and retrieved it with superhuman speed. He cut down every zombie before the infestation spread further than the foyer.

"Savannah!" shouted Rafe. "Help me!"

"No, Savannah," said Cinder. "Stay here with us. It's Rafe's job to protect us."

With a frustrated yell, Rafe charged into the living room, beheaded Daisy, and returned to the kitchen. Rafe spared the new vampires. With glowing blue eyes they sniffed the air, hungry for what few humans remained in the mansion.

"All of you come in here," said Cerberus, snarling. He herded the vampires into the room and turned toward Rafe. "Search for other zombies and kill them while I explain things to our new friends. If you find any humans, lock them up with the soldiers. We'll eat them tomorrow."

Rafe lifted his hand to strike Cerberus, but resisted when he saw the new vampires ready to attack him. He swung the sword toward the boy and let the tip rest on his small shoulder. Cinder and Savannah clung to one another, fearing for Cerberus' safety, afraid to challenge Rafe. Their pleading looks were all that kept him from killing the demon child.

"This is how things are going to be," said Rafe, angry. "From what I can tell, Savannah can't turn anyone into a vampire, she makes only zombies. But Cinder, Cerberus, and I can make other vampires, so we're the only three who can try it. The rest of you will share your food and kill what you eat. Savannah, no more attempts at making vampires. Ever."

"Don't be mad, Rafe." Savannah's voice sounded bittersweet. "We only did what we're meant to do. The new ones need something to eat. You're going to have to pick someone out and bring them in here. We'll wait."

Feeling like he was in a nightmare from which he would never wake, Rafe brought in the first person he found and left the poor soul with the demons. The task of finding people hiding throughout the mansion proved easy. When Rafe had gathered them all, he placed the scavengers in a room next to the soldiers. Rafe then looked in on the soldiers. Sarge was terrified. The soldiers heard the chaos in the kitchen and begged Rafe for their release.

"Don't try to escape," Rafe told them. "If you do, I may not be able to protect you. This place is now crawling with hungry vampires. I'm the only one who cares and I don't even know why, so don't make me do something we'll both regret."

"But Rafe, you've got fangs," said Sarge. "You're one of them."

"Yeah, I am."

Shutting the door, Rafe returned to the foyer. The new vampires had finished their prey and sat on the floor in front of Cinder and Cerberus. Savannah crept up the staircase, and Rafe went after her. He thought he had checked every room, but Savannah opened a door and screams shook the walls. She twirled into the room and jumped on the bed. Four people crawled out from hiding hoping to escape. Savannah looked under the bed, and pulled a fifth person out by their hair. The woman tore free, leaving a handful of blonde strands in the vampire's grasp.

"There are five lovely people here to eat," Savannah sang out. "Shall we share them or lock them up with the other cattle? Or will you turn another?

"I'd rather not," said Rafe. "I've seen enough tonight."

"You don't have the stomach for this," she accused. "Shall we let one or two escape to spread our little tale of horror? It might reach your precious Cadence. Oh, Cinder told me all about Cadence."

Rafe noticed that Savannah's dress was littered with bullet holes, yet her skin was perfect, unmarred.

"These people were your friends," said Rafe. "Just let them go. Let them go and spread the tale. That should appease your appetite for fear."

"People will hear of us and more will come to try and destroy us. Send them out. I won't say anything."

Rafe led all five humans out. The humans ran to their cars, except for one. He froze and stared at people he had known, peering out at him from the living room. Rafe took the terrified man by the arm and led him outside.

"Listen to me! You have to get out of here!"

"What are you?" asked the man, finding his voice.

"Not sure, modern vampires? I suggest you get into one of those cars, roll up the windows and get out of here. I'm not sure where Logan went, but I'd go south. Get on the highway and keep going, don't ever look back."

Chapter Sixteen

*H*ighbrow sat on a motorcycle peering through binoculars, studying the Broadmoor Hotel. Nomad perched nearby on a Harley. The Fighting Tigers sat behind them in a salvaged Jeep, waiting for Highbrow's decision. The luxury hotel was a disemboweled shell of former glory. The team came into town to find antibiotics for a boy who had broken his leg and was running a high fever. They saw the hotel on the way to the pharmacy and stopped to investigate.

Highbrow handed the binoculars to Nomad. "Take a look. Are they your people?"

Highbrow believed there were pockets of zombies lingering in the city and this hotel was prime for an attack if anybody was around. Nomad scanned the area and grunted.

"What do you think, Mr. Motorcycle? Friend or foe?"

"That's Logan's Hummer," said Nomad. He lowered the binoculars. "Look, you have every reason not to bring anyone else into your camp. I wouldn't blame you for torching the place, but you and I think alike. We believe every human is a soul that needs to be saved. Have it out with Logan later, but we need to make contact and convince any survivors to return with us."

"Oh, I'll have it out with that guy," said Highbrow, feeling his temper rise. "No doubt there, but he has to be crazy to stay around here."

"Men do strange things when they're desperate, son. If Logan's here, it's for good reason. There really isn't anywhere else to go, unless it's the middle of nowhere and game is scarce these days. Starvation and thirst are cause enough to remain in town. We'll have to be careful if we go inside."

"Is that what we're doing?" Highbrow chewed on his lip.

Nomad handed back the binoculars. "It's your call."

"We could use supplies, anyway."

Highbrow glanced back at his patrol. Freeborn manned the mounted M60 and Blaze commanded the wheel. Whisper rode shotgun with a constant eye out for any non-human activity. Dodger and Smack were just happy to be out on patrol and enjoying the ride.

Taking it slow, Highbrow led the team through a street framed by little houses that seemed untouched by time, a true picture of American life before the Scourge. A stray dog crossed in front of them, skinny, but alive. Rounding an overturned school bus, Highbrow and Nomad came close to slamming into a tank abandoned by the National Guard. Picking up speed again, they reached the pharmacy in minutes. The windows were broken, and trash littered the parking lot. Several cars had collided with each other and the corner of the pharmacy, but all seemed quiet otherwise. No zombies lingered, and there were no dead bodies anywhere in sight.

Highbrow and Nomad dismounted and paused to put on protective gear. Dodger joined them carrying a large duffle bag and filed in behind Nomad. Nomad raised his shotgun and walked through the frame of where the entrance once greeted customers. Glass crunched under their boots as they spread out to study the building. Dodger stayed behind Nomad, grabbing items off the shelves as they moved along. Highbrow brought up the rear, remaining vigilant. He knew they were never really alone.

"Hurry up," Highbrow called out. "This place reeks!"

Nomad reached back and grabbed Dodger by the arm. "Kid, get what you're going to get and move fast."

As Dodger scampered off filling his bag, Nomad walked the aisles, stuffing his pockets with more supplies. Highbrow moved with caution following Nomad, expecting a wanderer to appear any moment. Dodger slid behind the pharmacy counter where the best meds were kept. Within minutes, they had what they needed and a lot more.

"I really scored," Dodger grinned. "If we could sell this stuff, we'd be rich. I grabbed a few inhalers for Luna. She has asthma, you know."

Highbrow signaled thumbs up as a loud groan came from the back of the store.

Highbrow readied his pistol as Nomad and Dodger hurried through the shattered storefront. A grandma who never made it out of her curlers and slippers spotted Highbrow and moaned with hunger. She shuffled toward him as best she could with one eye hanging from its socket. Highbrow placed a bullet in her skull, splattering the shelves with black ooze before her face met the floor.

Dodger shouted at Highbrow and he spun in panic. Sneaking up behind him was a former baseball player, missing his lower jaw and an arm. Nomad pulled Highbrow behind him and put a round in the walker's ball cap. Black blood sprayed their goggles. Highbrow was glad for the protection and ripped the mask off in disgust.

"Sorry man, didn't mean to shout," said Dodger, fighting back panic.

"It's all good." Highbrow patted Dodger on the shoulder. "Thanks for getting my back."

"Let's get out of here. Apparently zombies like drugs," suggested Nomad.

They returned to their bikes, reloaded and did a quick wipe of their gear. Taking a moment to breathe in the cool air, Highbrow strapped on his riding goggles and scanned the deserted streets. Freeborn, Blaze, and Whisper were locked, loaded, and eyes peeled.

"Where now, boss?" Smack inquired. "All that gunfire is sure to bring in more. We need to get moving."

"We're headed to the Broadmoor Hotel," said Highbrow. "Nomad identified people he knows there. We don't know if they are in trouble or will cause it, so no screwing around. This is as close to a Code 4 as you can get while on patrol." He noticed movement on the street. It was the stray dog running from a slow moving group of zombies. "Let's head out."

The team threaded their way back to the main street. For a moment it was clear, then zombies came coursing out of doorways, appearing behind abandoned cars and dumpsters trying to corral them. Freeborn fired into the pack, cutting into their numbers as they cruised through town. As they approached the hotel, a few stragglers appeared and Freeborn dispatched them with pleasure.

Highbrow drove around and parked near the back door, while Nomad circled Logan's Hummer and a number of other vehicles parked near it. Blaze brought the patrol to a screeching halt near Nomad and jumped out.

"Did you see all of those zombies?" Smack exclaimed, chomping her bubble gum. "This place is crawling." Dodger punched her in the shoulder.

She returned the favor and snapped. "Stop that!"

"Knock it off, we're going inside. Get ready," said Highbrow. "Nomad, you can do the talking if we run into your friends. Freeborn, Whisper, stay with the vehicle and watch the perimeter. Blaze, bring up the rear."

Finding Logan, or anyone else, would be difficult and Highbrow knew it. Hotels were great locations for zombies to hide, and searching them was dangerous. They entered the demolished lobby, streaked with blood and signs of mayhem.

Dodger let out a soft whistle. He pointed his rifle toward a zombie missing the flesh from his face, staggering through a side hallway. Blaze stepped forward and engaged her crossbow, making her mark between its eyes.

"We'll search the floors in groups," whispered Highbrow. "Blaze,

Dodger, and Smack, you guys take the even floors. Nomad and I will search the odd ones. Don't waste time and don't take chances. We'll meet outside in thirty minutes."

"Let's just go honk the horn a few times," Blaze said. "If this Logan turkey wants to join us, then he'll hightail it or we'll leave him. Duh!"

Highbrow glared at Blaze, who made a face in return and walked away with Dodger and Smack. Highbrow and Nomad crept through the first floor, checking all the major dining rooms and event halls. Any zombie they found had been recently killed.

"As much as I dislike this guy, I respect how thorough he is." Highbrow walked out from a sports bar, gifting Nomad with a bottle of whiskey. "Just don't drink it until we get home. There's more if we want to make a trip back into town later."

"I prefer dirty martinis," said Nomad. "Ever have a Manhattan?"

"No idea what that is, unless you mean a girl from New York. Then the answer is no."

The first floor was vacant, so they took the stairs to the third floor. Lifeless zombies were strewn through the stairwell and into the hallway. Highbrow assessed the rooms on the right, and Nomad the opposite. In every room, Highbrow discovered a different scene. People had committed suicide, starved to death, or were rotting in tubs. Some had died as humans, others had experienced two deaths.

By the time Highbrow met with Nomad again, his new friend had picked up two more rifles, a backpack, and a loaded revolver. Highbrow didn't think to gather anything along the way. He was so used to the old rules that he let an opportunity slip by. Running footsteps brought Dodger their way. He was alone.

"We've got problems," catching his breath. "We looked out the windows from the sixth floor and all those deadheads we left back at the pharmacy found their way here. Freeborn and Whisper aren't where we left them either. We can hear gunfire, so I think they drove around the hotel and are circling back."

"Logan has to be here," said Nomad, then shouted as loud as he could. "Logan!" His voice echoed through the hallway.

"We need to make a run for it?" Dodger tapped the end of his revolver against his cheek. "Nobody is here. Let's take the Hummer and blow this joint. Blaze can hotwire anything with wheels. So?"

Highbrow looked at Nomad. "We can't wait for Logan and his buddies. I'm not getting pinned down in a hotel," He pointed to Dodger. "Go get the girls and meet us in the lobby. Get Whisper on the radio and tell them to go back to the motorcycles and clear out those zombies. We'll hold them off until you get back downstairs."

"Right!" Dodger took off.

As Highbrow and Nomad reached the first floor, they saw the faces of a hundred strangers, twisted and mangled, crowding the front doors of the hotel. At the back, they saw a mob of zombies moving across the field in the direction of Seven Falls, as if they could smell meat a mile away.

Smack, Blaze, and Dodger hit the first floor running. Dodger skidded and slammed into a wall, laughing. All three had picked up bags on their way and filled them with all manner of goodies. Blaze was wrapped in a gaudy feather boa with gold and silver chains beneath. Rings circled each of her fingers. Smack was holding a black mink hat to her head, and Dodger held up his arm to show Highbrow his new collection of watches.

"You guys are nuts," said Highbrow. "You get through to Whisper?"

Dodger nodded. "Yep, my walkie works fine. They're driving around to pick us up. Said they saw someone on the sixth floor we didn't see."

Heavy gunfire indicated the vehicle's location. Highbrow led them outside to see a throng of zombies in pursuit. The team fired on the creatures and helped clear a line to the Jeep. "Hey, Cap," yelled Dodger. "I have a present for you."

"I don't want a watch."

"I snagged a few comic books for you back at the pharmacy. One is a Superman."

Highbrow didn't think Dodger remembered stealing his comics in high school, much less caring about it now. He felt petty holding a grudge all this time. Being in a life and death situation brings perspective like nothing else, thought Highbrow.

Whisper pulled up close to the team, the motorcycles were surrounded by advancing zombies.

"After you, captain," said Dodger.

Highbrow climbed in back as the others squeezed in over top of each other. As Whisper began to drive away, Nomad noticed someone he recognized waving from a sixth floor window.

"That's my Betsy. We have to wait," shouted Nomad.

The Tigers continuing firing as zombies multiplied around the corner of the hotel. Stragglers appeared in the field behind their position. Freeborn fired the big gun until it whirred empty of ammo, then picked up her shotgun and never missed a beat.

"They better hurry and get down here," shouted Highbrow. "Circle the parking lot and give them some more time. These creatures are getting too close and we're running low on ammo."

The zombies' putrid march never ceased. Whisper drove around the large herd that was limping across the parking lot.

Gunfire from inside the hotel alerted the Tigers. They spun around to see Betsy and a group of armed scavengers making their way toward the vehicles in the lot. A man wearing a long, black leather coat walked toward the Hummer. He carried an extended barrel revolver in each hand and shot anything near him. In what seemed like slow motion, he reached the Hummer and slid behind the wheel.

"That's Logan." Nomad waved his arms and shouted, attracting the attention of every zombie in the vicinity.

Whisper wheeled out leading a caravan of six vehicles across the field. Logan brought up the rear of the convoy. The Tigers reserved ammunition as they passed the few zombies stumbling toward them. Whisper drove through the fence separating the field and main road, merging onto Cheyenne Boulevard and leading the group to Seven Falls.

Chapter Seventeen

"Make way!" Star shouted. "We've got wounded!"

Cadence broke from a crowd playing football and met the group of girls descending the long flight of narrow stairs. Star and Raven had joined the Amazons and Head Hunters scouting the Midnight Falls area, but it was clear they had taken some time to go swimming while there.

Two girls bleeding and crying were being carried by their friends. Barbarella was limping. A fourth was carried between Xena and Phoenix, the strongest of the Amazons. The girl they carried was covered by a towel, but Cadence could see by the white curls cascading down that it was Luna. Cadence sent the injured to her cabin. Raven was sobbing and remained with Luna's body as it was carried past.

"Puma," said Barbarella, limping by Cadence. "It got away."

Unbridled tears streamed from Star's eyes and she was covered in dirt. Someone had notified the Professor, and Cadence saw him running to her cabin with the soldiers that were picked up earlier at mid-camp, med kits in hand.

"What happened, Star?" asked Cadence. "Are you okay?"

"No, I'm not. Luna is dead. It was on us before we realized we were being hunted." She heaved for air. "Barbarella tried to chase the puma off, but it tore into Luna and Calypso. It dragged Calypso off into the trees. I think it has rabies, Cadence. It was frothing at the mouth and its eyes were blood red."

"What's wrong?" shouted Thor. He and Dragon ran to meet the girls, followed by the newly formed Elite.

"It's Luna," Star explained again. "We were attacked by a mountain lion at the pond. Calypso is dead, too. Barbarella was bitten, and so were Sheena and Skye."

Thor stepped toward Star. Dragon grabbed his arm, shaking his head.

"We will find time for comfort later," said Dragon. "We have a job to do. Commander, do we have permission to take the Elite and look for the puma?"

"Get on it and be careful," said Cadence. She watched the young men, and the newly formed Elite ascend the stairs. It was strange, yet satisfying for Cadence to watch a new force under her command move into action. The Elite were led by Uther, and had adopted Freedom Army uniforms as their own. Cadence turned back to Star. "Thor and Dragon will get the job done."

"They can't go up there. It's not safe." Star gasped for air again and wiped her face. "Something was wrong with that cat. We were all in the water, but it attacked us anyway. It swam out to attack Luna and Calypso, and it was strong, Cadence. Way too strong for a normal cat."

"It's infected with the virus," Cadence deduced. She lifted her voice. "Thor!" He turned to acknowledge her. "The mountain lion is infected with the virus! Not rabies!"

"Got it!" Thor yelled. He stormed the stairs, followed by Dragon, Uther, and the Elite.

Cadence embraced Star and saw that many had gathered on the porch. Teams still wore their old caps, which made it easy to identify them.

"This is a Code 2, people. We have a perimeter breach. If you see a wild cat, shoot to kill. I want the Blue Devils and Bull Dogs walking the road. Panthers, take a vehicle and go tell everyone at the entrance what's happened. Black Beard, take the Buccaneers and guard the stairs. Make sure that cat doesn't get down here. Get moving people. You have your orders!"

"It's not your fault," Cadence said, hugging Star. "I'm just glad you're okay. Why would you go swimming when you know the camp isn't secure yet? Didn't you post a lookout?"

Cadence received no answer, and she knew her questioning was making it worse. Star was in shock.

Cadence instructed someone nearby to get Star something to drink and find the rest of China Six, then walked Star to a bench to sit down. Some members from the Monster Squad joined them. They were the youngest patrol in the camp and struggled to find their place in all the fighting and tension.

"Hey guys, stay here with Star," said Cadence. "She needs some friends right now." She looked to Star, "I'll be right back. Stay here and take a minute to gather your thoughts. We're going to get through this somehow."

Cadence found the Green Hornets standing guard at HQ. She entered expecting to see Luna's body. People lined the sides of the room as Sterling, Wizard, and Dill cared for the wounded. The Professor, Xena, and Phoenix stood over Luna's body. Raven crouched in a corner, sobbing.

Cadence pushed in to stand beside the Professor, watching as the beach towel was pulled back from Luna's body. Her torso was ripped open, exposing what remained. Sterling quickly covered her body again.

"She's dead," howled Raven. "Luna is dead!"

"I tried to keep Raven out," said the Professor. He put his arm around Cadence. "I'm so sorry this has happened. I don't know much about mountain lions, but I've never heard of one attacking without reason. Did any of you notice any cubs about? A mother might protect her young and attack out of fear."

"I don't think that was the problem," said Cadence.

The Professor released Cadence and put his hand on Xena's shoulder. "Tell us what happened. No one is angry with you, Xena," said the Professor. "We just want to know about the cat that attacked you."

Cadence knelt and put her hand on Luna's arm. It was still warm.

"Barbarella, what happened up there?" asked Cadence. "Star said the puma had rabies, but it sounds like it had the virus."

The leader of the Amazons wasn't quick to answer. She was not easily rattled. "I don't know, commander. We were all swimming when we heard this horrible roar. The cat swam out and attacked Luna, first, then Calypso. Raven and I both shot it. It started dragging Calypso into the trees and then attacked me. Sheena and Skye got in the damn way trying to help me and the thing bit all three of us, then dragged Calypso's body away. I know Raven and I shot it more than once. I don't know if it had rabies or something else. We didn't stick around to find out. That's all I know."

"The cat was messed up," said Sheena. "Rabies or something. We didn't do anything to make it attack and there weren't any cubs." She slapped Dill's head as he bandaged her leg. "Ouch! That hurts, you know."

He apologized and finished the binding.

"Is that it?" asked a worried Skye. She pushed back a strand of hair from her eyes. "Don't we get a rabies shot?"

Barbarella glared at her teammate. "Your voice is piercing, Skye. Bring it down a notch." She turned back to Cadence. "I've never seen anything like it. Back home I used to go hunting with my dad and brothers all the time. This animal moved like it was possessed. We're lucky any of us survived."

"Thor and Dragon went to hunt the cat," said Cadence. She put her hand on the big girl's shoulder. "You need to rest, Barb. We'll get this sorted out. The rest of you girls don't need to be in here. Xena, Phoenix, take charge and clear this room. I'll leave the Green Hornets outside as guards. Go get cleaned up and find me later to fill out a report."

"Thanks, commander." Barbarella collapsed in a chair and hung her head.

Sterling approached Cadence and gestured for her to walk with him outside. They walked to where Star sat, and seeing her team surrounding her, gave the group a wave and continued on to the snack shop.

"What is it, corporal? I remember you. I didn't know you were a medic."

"That's right," he said. "You did me a favor."

"If you can call saving your life a favor, then yes, that's what I did. I hope your name means you're of sterling character, trustworthy."

"Nightshadow thought so. If a man can't be honest, he's nothing in my opinion. I try to live up to it."

Cadence liked his response. "What did you want to tell me, Corporal Sterling?"

"Everything we touch is toxic. We need to be more careful. The slightest cut or blister can be a gateway to infection. The Professor told me the virus is mutating. Of course he asked me not to tell anyone, but seeing you're the new commander . . ."

"I already know," Cadence said. "We can't be sure of anything until Thor brings back the carcass."

"My point is that three girls were bitten, and two are dead. The injured won't die of the bites, but there's still risk of infection. If its rabies, I can treat them. If it's anything else, I'm not sure they'll recover. I'm also not sure they won't show signs of aggressive behavior and attack like the puma. I heard you put Freeborn in charge of security. You may want someone with a little more experience to have that job."

She narrowed her eyes. "And I suppose you want the job."

"I'm not only a medic. I'm also a soldier." Sterling's dark eyes were intense. It was no wonder he had survived the Peak to live another day. "People are starting to drop around here, commander. What are you going to do about it? Pass out aspirin and disinfectant wipes?"

Cadence was shocked by his assertiveness. "An infected puma attacked my friends. It's not like I could plan on something like that occurring."

"As the leader you have to plan for everything, especially the unthinkable. You have to be ready for an attack at any moment of every day. There's no rest for those in command. The Captain did his best, but didn't survive. He was the best of us and now he's dead."

"Look, corporal, I bust my butt around here, in case you haven't noticed," said Cadence. "If you want me to start thinking of everything, then we might as well shoot every animal we see. The Captain was a good man and I'm sorry he's dead. If you believe you can handle security better and make this place safer, let's hear your ideas."

"Placing guards at key strategic points twenty-four-seven would be a good start. When guards break for meals, no one takes that duty. That has to stop. And no more hikes or swims. We all stay at the camp. A team can stand guard at the top of Midnight Falls. Station teams in shifts. When we get the electric fence up, we can adjust. Sound good?"

Cadence nodded. "Yeah, it sounds good."

Sterling was right about everything he said. The loss of life was unacceptable. Cadence was responsible. *Plan for the unthinkable. An impossible task*, she thought. Being in command was difficult, but Sterling seemed willing to help.

"Anything else?" Cadence asked.

"Some of you have seen more combat than a lot of vets. I was in Afghanistan for three years and I knew men like Sarge. Now that he and the Captain are gone, I'm the one on your team with the most experience. I can help Captain Highbrow with the patrols and assigning new officers in the Freedom Army."

"I'll bring it to Highbrow and let him decide how to best use your skills. I appreciate you stepping forward. I'm sure this flip-flop in command is difficult for you."

The sound of vehicles approaching alerted them both the scout patrol was returning. Cadence and Sterling rounded the building and headed toward the path. The Vikings and the Green Hornets formed a defensive line behind their commander. The team stopped in front of Cadence.

Highbrow jumped out. As always, seeing Highbrow made Cadence relax and she wished she could throw her arms around him.

"We got everything on your list and more," said Highbrow. He looked around, noting the guards and met her gaze. "What happened?"

"A lot."

Cadence tried her best to sound normal. Nomad walked up behind Highbrow and held up a backpack.

"Great," said Cadence. "Take those to my cabin, Nomad. The Professor needs whatever you've brought us." She took Highbrow by the hand. "I don't know how to say this, so I'll just say it. Luna is dead. So is Calypso. They were killed by a mountain lion. Luna is in my cabin, but the puma dragged Calypso off. Three other girls were injured, including Barbarella."

"What? I'm so sorry," Highbrow said. "Luna was your friend."

"The puma is infected," interrupted Corporal Sterling.

Cadence dropped Highbrow's hand and gestured toward the soldier. "You met Corporal Sterling last night. I'm putting him in charge of security. He's a combat veteran with more experience than any of us. I believe he can help us in that area. I'll inform Freeborn."

"We saw a little action ourselves," said Highbrow. "You might want to send Sterling to the front entrance. We were followed, and not just by zombies. We've brought a few people into camp. They're scavengers, Cadence. We found them holed up at the Broadmoor Hotel. Their leader, Logan, came with us."

The convoy of vehicles pulled up. Cadence watched a tall man climb out of a Hummer. There were about ten scavengers in total. Sterling bristled at the sight of them.

"Is this their leader?" Cadence kept her voice low.

"Yep, that's Logan," said Highbrow. "He's a friend of Nomad's. He says we can trust him."

"Trust the man who led the attack against our camp because one of his men said he's trustworthy? Highbrow, how could you bring them here?" Cadence let out a sigh. "What am I saying? Of course you rescued them and brought them here where it's safe. I won't ask what happened. I'm sure you did the right thing."

Cadence looked at Sterling. Logan and Sterling were sizing each other up. Both were tall men and powerfully built, but arrogance seized Logan and made its presence known.

"Corporal Sterling, take the Vikings to the entrance," said Cadence. "Secure the barricade. Recruit whoever you need."

He nodded. The Vikings lined up with a few more strong recruits and they moved out. Cadence watched as they made their way to the entrance, and then turned to face the scavengers.

Chapter Eighteen

"So this is the famous Commander Cadence!"

Cadence stood her ground. She discerned the man was conceited, unpredictable, and therefore dangerous. His eyes were full of malice, and she disliked him at once.

"You're Logan, right?"

"This is Commander Cadence," said Highbrow, "and I'm Captain High—"

"I'm sure you are," Logan interrupted. He extended his hand, adorned with a silver skull ring. "Not going to shake? I don't bite." He lowered his hand. "You're a little young to be in charge, but then, most of your soldiers are nothing more than kids. I expected someone other than a pretty little girl."

Cadence glared at Logan, unimpressed. "You must not get it, Logan. Because of you, a lot of people have died. Our camp was destroyed and now we've got zombies coming to our new site. Honestly, I'd like nothing better than to shoot you. All you had to do was contact our captain and ask him to let you through the gate. Cross me or try to injure anyone in this camp and I will decimate you."

"You always like this?" Logan sounded amused.

"Pissed off and mean? Yes, always! I thought I told you to bring a flag."

Logan held up his hands. "I surrender!"

Cadence fumed.

"The last thing we want is more trouble," said Logan. "Okay, so I didn't handle things right and the Peak fell. I admit I was wrong. I'll even admit I deserve to be shot and tossed out to the zombies, and you almost got your wish. If Nomad and your pal, Captain Highboy, hadn't shown up and saved our asses, you wouldn't have the pleasure of meeting me. But hey, it's been a rough couple of days and I'm throwing myself at your feet."

"Charming," said Cadence. "This is Captain Highbrow. Show him respect and knock off the cute remarks. Highbrow saved your lives. I hope it was worth it."

Logan held his hand out again. His confidence was infuriating. She ignored the offer.

"Get your gear and set up camp in the tunnel, Mr. Logan. We have cots and sleeping bags in there. All other buildings are booked solid. Sorry."

"It's just Logan. My last name is—"

"We have no last names here. I don't want to hear it."

"Not a problem. Nor are your rules, commander."

Whisper and Freeborn led the newcomers to the tunnel. Logan and Nomad shook, glad to see each other again.

"Welcome home, you scallywag," said Nomad. "You smell horrible."

"Not as bad as you." Logan laughed. "Seems you found the perfect spot to camp. One entry point cuts down the odds of probability. No matter what happens, I can always rely on you to land on your feet."

"I'm part cat." Nomad quipped.

Cadence found the comment in poor taste. They were not aware of what had happened, but it still pissed her off. When the two men started chatting as if she and Highbrow were invisible, she considered tossing them both out of camp.

"Did you see the corporal? He's a hard one," said Logan. "Pure army. Several generations I'd wager. Pity I didn't get a chance to shoot him last night."

Cadence didn't let the remark pass. She turned and put a foot in Logan's gut. He let out a woof and bent over, coughing hard. Nomad stepped between them, lifting his hands high.

"Tell your friend to mind his mouth," said Cadence. "If he causes any trouble, any at all, he's out the door along with the rest of you. You're an okay guy, Nomad, but I'm not in the mood for games. It's my way or leave."

Highbrow cleared his throat. "Nomad," he said, in a soothing voice, "please explain to your friend how things work around here. Cadence means what she says. He'll need to learn that fast."

"Logan, tone it down. We don't need any trouble," Nomad grizzled. His expression changed and he let out a shout as he looked past Logan. "Betsy! You beautiful, crazy dame! You made it! Come give me a hug!"

With a belly laugh, Nomad ran forward with open arms and embraced a woman with the scavengers. Betsy returned the gesture and the two met with excitement. He lifted her into the air and spun her around. When Nomad set the wild blonde down, he gave her a kiss that left everyone watching feeling lonely. Cadence couldn't help but like the guy. Logan didn't realize how close he was to exile. Nomad was his saving grace.

"Wow," Betsy blushed. "You really did miss me!"

"We'll catch up later," Nomad gave her a wink. "I'm having a chat here with the command team. Go join the rest of the gang and tell them we've found a new home."

"Where's Savannah?"

Nomad's smile faltered, but he gave her a comforting hug. "It's going to be all right. Promise."

As Betsy turned to leave, Sturgis met up with her. They walked away giggling and chattering as if nothing in the past twenty-four hours had happened.

"We need to talk, Commander," said Logan. "In private, if you don't mind."

"Why?" demanded Cadence.

"What I have to tell you might cause a bit of a panic."

"If you've got something to say, then you can share it with my team," said Cadence.

She led Highbrow, Nomad, and Logan to a table under a tree. Nomad plopped down on a bench beside Logan.

"So?" prompted Nomad. "What happened to you after I last saw you?"

Logan fumbled with his hands for a moment. Cadence noticed the tattoo of a snake that curled around his neck. She was scrutinizing too closely and letting her emotions rule.

"I don't have all night, gentlemen." Cadence's voice was sharp.

Logan stared at her long and hard before he shared his experience at Miramont Castle. He spoke of Rafe and two demon children. Cadence recognized the children he described as Cinder and Cerberus, sharing an alarmed look with Highbrow.

"Is Rafe a friend of yours?" chided Logan. "I take it by your reaction that he is, or rather was, a close friend of yours."

"Rafe was a former love interest," said Highbrow.

Cadence nudged him. "Must we?"

"The two kids you mentioned showed up during the battle," said Highbrow. "Cadence observed them as they destroyed over fifty zombies in less than a minute. What you've described are vampires. Of course, they're not really vampires. I mean, there's no such thing as vampires. Zombies aren't the zombies from movies, either. They're humans with a disease that can only be remedied with death. We call them that because they're easier to kill if we think of them as, well, zombies."

"Call them whatever you like, Captain," Logan said with a shrug. "They had fangs, claws, and moved with lightning speed. They sucked blood and enjoyed it. Sounds like a vampire to me." He took a deep breath. "And let's be clear on what happened before Pike's Peak fell. I had two hundred fifty-three people under my care. I did contact your captain and he told me that you didn't have the resources for more survivors, so he turned us away. Now, I wouldn't have come in guns blazing if we hadn't been desperate. I did what was necessary to give our people a chance to survive. Sure, you took a loss, but I'm down to only twenty souls in less than two days. I had forty of my own people, and nine soldiers when we arrived at Miramont Castle. The soldiers may or may not be alive. I'd be dead if Rafe hadn't thrown me out the door. Maybe I'm wrong, but I don't think he's a killer. Betsy said a fourth vampire tried to kill her. Some girl with long, red hair. I think it was Savannah, but it was all a blur. The way I see it, the vamps pose a bigger threat than zombies."

"Savannah is alive?" Highbrow turned bright pink. "She's a vampire?"

"Yeah," said Logan. "With big teeth. You got a thing for her, pal? Trust me, she's not capable of a long-term relationship. She's a monster now."

Nomad sat back, taking the news pretty hard.

"Stay calm," said Cadence as Highbrow got up from the table and started pacing. "We already know about the two kids. We just didn't know they were vampires. But you said Rafe saved you? That's not like him at all. When Rafe was human, he only cared about himself."

"From what I saw, those kids intend to make an army of vampires. Rafe is the only thing that kept them from killing all of us. Maybe he wasn't such a great soldier, but he makes a damn good vampire. I like the guy."

"Like him?" Highbrow quivered with anger. "It's because of him that Savannah was taken!"

"Son, try to keep things in perspective," said Nomad in a fatherly voice. "I'm sorry about Savannah, but if the virus can turn people into zombies and vampires we're in big trouble. Both multiply fast."

"That's not the only thing out there," said Cadence. "Animals are being infected now. An infected puma attacked two of our teams up at Midnight Falls. Two are dead and three were bitten. Thor and Dragon are tracking it down."

Highbrow turned and faced the table. "How can you be so sure the mountain lion is infected if they haven't caught it yet? Maybe it is rabies?"

Not wanting to argue, Cadence gave Highbrow a stern look. He sat back down, but refused to look at anyone. His inability to act professional had Logan amused.

"I'm sure that animal has the virus," said Logan. "I've seen this before. I think you'd better put the injured girls in quarantine, commander. They're about as safe as a pet zombie and if you don't want anyone else hurt, you should keep them in a cage."

"I can do that," said Cadence. "I'm sorry Highbrow, but Savannah isn't our main concern right now. Nor are the vampires at Miramont Castle. If you'll excuse me, I need to check on my friends and find a way to quarantine them."

"It's nice to know that one of you has brains," said Logan with a know-it-all tone. "I've been killing things weirder than zombies and vampires since I was a kid. My dad was a cop. We tracked down things that aren't supposed to be real, so trust me when I say I know what I'm talking about. Once bitten, even if killed, they'll come back in the form of whatever bit them. With your blessing commander, I think Nomad and I should go up to Midnight Falls and take a look around. I know how to deal with therianthropes."

"Is that what you call them?" Cadence got up from the table. "Fine. You have my blessing. Track that puma down, kill it, and bring it back.

I want to be sure it's a . . . whatever you called it before we start freaking out every time a squirrel runs by."

Logan stood up. "You might want to know how to kill therianthropes and vampires," he said. "A bullet through the heart or head is all it takes. I came loaded with silver bullets, but lead works just as well on a werewolf. Or a werepuma. Hopefully you won't need that when your dead girl gets back up."

Highbrow glanced toward the cabin. "Luna's not dead?"

"The ones that die and come back are the strongest," said Logan. "Come on, Nomad. Let's go find these Vikings and show them how professionals hunt."

"You got it," said Nomad.

A scream filled the air. Whether cat or human, Cadence couldn't tell. More screams escaped her cabin, followed by gunfire. She raced toward HQ with three men on her trail. She imagined Luna and the injured girls as something much more dangerous than she had last seen them.

Chapter Nineteen

Rafe and Savannah watched the soldiers burn the dead from the porch of Miramont. It had taken all day for the humans to clean inside the mansion, scrubbing blood off the walls and furniture, but nothing could be done about the smell of death. The windows on the first level were kept closed. Vampires with sunglasses watched from second story windows, keeping their eyes on a large group of zombies following the scent of burning flesh. When a zombie came within range, vampire snipers ended their hunger.

"I was thinking I might go into town and find supplies for the prisoners later," said Rafe. "Living on dog food isn't going to cut it. These people need food. I know a few places in town where I can get my hands on some canned goods. You want to come with me?"

"This used to be such a pretty place," said Savannah. "I don't want to go into town. It's depressing. Besides, if we both leave there's no telling what Cinder and Cerberus will do to the prisoners. There are far too many vampires here now, and not enough food. You should be looking for survivors, Rafe, not worrying about feeding the ones we're going to have for dinner."

"What made you so unpleasant? You get bullied too much as a human or did you always want to be a bitch?"

"Where are you going?" asked Savannah. "The sun is up."

Rafe didn't bother pointing out that they were standing outside and not turning to ash. Sunlight didn't affect vampires, but the queen and lord remained locked away in their new bedroom refusing to come out.

Annoyed with the entire situation, Rafe walked down the steps carrying an automatic rifle and walked the street that led to Miramont Castle. The snipers stopped targeting the zombies. Left on his own, Rafe began mowing down the mangled-faced corpses lumbering toward him. The road leading to the mansion was clogged with zombies. A staircase near the castle met a path leading back to the main street in Manitou Springs. If he was to visit town tonight, Rafe would need to take the alternate path. He trotted back toward the prisoners.

"We're done with the bodies," shouted Sarge. He kept his expression blank when Rafe approached. "What now? Do you want us to help take out those zombies? If you don't do something about them, they'll overrun this place before dark."

"Or you could let us go," said Destry, his head wrapped in a bandage.

Rafe had rounded up eight more soldiers the past few days, increasing the group to seventeen. The vampires decided to eat the scavengers first and were locked in the basement.

"The road is blocked," said Rafe. "You can't drive out of here. The only way out is by foot and take the stairs. There's no telling how many zombies are in Manitou Springs. If you find a car that still operates, you won't have much gas to get far."

"You know Cadence moved the camp," said Destry. "We'll head to the Falls and take our chances with the gas. It's better than staying here. Come on, Rafe. Help us out."

Sarge bristled. "You're still nothing but a punk. Where's your spine, soldier?"

A zombie wandered from the group to sniff out the remains of a car wreck. The body inside had already been picked clean. The creature turned toward Rafe and the soldiers and expelled a hungry moan.

"Keep your rakes and shovels for protection," said Rafe. "Take the stairs and don't look back. I'll try to give you a few minutes, but the newer vampires might decide to follow you, so don't stop for anything. If you're lucky, you'll find weapons among the dead in town."

"You mean you're letting us go?" Destry motioned to the soldiers. He was surprised when Rafe handed him his rifle. "Why don't you come with us?"

"I'm a vampire," said Rafe. "I don't think Cadence would want me around. Just get going. If you make it to the camp, tell Cadence where I am. Tell her I'm okay." He grabbed Sarge by his collar and pressed his lips to the man's ear. "Tell her I want to meet her Friday night at Midnight Falls. At midnight."

"I'll try to remember that when we're knee-deep in moving corpses trying to get out of here," snapped Sarge. He pulled away from Rafe. "Move out, men."

The soldiers shadowed the side of the mansion and disappeared around the corner. Rafe could hear them running down the stairs. The zombies noticed them and stumbled toward the parking lot. Rafe waited at the door, watching the monsters fill the lot. Only a few figured out where the soldiers had fled and followed them. When the creatures reached the porch, Rafe went inside, locked the door behind him, and retired to his room.

Savannah sat in front of the vanity, gazing at her reflection in a mirror. She had changed into a lavender dress, braided her hair, and was toying with jewelry that didn't belong to her. Being a vampire brought out her natural beauty and amplified it. He figured it was the amount of blood she consumed that added a blush to her cheeks. She turned and held her arms open.

"Come here, my handsome man," she enticed. "Kiss me and tell me something nice. Stay here. Don't go into town."

Despite her beauty, Rafe found his hatred for Savannah grew. "You want a kiss? What about all the other boys? Isn't there someone else you want more? They all flirt with you. It's pretty obvious I'm not your first choice. How many did you seduce before me?"

"There isn't anyone I want more than you. Why do you have to be so mean to me? Why can't you be happy like me? We have everything we want right here."

"I was never a nice guy, Savannah. I loved one person and I couldn't even be faithful to her, so stop pushing. Getting serious is the last thing I want. Whatever this is between you and me is temporary."

Rafe shrugged out of his jacket and moved to kiss her. She wrapped her body around him, pulling herself close. He allowed his thoughts to imagine Cadence.

"I want you," he whispered. His hands caressed her body. "I want you so much, Savannah. Right now."

"But it's still daylight," she said, kissing him. "Shouldn't we be resting?"

"We're not vampires, Savannah. Not the kind you're fantasizing about. Sunlight doesn't burn us and zombies like the way we smell. There is a multitude of them outside, too many for me to kill on my own. If they get inside, they'll eat us all."

"Talk about something else or I'm not going to be in the mood."

A wicked smile seized Rafe's face as he continued to seduce her. He played his kisses along her cheeks, pressing his lips into her neck, and across her collarbone. Her soft moans convinced him she bought his game. Rafe felt her soften against him. He slid his strong hands around her head and whispered in her ear, "Look at me." As Savannah met his gaze, a single, violent twist snapped her head from her shoulders. Rafe's chest was splattered with blood as her body fell to the floor. Without regard, he tossed her head in the fireplace.

"I've wanted to do that since I turned you."

Not wasting another moment, Rafe sped to the small room that imprisoned the scavengers. His only concern was free the prisoners and leave Miramont forever. He opened the door quietly and stared into the darkness. Twelve scavengers crammed into the tight quarters. A few were bitten, but had not yet turned. Sampling humans was the only way to ensure they didn't turn.

"Stay quiet," Rafe told them. "I'm letting you go. Zombies are outside, but if you take the stairs you may be able to catch up with the soldiers. I set them free a few minutes ago. Go east and head to Seven Falls. That's where the survivors have relocated. If you're lucky, you'll reach them."

Rafe led them out into the hallway. He walked beside them, aware vampires were present in both the living room and study. Seeing Rafe with the humans, the vampires paid no mind as they exited through the front; however, zombies were waiting with singular intention. Some of the humans made it to the side of the house, and Rafe gave no further thought to their safety. He left the front door open wide and rushed through the mob of zombies, pushing them aside as he ran to the street. He turned back when he was clear of the throng and witnessed them pouring into the mansion. Screams of vampires filled the night. Rafe laughed as he turned to run.

He found a black Mercedes parked on a side street with the driver's door open. Rafe climbed in and found the keys still in the ignition. If there was a God, he was responsible for the engine roaring to life. Rafe raced toward an unknown future. He wasn't sure where he was going, but he knew what he'd left behind.

Highbrow was greeted by the very scene he'd imagined, yet far more vivid and painful to see. Luna, Barbarella, Skye, and Sheena were gone, a wake of destruction remained. The Professor was dead, along with the six members of the Green Hornets and the two medics. They had been shredded, and the evidence covered the floor and walls. Highbrow assumed the four girls had fled to Midnight Falls, but knew the dead here would rise again.

Logan pushed in behind him and took a quick look around before glancing at Nomad. "We have werepumas, brother," said Logan. "Just like I thought. We're going to have to go hunt them down or they will return."

Cadence stood at the entrance, unable to come further into the cabin. Highbrow wanted to comfort her, but Logan beat him to it. The scavenger put his hand on Cadence's shoulder.

"I know you want to cry," said Logan, "but don't. Your entire camp is at risk. This is the world I grew up in. It only gets weirder from here."

"The Professor is dead," said Cadence. "There is hardly anything left of him. Are Luna and the other girls dangerous? Will they come back and attack others? I thought they could only change at the full moon?"

"These creatures are different from the Old Ones," said Logan. "Old Ones are werewolves from the darkest forests of Europe. Not many of their kind are left in the U.S. I know. I hunted them down and killed them. Old Ones can only change at the full moon, but this is a new virus. I'm not sure if the girls will remember who they used to be. Now they've tasted human blood, they may want more. It's hard to say."

"Enough of this," said Highbrow. He pushed Logan aside and pulled Cadence outside. "It doesn't matter if Luna and Barbarella remember who they were. They're infected. We have to kill all of them. The safety of the camp comes first, and you know that."

"But if they're still human and they remember, they might not be dangerous. I don't want Luna and the others harmed. I only want the infected puma killed. That's a direct order."

Highbrow wasn't pleased when Logan and Nomad joined them. He wanted to talk to Cadence in private, get her calmed down and make sure they were on the same page before taking action. But she'd given a direct order. If he didn't follow her order, he knew there would be consequences.

"You say you can kill those things?" snapped Highbrow. "Get up to Midnight Falls and locate Thor. Let him know what's going on. He's already up there hunting for the infected puma with Dragon and the Elite. Only," he glanced over his shoulder at Cadence, "no harm to the four girls. Cadence doesn't want them killed. I disagree with her, but I support her decision. We'll deal with Luna later."

"You got it, captain. You don't need to tell me twice," Logan said. He and Nomad turned and quick-paced to the stairs.

Highbrow put his arm around Cadence and led her to a railing beside the stream. He had never seen her so upset. She was holding back emotions, but she wasn't handling things well. Highbrow felt there was some way he could step in until she was able to lead effectively again without making a permanent change in command. It wasn't like they had a rigid command structure. They were doing the best they could with what they had.

"I think you better let me handle things," said Highbrow, softening his tone. "At least for now, until you feel better. I'll get a team in here and have the bodies burned. We don't want the Professor and the others growing fangs and tails. Sit down and rest for a bit. I won't be gone long."

She stared at him as though he were a void.

"Cadence, did you hear me? I said go sit down and turn your mind off for a minute."

Instead, Cadence removed her katana from her sheath and walked inside the cabin. Highbrow gave chase. She seemed far too calm as she began slicing the heads off every dead body. Highbrow turned away when she stood over the Professor. It was too much to believe the one man they needed most was no longer alive. He took it hard, but he believed Cadence was losing the capacity to cope.

Cadence walked outside, wiping her blade with a towel. The Blue Devils and Valkyries arrived to give an update on their progress. Highbrow informed them of what had taken place and instructed them to begin cleaning the cabin. He followed Cadence and sat with her.

"Feel better?" said Highbrow, angry. She sighed and he softened his tone. "I'll handle things from here, Cadence. You rest. I mean it. You're not thinking clear right now and I can't be worrying about what you'll do next."

"We're way out of our league, Highbrow. You saw what those things did."

"You gave orders not to kill Luna and the others. Did you change your mind?"

"No. I'm going to sit here a while. Just sit." She fell silent.

Taking charge was the only thing Highbrow knew to do. He established teams, briefed everyone on safety measures, and assigned duties. He sent runners to find Star and the rest of the Fighting Tigers. Highbrow wanted to surround Cadence with her team. Everyone was hustling according to their assigned tasks, and the fire to burn the remains of their friends raged fierce.

The Fighting Tigers arrived without Star. Highbrow wasn't surprised as Star was grieving Luna's death as well and needed distance. Blaze and Freeborn sat on either side of Cadence, while Dodger and Smack leaned against the railing, rifles in hand. Highbrow knew their senses were heightened and ready for another attack. Whisper sat silent.

"Is she going to be okay?" asked Highbrow.

"What do you think, Highbrow?" Freeborn responded.

"Not good," said Whisper.

Highbrow heard voices at the waterfall and hurried to the stairs. Thor, Dragon, and the Elite were exhausted and empty-handed. Dragon was the first to meet Highbrow.

"No luck?" asked Highbrow.

"The trail went cold," said Dragon. "That cat is long gone."

Dragon spotted Freeborn and joined the Tigers. Thor met with Highbrow as the Elite passed by. Raven pushed through the Elite and threw herself into Thor's arms. Her sobs were unfiltered and heart-breaking. The Vikings stood back as Thor held her tight. He looked over her head to meet Highbrow's gaze.

"Did you spot Luna? She and the injured girls turned," Highbrow said, trying to sound calm.

Shock rippled across Thor's face. He set Raven back and stared at Highbrow as if he were mad. "Excuse me? Turned into what?"

"Mountain lions, or, werepumas as their being called."

"Have you gone crazy, or are you serious? Luna turned into a cat?" Thor wrestled with belief.

"I know it sounds crazy, but Luna, Barb, Sheena, and Skye changed. They killed the Professor, the medics, and all of the Green Hornets, but they won't hurt anyone else. Not with their heads cuts off."

"That's messed up," said Thor. He looked at the cabin and held Raven tight. "We'll go back and look for the puma after we take a break. Raven isn't in any shape to help, and I'm sure Cadence and Star are taking this hard. You and I need to step up, Highbrow."

"I'm captain," said Highbrow. "I'm in charge. You do what I say. Got it?"

Thor laughed. "Man, you need to step off. Don't go lording over me now, Highbrow. You're ego is way too big for your own good. Dragon, Uther, and I will go back and look for the puma like I said, and you can take care of the women. It's what you always wanted, right? Take care of Cadence and play house."

"Where is Cadence?" said Raven, lifting her head. "Why isn't she here taking care of things? You two can't be in charge. You're both idiots."

Highbrow held his tongue. Thor laughed.

"You two are horrible," said Raven. She pushed Thor back and her temper flared. "Cadence is carrying a heavy load. She can't do it alone. You know how she felt about Rafe and . . . and now, Luna. I loved Luna, but they were best friends. Both of you need to show some compassion. It's no wonder if she's cracking. I'm surprised it hasn't happened sooner. If she cracks, we all crack. She's the only thing keeping this camp together. You two sure can't."

"Go check on Cadence," Thor said. "Maybe you should take her to see Star and the three of you can hang out for a while. I know you're hurting, and I'm sorry. I really am. I'll take the Vikings back out with me."

Raven nodded.

Thor motioned for Highbrow to follow him. They walked the wooden porch past HQ, and kept walking.

"We looked everywhere for that cat," said Thor. "It's long gone. But we did run into Nomad and the new guy. They may have better luck than we did. I didn't want to say anything in front of Raven, but we may need to kill the werepumas."

Highbrow accepted the cigar Thor offered. He didn't smoke, but it seemed like a good day to start. Thor lit the end for him and then lit his own.

"I don't know what to do," said Highbrow, drawing on the cigar. "Cadence is in shock. I hope Raven and Star can snap her out of it. But hell, they're in no better shape than she is. If it wasn't for you and Dragon, I'd be lost."

Thor scratched his jaw, realizing it had been days since his last shave. "First things first," he said through the thick cloud of the cigar. "Nomad and this Logan can track down the puma. As for us, we can work on bringing order back to the camp. I regret giving you so much crap in the past. You're doing fine as Cadence's second. But that's just it. Cadence is the commander and she's out of commission for now. You need to start appointing new officers before it catches up with you."

"Okay, you're a corporal." Highbrow didn't take Thor serious. They never liked one another, and Highbrow wasn't ready to start now.

"I don't want to be a corporal," said Thor. "I need more power than that if I'm going to get things done. I'll help you figure out what to do about the puma problem. Have everyone sleep in the tunnel tonight and post squads at the entrance. Whisper and the other snipers can stand guard at the lookout point. Hell, I'll take first watch with my team, then Dragon's, and then yours."

"Wow, you just eliminated the leaders of two of those teams. It's Star's team and Cadence's team."

"No, it's the Freedom Army, and you assume command when she's not able to." Thor blew smoke into the air. "I know things are bad. Trick is not to feel guilty about who lives or who dies. I'm sorry about the Professor. We needed him, but he's gone. All you have to do is make nice and get everyone in line. People need a leader, Highbrow. Right now, that's you."

"You're handling this better than me. Why don't you do it? I quit."

"Grow up," Thor gruffed. "Dragon and I have been searching those trails for hours without a rest. We're worn out. I'm too tired to lead. That's your job. Send Whisper up to Eagle's Point to watch for intruders and deploy security teams. Appoint officers and rely on them to carry out your orders. Get it together, Captain. Right now, I don't think you're in any better condition than Cadence to lead this ragtag group."

Thor blew smoke in Highbrow's face. Highbrow stepped away, coughing. He looked at his cigar and tossed it with an angry flick. Highbrow was fuming inside, but held it in and stared at the ground.

"Hell, there's no fight left in you," said Thor. "I'm going to do you a favor, Highbrow, and give you some suggestions. First, get your butt down there and attend the funeral. They're burning the Professor and the Hornets, and you need to say a few words. Then, go talk to the Head Hunters and Amazons. Combine their teams and put Xena in charge. They don't need to sit around moping, so have them patrol the park road. Ask the Valkyries to patrol with them. Seeing those hot girls walking up and down the road carrying swords and battle axes, wearing their weird helmets and breastplates, will boost camp morale. You've got to get people's heads up and create some harmony. Work with what you've got and roll with the punches."

"You've changed since the last time I saw you," said Highbrow, impressed and humbled. "I feel useless. I found strength in the Professor and Cadence. I'm lost when she's down. I love her."

"Yeah, well, we're not all perfect. Suck it up and be a man. I'll go back to Midnight Falls and you get out there and act like you're in control. Fake it if you have to, Highbrow, but get out there and keep it together. Cadence will snap out of it."

Thor gave a whistle and the Vikings joined him. Dragon kissed Freeborn and joined them as they departed for Midnight Falls. Highbrow sent a runner to find Xena and Phoenix.

Highbrow took a walk around camp, encouraging everyone and reassuring them everything would be okay. Several people called out 'captain' and grinned when they saluted. Highbrow saluted back, and felt good about it. He hopped on a four-wheeler and rode down to the bonfire. The Valkyries passed him on their way up to the main camp, leaving the Panthers and a handful of others to watch the fire. No words came to Highbrow. He didn't make a speech, but he remained until there until the fire turned to embers and helped the Bull Dogs fill in the pit.

By the time Highbrow returned to camp, the sun was setting. Tents had been set up under the trees, and everyone was settling down for the night. Campfires were burning, a group was tossing a football around, and morale seemed up. Highbrow located the Tigers and found Dodger, Smack and Blaze tidying up and putting away their gear. Freeborn sat on a blanket, cleaning her shotgun.

"Hey," said Whisper, walking up behind Highbrow. "It's not so bad right now. Saw you talking to the patrols. Did good."

"Think so?" Highbrow wasn't used to hearing Whisper talk. It was even stranger receiving a compliment from him.

"Yeah. Saw a honeybee earlier today. Haven't seen one since spring. Good omen. There's hope. Anyway, that's what Freeborn says."

"We survived," said Freeborn, looking up.

"And we're still together," Smack added.

Highbrow returned to HQ and found the Bull Dogs waiting for him. After spending some time with them at the fire, he decided to make them his personal guards. The former captain had his own guards, so it seemed like a good idea. Highbrow entered the cabin and found it clean. Apart from the boarded up window, there was little evidence to suggest a massacre had taken place here. Rugs were brought in from the old trading post and covered the floor, and a new blanket covered Cadence's cot.

Someone lit a few white candles and some incense and placed them on the table. It was a nice touch, thoughtful.

Star and Raven appeared in the doorway supporting Cadence between them. The girls had been drinking and were giggling as they led Cadence to her cot and plopped her down. Cadence lifted a boot for Star to remove, then the other for Raven to pull. Star removed Cadence's sword and weapons belt and slung them over a chair. Cadence threw herself back and spread out her arms.

"Are we going to have a party?" asked Cadence, drunk. She patted the bed on either side of her. "What's the problem? I want to party. Where is the rum?"

"She's had enough," said Highbrow. "Why don't you two call it a night and go back to your tents? I'll take care of Cadence. Thanks for letting her drink so much."

"Our pleasure," said Raven. "Star and I will go play with the Tigers if you won't let us stay here. They always have the good stuff."

Highbrow closed the door as they ushered out. He slid out of his coat and laid it over a chair.

"You staying the night with me?" said Cadence in a husky whisper.

"Yes." He removed his boots and sweatshirt while she watched. "I don't think you need to be alone tonight. I don't want to be alone either."

Sitting down beside Cadence, he reached up and ruffled her dark brown hair. They had never been alone together like this, but he felt comfortable with her.

"I wish you hadn't cut your hair so short. It was pretty."

Cadence smiled. "Compliment or insult?"

"Compliment. You're amazing, beautiful inside and out. Strong, confident, and incredibly fragile at times. A bit hot-tempered too, but you always manage to figure it out and keep it together." Highbrow moved a little closer. "I know it's been hard on you, but I'm here to help carry the burden. I've always been here, Cadence. I've just been waiting for you to tell me what you need from me."

"You mean you want me to tell you how I feel about you. Really?"

"Really. Now is the time, I think," said Highbrow, reaching over to fiddle with the buttons of her jeans. Her hand settled on top of his, holding him still. He met her green eyes and sighed.

"This is a big step," said Cadence.

"I'm not good at saying how I feel, but I try to show you. I admit I'm a little scared of you, and of how I really feel about us. I love you, Cadence. I think I've loved you from the first moment I saw you."

"I don't love you."

Highbrow felt his heart pound in his throat. "You don't? But I thought—"

"I'm in love with you," Cadence said. "I'm drunk enough to admit it, but I didn't know until I thought I'd lost you. I need you, and if tonight is to be our last night on earth, I want to spend it with you."

She pressed into his arms. Passionate kissing brought an end to her drunken conversation. They had all night together.

Chapter Twenty

*T*he morning sunlight streamed in through two windows. Cadence found Highbrow attractive as the warm beams of light fell across his skin. He licked maple syrup from a plastic fork and punched it into a stack of pancakes they shared. His muscular body was a delight to take in while having breakfast in bed. They shared a feeling of contentment after their night together. In this moment, everything was okay.

A thick, black string weighted by a bear claw hung around his neck, same as the one she wore. Highbrow stabbed another stack of pancakes as Cadence reached over and lifted his claw.

"Once a Tiger, always a Tiger," she said.

Highbrow set the fork down and leaned in close to tickle her.

"Why do you make that funny little *oomph* sound when I touch you in certain places? You sound like a little gremlin. I can't tell if you like it or not." Highbrow continued tickling her while she laughed. She ended their sport by pinching him. "Not fair!"

"I don't make that sound," said Cadence. Highbrow moved their plate out of the way as he pounced on top, his tickling evolved into kissing. She giggled and removed any space left between them. Neither of them noticed the door open until a figure was already stepping through the doorframe. Cadence froze, seeing Logan standing there watching.

"What the hell do you want? Can't you knock?" said Cadence.

Highbrow spun around and threw a blanket over Cadence. Logan remained in the doorway as they both dressed at a frantic pace.

"Man, you have some nerve," said Highbrow. "This better be good, Logan. You have something to report?"

"Isn't she the commander?" asked Logan, smug. He glanced at Cadence and let out a sultry whistle. "You sure are pretty when you relax a little, commander. I wonder—"

The punch from Highbrow sent Logan tumbling. Cadence finished dressing as Highbrow landed a second fist. She strapped on her sword as Highbrow stepped back in the door. Logan lay still on the wooden deck, eyes closed.

"I hit him hard," said Highbrow.

"Get dressed and come back out."

Cadence shut the door and knelt toward Logan. Her first inclination was to kick him in the side. She noticed blood on his jacket as she placed her hand on his forehead.

"You okay?" Cadence leaned closer and breathed into his face. "Sorry you didn't get any pancakes. They were delicious."

Highbrow walked out, frowning.

"Let's hear what happened, Logan. Did you catch the puma?" Cadence demanded. "Did you see Luna? I gave orders not to harm her or the other girls."

"God, you're all business." Logan got to his feet and gave his jacket a shake. "We killed a big one, but it didn't turn back into a girl. We cut it open and didn't find much, although it was curious to find it rotting from the inside. I'm not sure what would've happened if we hadn't shot it."

"Did you haul the carcass back to camp?"

"Burned it. We set up a few non-lethal traps on the trails. You gave orders not to kill Luna. It's a safe bet they moved into high country. I'll go back and see if we caught anything, after I have some of those delicious pancakes and a cup of coffee." Logan winked. Nomad is waiting for me in the mess hall."

"Those werepumas are my friends," she said, defensive. "I don't want them hurt."

"Correction. They were your friends and now they are infected. If they retain any connection to their human lives, they might return here. I don't think you want them here if they've gone feral."

Highbrow remained silent while Logan spoke. Cadence put her hand on his arm. He looked way from Logan and gave her a thin smile.

"I assigned Corporal Sterling as the new security chief," said Cadence. "I'd appreciate it if you spoke with him about security for the camp."

"It's Sunday," said Highbrow. "Did you forget? It's the only day of the week we get to sleep in until nine."

"Patrols used to sleep in, not soldiers. We're all soldiers now, so go find him and make sure the entrance is secure. Sterling suggested we retrieve the fence sections and use them to surround the box canyon. Sort out the details and make it happen."

With Logan watching, Highbrow planted an awkward kiss on Cadence before jumping on a four-wheeler and speeding off.

"That boy is too young for you," Logan said, when the competition was gone.

Cadence glared at him and crossed the porch to the stairs. He followed.

"You actually made Highbrow your captain? How old is he? Sixteen? Seventeen? Does he even shave? I'm pretty sure I saw him on the news about a year ago. Something about a Colorado senator embezzling money. I can see the dutiful wife and son standing on the steps of the courthouse."

"Leave him alone. Leave me alone."

Logan blocked her path.

"Highbrow is Senator Douglas Powers' son, right? The son graduated a year early from high school and entered the AFA on a full-scholarship when the scandal broke. Shame he'll never get to be a fighter pilot. What about you? Did you graduate before the Scourge happened?"

Cadence wanted to shut Logan up fast. People were drifting into the mess hall and the morning patrols were reporting to their assigned posts.

"The first rule here is the past no longer matters. We don't talk about who we were, what we did, or discuss our families. Camp names are given to protect people from any stigma they may have brought with them and gives everyone a chance at a new start. The simple fact that you are here puts a strain on my ability to maintain law and order. Quite a few people would love to feed you to the zombies, and right now I'm starting to like the idea myself. You either make yourself useful or move on, but don't think you can come in here and start trouble."

The sound of an insect buzzing around her head distracted her. She glanced down at a clump of wild flowers growing, and watched a honeybee flitter from flower to flower.

"If those are the camp rules," said Logan, "I guess who I was before coming here doesn't matter. The slate is wiped clean, unless you have dual standards. You should be able to overlook what I've done in the past and let me start fresh." He stepped closer. "You should trust your instincts. Keep away from me if you can. Not going to be easy, but try."

Cadence kept her back turned. Logan was an unknown element, and that was a signal to stay clear. She was not going to wind up as one of his games to be played.

"Not interested."

Chuckling, Logan turned toward the mess hall. Cadence walked in the opposite direction through the maze of tents set up along the creek. It was a beautiful morning and she let the sun wash over her. Her worries melted for a moment as she approached the Tiger's tent.

"Morning, commander." Whisper looked up from the small campfire. A grate over the flames held a coffee pot. "Cowboy coffee?"

"Sure," said Cadence. "Thanks."

Whisper handed her a cup, put a sock on his hand to lift the pot, and poured a serving of tea-colored coffee. Cadence saw another sock hanging out of the pot.

"Did you put the coffee grounds in your sock? They better be new."

Whisper smiled. He smiled a little longer when Blaze emerged from the tent wearing only jeans and a bra. She stretched her arms and fetched her freshly-washed sweater from a tree. Satisfied it was dry enough, she slipped it on.

Shouting came from the creek. Dodger and Smack fought over a tube of toothpaste as they popped each other with towels.

"Those two are so annoying," said Blaze.

She accepted a cup of coffee, thanked Whisper, and sat down on a log to put on her boots. The snap of a twig turned their attention. Freeborn approached the tent, looking like she hadn't slept. Dark circles sunk her eyes and she moved sluggish.

"Sarge and Lieutenant Destry just arrived at camp," Freeborn told Cadence. "They brought about fifteen soldiers and some scavengers they met on the way here. Highbrow and Sterling are talking to them. Let me drink some coffee and we can go meet with them together."

"Sarge?" Cadence set aside her coffee cup. "Is the Captain with them?"

Freeborn shook her head as she took a cup from Whisper. She took a sip, spewed, and handed it back to him. "Cowboy coffee? Tastes like a foot. Sarge wants Destry to be in charge. Better have the team follow us. When you're ready, commander, I have an ATV parked on the road."

"Get up there as soon as you can guys," said Cadence.

"We'll be there in a few minutes," said Blaze. "Dodger! Smack! Stop screwing around and get dried off. We've got to go."

Cadence and Freeborn drove through the winding road, flanked by the majestic cliffs and trees. They arrived at the new barricade that stretched from one end of the canyon to the other, cutting off the main road leading into the park. Four school buses and a fire truck were parked bumper to bumper to block the road. Giant trash bins, wooden crates, and even furniture wove together with barbed wire filling any gaps. It wasn't quite what Cadence imagined, but it would do for now.

"You need to assert yourself," Freeborn warned. She slid off the ATV after Cadence, assessing the situation. "How bad do you want to stay in command? From what I see, you're going to have to fight to keep it, commander."

Several patrols stood guard behind the barricade and on the buses, watching between the road and the conversation heating up between Highbrow, Corporal Sterling, and the new arrivals. Some of the soldiers were injured, and one was guarding a group of scavengers huddled together. Sarge was angry and had the soldiers agitated. He and Destry were the last two soldiers Cadence ever wanted to see again, and now they were in her camp.

"Hey, Freeborn! What's up?"

Black Beard and his Buccaneers were adding a cement table to the barricade. They finished and joined Freeborn, who filled them in. As Cadence walked toward the soldiers, she saw the Blue Devils leaving their positions at the barricade. Led by Echo, a stocky, red-haired girl, they joined Cadence's growing entourage.

"What's the situation?" asked Cadence, turning to Echo.

"Sarge arrived a little while ago. We had to kill a group of zombies before we could let them in," said Echo. "Don't worry, commander. We're not letting them take over our camp. The Panthers and War Gods are with us. Kahn and Caesar have their eyes on Sarge and Destry." She indicated the two patrols standing on top of the buses. "Give the word and we'll drop them both."

Freeborn readied her shotgun. "Dragon is bringing the rest of the camp," she said. "This may get ugly."

"Stay beside me and say nothing," said Cadence, as she waved Black Beard over. "Have Drake get on his radio and make sure every patrol is coming here. I'm not letting Sarge and Destry take control of this camp. We took it. We're keeping it."

Lifting her chin, Cadence and Freeborn marched over to the soldiers followed by the Blue Devils and Echo. Sarge nudged Destry. Highbrow and Sterling turned around, but only Highbrow looked relieved and saluted.

"Commander," said Highbrow.

Cadence saluted Highbrow. Not one soldier saluted her, including Corporal Sterling, making her regret his promotion. There were more teenagers than soldiers, but Sarge and a few of his men were armed. Cadence did not want things to escalate, but backing down was not an option.

"Good morning, Captain Highbrow, Corporal Sterling," said Cadence. "How many people arrived with Sarge and are any infected?"

"Twenty-five, including the scavengers," Highbrow reported. "As far as I can tell, no one is infected. The soldier on the stretcher fell down a flight of stairs. He probably broke some ribs, but he wasn't bitten. I checked him." With a quick glance at the growing number behind Cadence and Freeborn, he began to calm. "How do you want to handle this?"

"Lieutenant Destry, as senior officer, requests he assume command immediately." Corporal Sterling gave Cadence a look she couldn't quite decipher. "I explained that you've replaced the Captain as commander."

Sarge was pacing and rubbing his hands together. Cadence saw that he was close to cracking. Whatever had happened since the Battle of the Peak, they had not fared well. Most looked banged up and exhausted, and not in any shape to fight. Destry's face was contorted as he glared at Cadence. He wasn't man enough to talk for himself in the presence of the soldiers.

"We're not taking orders from a little girl," shouted Sarge. "Corporal, are you siding with these punks? Highbrow, you're no more a captain than I am and I'm certainly not going to call that one commander.

211

Lieutenant Destry is the rightful commander and we intend to take charge of this camp. The first thing we're going to do is hang every last one of these scavengers."

Freeborn bristled. "Not gonna happen, Sarge. Cadence is our commander."

Shouts fueled the air behind Cadence. The teenagers weren't going to back down without a fight. The soldiers noticed those at the barricade were aiming at them and grew nervous.

"This is my camp, gentlemen," Cadence asserted. "We are not at the Peak and the Captain is dead. I'm in command. If you don't like it, leave. It's that simple."

"What about the scavengers?" demanded Sarge. "Do they get to stay?"

"Looks like the scavengers have been through a tough time of it, commander," said Freeborn. "We need to be sure they're not infected. Best to have them strip down and check for bite marks."

Destry looked offended but nervous. "None of us are bitten," he said. "It's not zombies you have to worry about, Highbrow, but the monsters at Miramont Castle! If Rafe hadn't helped us escape, those creatures would have fed on us. You kids have no idea what you're up against. Those little demon children turned a bunch of scavengers into vampires and they're coming here next. Rafe said they might follow."

"You will address Commander Cadence directly," said Highbrow. "As for the vampires, we already know about them. The zombies remain the greater threat. If any followed you here, we're going to have a bigger problem on our hands."

"Oh, we don't have a problem." Cadence smiled wide. "I know precisely what I'm doing and how to handle these jokers."

The roar of ATVs and vehicles filled the canyon. At a nod from Cadence, Black Beard instructed the arriving patrols to join the others flanking their commander. The Fighting Tigers, China Six, Vikings, Bandits, Panthers, Valkyries, Razorbacks, and Bull Dogs fanned out, aiming at the soldiers. The Elite were missing and Cadence assumed Uther had taken his team to Midnight Falls to join Logan and Nomad in their search.

"Corporal Sterling," ordered Cadence, "relieve Destry of his weapon. The rest of you will place your weapons on the ground and take three steps back. Captain Highbrow, draw your weapon and shoot Corporal Sterling in the leg is he refuses to follow my orders."

Several in the crowd gasped.

Highbrow drew his gun and pointed it at Sterling. "You heard what the commander said Corporal Sterling. Take the man's weapon. The rest of you lower your weapons and move back three steps or else."

"Or else what?" Sarge snatched the rifle from Destry and aimed it against Highbrow. "You're not going to do anything! None of you move or Highbrow's a dead man."

In a rush of surprise, Sterling drew his pistol and leveled it at Sarge. Highbrow kept his own weapon aimed at Sterling. The corporal removed the weapon from Sarge and handed it to Highbrow. Sarge stepped back, confidence shattered, and motioned for the soldiers to lower their weapons. Every soldier placed their weapons on the ground and, except for Destry, took three steps back. Corporal Sterling stepped in and backhanded the lieutenant. Destry twisted backward from the strike and stumbled.

"I'm the new commander," said Cadence, "Captain Highbrow is my second. Destry, you are demoted to the rank of private. As for you, Sarge, the only duties you will have are those I assign you. Corporal Sterling, escort Sarge and lock him inside the storage shed so he can reflect on things. If anyone would like to join him, please raise your hand. Otherwise, you will acknowledge me as commander or you can get out of my camp."

"You can't do this," protested Destry. "I'm in command! I'm next in line!"

Echo moved to Destry and snatched the Freedom Army beret from his head. The Tigers gathered the surrendered weapons, and the patrols let out a cheer. Corporal Sterling apprehended Sarge and walked through the patrols.

"Make sure Sarge is locked up and post guards," said Cadence to Echo. The leader of the Blue Devils signaled her team and they followed Sterling and Sarge to the shed. "Whisper, have the Tigers take the scavengers to the tunnel. Conduct a strip down and let Raven check them for bite marks. Give them food and water and assign them a place to sleep. Stay with them until you hear from me. Turn the weapons over to China Six before you go."

Everyone carried out their orders as fast as they could move. The Bandits moved into position and replaced the Blue Devils at the barricade.

Highbrow holstered his pistol. "What about the rest of the soldiers, Cadence? We could use their help. Sarge and Destry are the only troublemakers. They look tired and hungry."

"So what," Freeborn muttered under her breath.

"Black Beard." Cadence motioned for him to come closer. "See that the soldiers strip down check them for bite marks. If anyone is bitten, leave them here for Captain Highbrow to deal with. Anyone with a noninfectious wound is to see Raven for medical aide. Get the Panthers and Razorbacks to help you escort the soldiers to the mess hall and get them something to eat. Keep them there under guard until I decide otherwise."

"You got it," saluted Black Beard. The Buccaneers approached the soldiers and soon had them stripping down.

Feeling a little unsure of himself, Highbrow put his hand on Cadence's shoulder. She didn't shrug him off. "Hey, it's all under control," he said. "I'll handle things up here. For a minute, I thought you really wanted me to shoot Sterling in the leg. Did you mean it?"

"Yeah, I meant it," she said. "Ten to one, you can bet zombies followed Sarge to our camp. Keep as many teams as you need, but make sure this barricade holds. We're in this for the long haul, Highbrow. We're going to have to do things we never thought we would. Keep your eye on Sterling. I didn't like how he hesitated when I gave him an order. The older soldiers can work with us or leave camp. If you need me for any reason, I'll be in HQ. Come on, Freeborn."

"What do I do if someone was bitten?" asked Highbrow.

Cadence lifted an eyebrow. "Shoot them and burn them."

Leadership was not supposed to be easy, but Cadence felt she had been hard on Highbrow as she walked away. Part of her doubted Highbrow would have shot Sterling if ordered. If Highbrow would not follow her orders, why would anyone else? He thought she was weak because Luna's death affected her so deep, but it was the last time she would ever let her emotions rule her. Life would never return to normal. It was sink or swim from now on, and Cadence intended to swim hard.

Chapter Twenty-One

*H*ighbrow spent the following morning observing the patrols train under their new instructors. Whisper had team snipers working on range and accuracy. Dragon and Xena were instructing hand-to-hand combat exercises and swordplay, while Blaze led archery lessons. Phoenix and Calico Jack were rotating group cardio and kick-boxing sessions.

Near lunchtime Highbrow found Cadence unlocking the storage shed. Dodger, Smack, and Freeborn surrounded with Raven and Star nearby. Sarge was shouting from inside, and as Cadence opened the doors he charged through, knocking her to the ground. He descended on her and pushed a knife to her throat. Cadence caught his arm, but he was too strong. She was losing her hold.

"Help her," shouted Smack.

Freeborn clubbed Sarge over the head with the end of her shotgun and the big man collapsed on top of Cadence. Freeborn pulled Sarge off and helped Cadence to her feet.

"Are you okay?" Highbrow hurried over. "Why did you let him out?"

"Because he's been shouting Rafe's name for hours," said Cadence. She brushed the dirt and grass off. "Take him inside my cabin and tie him to a chair. Raven, get a sedative ready. I want to question him about Rafe."

Highbrow sent the Bull Dogs to the mess hall and followed Cadence into the cabin. Freeborn and Dodger muscled Sarge into a chair and tied him down. Twenty-four hours in the storage shed had broken Sarge. His eyes were wild and he fought at the ropes as he began to wake.

"Give him a dose, Raven," said Cadence, taking a seat.

"Keep him still," said Raven, as she administered the shot. "This is a mild sedative and it works fast. His pulse is a little high, but I think he's calm enough to answer a few questions."

"Star, you handle it," said Cadence. She motioned for Highbrow and smiled when he leaned down to kiss her. "Come on. This is serious. Don't do that in front of everyone."

"Can't help it." Highbrow leaned against the desk. "What's this all about? Logan told you everything about Miramont Castle. I've already questioned Destry and the rest of the soldiers. So did Sterling, and the stories lined up. They didn't see much, and everyone said Rafe let them go."

"I want to find out what Sarge knows about the vampires," said Cadence. "Logan seems to know a lot about vampires, but I want hear what Sarge says. Plus, Echo said he refused to eat last night. I can't let him starve in there."

"I'm going to ask you about Miramont Castle," began Star. "Tell us what you saw. Who turned the scavengers into vampires? Was it Rafe? How did he do it?

"Maybe." Sarge lifted his head. "Rafe let us go. I never saw him bite anyone."

"Who did you see biting people?" Star was calm and patient.

"The girl named Savannah and the two Little Leaguers. They're vampires."

Cadence glanced up at Highbrow. He still felt responsible for Savannah's capture. He promised to protect her and now she was beyond help. Sarge started mumbling. Star lifted his head and leaned in to hear what he was saying. Freeborn braced his shoulders.

"Savannah killed most of the scavengers," said Star, looking back toward Cadence and Highbrow. "Sarge didn't see it, but he heard the screams and knew what was happening."

"Keeping him locked up overnight brought it all back to him," said Raven. "He's definitely experiencing post-traumatic stress. I haven't seen signs of it in any of the other soldiers. I think more will probably come to Sarge as time goes on. Corporal Sterling asked if I'd clear them for active duty, but I don't think Sarge is in any condition to return to his former duties."

"No one was infected?" said Cadence.

Raven shook her head. "Fortunately, but letting those people in without quarantine and examination was a stupid thing to do. Some of the old rules have to be followed and that's one of them."

"Why is Star handling the interrogation?" asked Highbrow.

"Because Sarge doesn't like me," Cadence said. "He also tried to stick me with a knife. Now sit down and be quiet or get out of here."

"Tell us again what happened when Savannah bit the prisoners." said Star. "You were able to hear the vampires, Sarge. What did they say?"

"Rafe told Savannah to stop trying to turn humans into vampires," said Sarge, slurring. "He said he could do it, that he made her, but Savannah was different. Rafe said she needed to kill her prey or they'd turn into zombies. He killed everyone bitten by Savannah. Their screams . . . The next day we had to burn them, all of them. That brought more zombies. Rafe came out of the house and killed them, and then he let us go."

"What a crock," said Highbrow. "Sarge didn't see it, so he doesn't know what he's talking about. Savannah was kind, she wouldn't have killed anyone. He's making this all up. You're not going to get the truth out of him. Let's bring Destry in here and ask him the same questions."

"Shut up," said Raven. "He's talking and you're talking, and I'm trying to listen."

"I'm telling the truth," said Sarge, licking his lips. "Savannah and those two little monsters killed and killed, and Rafe made us clean it up. We scrubbed the blood off the walls, down the hallway, and then . . . all those decapitated heads. Me and Destry picked them up and added them to the pile of bodies burning outside."

"What did they do then?"

Sarge shivered. "They watched us from the upstairs windows, but they wouldn't come out in the daylight, so they made us do it. They made us do everything."

"It's going to be okay, Sarge," said Cadence, standing. "You're safe here. No one is going to hurt you. They don't know you're here."

"Yes, they do. They do," said Sarge, groggy but anxious. "All those signs you put up outside of Manitou Springs, they saw them. We saw them and knew you were here, and Rafe knew you were here, so that means the vampires know. There were lots of them that morning. They had fangs and glowing eyes. Had to be fifteen or twenty or more vampires. Destry and I begged Rafe to let us go, so he did. He let the scavengers go, and they found us in town and came with us. That's all I know. All I know."

Sarge started screaming uncontrollably. Raven didn't wait for an order from the Cadence. She got up, prepared another syringe, and gave Sarge a second shot. Highbrow couldn't see what she was using, but Sarge quieted down fast and sat like a lump in the chair.

"Is that necessary?" asked Highbrow.

"Yes," said Cadence, Raven, and Star in unison.

"Tell us about Rafe," Star continued. "You were talking about him earlier. You said he wanted to meet with Cadence. What did he tell you? Why does he want to meet her?"

Sarge drooled over himself. "Yeah. Rafe. He's a great guy. He put his neck on the line for us. Yeah, that's what he did. He's the only one that went outside in daylight. He's not afraid. He's not afraid of anything. I always thought he was a coward and he was a coward, he really was, but he's not now."

Star gave Sarge more water to drink and cleaned his face. Wanting to finish the interrogation, Highbrow walked over and knelt beside Sarge, watching the soldier with concern. Star sat back in her chair without saying a word.

Sarge frowned at Highbrow, his eyes swimming. "Rafe told us to take the stairs and come to your camp, so that's what we did. We just kept running and running, and then we found a truck. A blue truck. It was a nice truck. And then we came here, because Rafe said that's what we were to do. Rafe said he was sorry, said he wanted to see Cadence, and wanted to be friends again."

"Like that's going to happen," said Highbrow.

"What do you take me for?" Sarge's anger seeped through his slurred words. "I'm not lying. Rafe . . . I called him a punk . . . and he gave Destry a gun . . . and then he let us go."

Highbrow had heard enough. "Shouldn't you be questioning Logan? Logan was there. He heard as much as Sarge, maybe even more. He's the one you should be talking to. Where is Logan anyway?"

"I already told you where he is," said Cadence, annoyed. "Logan and Nomad came in earlier. We had breakfast and talked about Rafe, Cinder, and Cerberus."

"What are you going to do with Sarge?" asked Highbrow. "He's a wreck and whatever your shooting him up with isn't helping."

Sarge had fallen asleep and was snoring.

"Sarge will remain locked up," said Cadence. "We can't let him out. Put the other soldiers to work, but you're responsible for them, Highbrow, not Sterling."

"If you don't like the guy, why did you make him the security chief?"

Cadence waved Highbrow silent. "Sarge? Hey, Sarge? Wake up," she shouted. His head rolled around and he looked up at her, unable to focus. "What else did Rafe say? Tell me and I'll let you get some sleep."

"Rafe wants to talk," said Sarge. "That's all. Just talk. He wants to meet you alone. Friday night. Is tonight Friday? At midnight at Midnight Falls. That's all I know. Destry might know more. Yeah, Destry might remember. Destry knows everything."

"Destry doesn't know anything," said Highbrow. "I already talked to Destry and everyone else who was with you, Sarge. No one heard Rafe say anything about meeting Cadence Friday night at Midnight Falls. You're the only one he told. Did you talk to Rafe? Did Rafe tell you this or are you making it up?"

"I think so," said Sarge. "I can't remember, but I think so."

"You better ask Destry about the meeting," said Star. "If he can't confirm it, Rafe may have talked to Sarge in private. Let Sarge rest. We need to find a permanent place to keep him. If we clear out the merchandise from the toy store, we can keep him in there for now."

"Dig a hole and stick him in it," said Raven. "I'm not a babysitter and this man requires twenty-four seven. He also needs a bath. I'm not doing that, either."

"Fine," said Cadence. "Star, have China Six get the toy store ready and take him when you're ready. He can sleep here for now, but he needs to be kept sedated temporarily and that means you, Raven. He's your patient." She turned toward Highbrow. "Outside. I want to talk to you in private."

Highbrow nodded, opening the door, and Dodger moved. Cadence barged out, the rest of the Tigers scurrying out of the way. She stomped toward the waterfall, and Highbrow hurried after her. He knew he had pissed her off, but he was determined not to let her go meet with Rafe.

"Don't be angry," said Highbrow. "I'm sorry for interrupting back there, but I felt bad for Sarge. He's been through hell, Cadence. You didn't question anyone else like that. I know you don't like the guy, but he doesn't deserve to be treated like a war criminal."

"I know what I'm doing," she said. "You have to trust me."

Highbrow was surprised when Cadence pulled him in and kissed him. His head swam with visions of their future together. He kept hold of her hand when she drew back.

"Midnight at Midnight Falls," said Cadence. "Poetic, isn't it? I know you'll try to convince me not to meet Rafe, but if Sarge is telling the truth, I'm going. We need to know more about the vampires. I'm hoping Rafe wants to help out."

"Help out? Rafe can't be trusted. He is a vampire. He wants to make you one of them. Besides, the werepumas are up there. You can't believe anything Sarge said. For all we know, this is a trap."

"Then come with me and bring friends," said Cadence. "Rafe can't expect me to come alone. I'll talk to him, but he won't bite me. You'll make sure of that."

"Is this really because you want Rafe to help us? You're not feeling sorry for him, are you? Please tell me this isn't about something more."

"What a thing to ask."

"Well?"

Cadence shook her head. "I love you. But I do care about Rafe. I know you're worried, and so am I, but this is important. We need to know all we can about how the virus is mutating. A few days ago there weren't any vampires or werepumas. I need to be able to anticipate what comes next. That's why I have Logan searching for Luna. My hope is that Luna and the others haven't lost their humanity. I want to believe it's the same for Rafe. I have to believe it, Highbrow."

"I hope you're right. Let me talk to Sterling and arrange things. If we're going to do this, we need plenty of backup."

Later in the evening, Highbrow returned from his rounds and found Cadence in her cabin. She wasn't alone. The Vikings were standing outside. Thor, Star, Raven, and Dragon were inside with the Tigers. They were gathered around a desk with a large map of the hiking trails spread out. Whisper looked up at Highbrow, smiled, and motioned him over. He nudged between Whisper and Smack, scanning the map. Midnight Falls was circled in red ink.

"Highbrow, good. I'm glad you're here," said Cadence. "I've told everyone what we're planning tonight. Thor thinks the Vikings should stay at camp to protect the children, so we're taking the Fighting Tigers and China Six with us."

"Corporal Sterling has Destry and the soldiers at the barricade," said Highbrow. "We've positioned patrols along the road and throughout camp. Nomad and Logan aren't back yet, but the Elite have returned. I'll post them at the waterfall."

"What about the scavengers?"

"Sturgis and Betsy have asked to help out," Star said, glancing at Thor and back to Cadence. "They've set up tents outside the tunnel. Betsy suggested keeping the little ones inside with her. She has been a big help with them today. I think we've found our new school teacher."

Thor crossed his arms over his chest. "I hope you know what you're doing, Cadence. We're trusting scavengers, and now a vampire. I'll hold things down here while you're both playing nice with Rafe, but I'm not taking orders from Corporal Sterling, just to be clear."

Cadence didn't blame him. "Fine. You're the new acting camp sergeant, Thor."

"About time, too. We've got two hours to go. I suggest you go and get your teams in place. We'll do the same here. If you run into problems, contact us and I'll send in the Elite."

"You sound like a sergeant." Raven grinned when Thor blushed.

Everyone filed out of the cabin. Highbrow hung back while Cadence geared up. He wanted to hold and kiss her, but she didn't seem interested. He waited until she was ready to see what she would do. Cadence moved around the desk to him, and slid her arms around his neck. He embraced her.

"I love you," said Highbrow. "I won't let anything happen to you."

"Is that a promise?"

"Yeah," he said, and kissed her.

Chapter Twenty-Two

*L*ate Friday night the lights came on in Colorado Springs. Rafe didn't know who restored power, but it was working. Rafe cruised through the city in a Ferrari he took from a dealership display floor. The lights turned red and he sped through, laughing.

Rafe went to Colorado Springs after leaving Miramont Castle and spent hours walking through a shopping mall, waiting for Friday night. He killed several zombies and made a meal of a stray dog. He felt guilty, but not enough to kill it afterward. He would be hungry again soon. His thirst was already growing again.

He knew the demon children and their new vampire family would be looking for more survivors. Rafe had to warn people about vampires.

An idea occurred to him.

He drove to the historic old town of Colorado Springs and parked outside the local radio station. The front doors were locked, and a window was open on the second floor. Taking a step back, Rafe jumped to the window and pulled himself inside.

Security lights were on, casting a dim, red glow through the station. He found a zombie in the control booth, still trying to talk to his audience. He wore a cowboy hat and sat close to the mike, chewing on the sides of his mouth. Now and then the DJ's garbled sounds came across the speakers inside the station, making no sense.

Rafe entered the control booth and ripped the DJ's head off with a clean twist. He tossed the head into a trash can, pushed the remains of the body to the floor, and slid behind the console. His fingers sped across the controls, pushing buttons and arranging sliders, until he familiarized himself with the system. He fiddled through the CDs until he found something he liked and let it rip, at least in the station.

While the music played, Rafe clicked the microphone with his thumb and smiled when he heard it reflected back in the speakers. The station he selected was a local favorite and hoped someone was listening. He turned the music down.

"Hello, Colorado Springs," Rafe announced, grinning when he heard his voice over the speakers. "This is Rafe, proud new owner of Wolf Radio. If you're catching my show tonight, you're probably huddled in a room sealed off from the outside world wondering if the zombies will ever go away, or if the sun will rise in the morning. Well I'm here to tell you, dear humans, your nightmares are not over. Zombies are out and vampires are in."

He leaned back in his chair.

"Oh, I don't mean the Bela Lugosi type. Holy water and crosses don't work on us. Sunshine doesn't set us on fire and we can see our reflections. New vamps, as I like to call us, are fresh on the scene. It seems swallowing zombie blood changed a few of us, but only a few of us can make other vampires. If you're already a vampire, don't try to turn a human or you'll end up with a zombie. Why? I don't know, but be warned, there are a lot of new vamps here in Colorado Springs. We have the need to feed too, only we're a lot better looking than zombies."

Rafe changed the music to something harder. The music made him smile. He soaked in the drum beat, hypnotic and dark, thinking what he wanted to say next. The song was into its chorus when he cut back in.

"I'd like to invite all vampires to come to Colorado Springs and join me in establishing law and order. We have a vicious little queen, named Cinder, and her hellish consort, Cerberus. They consider humans as cattle. You can find them at Miramont Castle if you're brave enough to enter. For the rest of you fang bangers, I suggest you call in and set up a private one-on-one meeting with me."

When the phone rang, it was the strangest sound in the world. Rafe lowered his legs and sat up straight. All eight lights were blinking red. He tried to sound calm when he spoke into the microphone.

"Damn, well, I seem to have aroused someone's attention. Let's listen to our first caller."

It took him a minute to figure out what he was doing, but soon heavy breathing filtered through from the other end of the phone. Rafe lit up a cigarette.

"This is Rafe. Who am I talking to?"

"*Son, you're messing with the wrong sort of people,*" said a man with a deep voice and a distinct southern accent. "*Someone got the phones working. That same someone has control of the city. That means someone bigger and badder than you is in charge. I suggest you—*"

Feeling a little freaked out, Rafe hung up.

"Come on," Rafe said. "I want vampires who want meaning and purpose to their miserable lives to come to the Springs. So thank you to whoever got the lights back on and the phones working again." He chose another line. "This is Rafe. Talk to me."

"*Are you serious, man? Like, you're on the radio broadcasting?*" The man on the other end of the phone sounded young and scared. "*I thought the phones were down. How come we can call in now?*"

Rafe blew out a cloud of smoke. "According to the last caller, we have a new town mayor. What's your name, pal? You got a story to tell or am I wasting my time?"

"*My name is—*"

"Boring." Rafe disconnected and chose line four. "This is Rafe. Whatcha got for me?" He spun around in his chair, waiting for the voice on the other end of the phone to speak. "Come on. Don't be shy."

He paused.

"This is Rafe. Say something I want to hear."

"*Rose is the name. I'm a vampire.*" Her voice was sexy and self-assured.

Rafe laughed. "Now we're talking. Honey, where you at?"

"*In the city. It's not safe for you to be on the radio, Rafe. You're playing with the wrong sort of vampires. The ones in power are dangerous.*"

"Are they the ones who got this city rocking again, baby girl?"

"*Yes. They are called Shadowguard. The vampire in charge is what we refer to as the Kaiser, and you don't want to get on his bad side.*" The woman paused. Someone was talking to her. When she spoke again, she was panicked. "*Take me off air, Rafe. What I need to say is private.*"

Rafe picked up the phone and put the receiver to his ear. He let the music roll on-air, and addressed his caller in a more serious tone.

"Rose, what's going on?" asked Rafe. "Talk to me, sweetheart."

"*You're in danger. Get out of the station and meet me on the corner. I'll come for you in a limo. You have less than a minute to get out of there. Move.*"

"Baby, who are you?" Rafe leaned forward. "Who is this boogie man you're talking about?"

"*Lieutenant Aldarik and he's already inside the station. Run, you idiot. They're coming for you.*"

Rafe shot like lightning from the sound booth and stood at a window. He used a chair to break the glass. On the floor above, he heard the sounds of crashing and footsteps, and a man's voice barking orders. He leapt out the window and landed on the roof of a bus. His eyes focused on the intersection as he dashed forward. A limo pulled to the middle of the intersection under the street lights. A door opened and someone motioned Rafe inside.

Rafe jumped in and slammed the door as the limo sped forward. Turning toward the occupant seated next to him, Rafe beheld a pale, slender woman who looked to be about thirty with long blonde hair. Rose wore a black jumpsuit and high-heeled boots. Her makeup was flawless, with a soft shade of pink lipstick offsetting her glowing, violet eyes. She was breathtaking. Her driver was slick and proper, and an Asian with the tattoo of a green sea serpent sat in the passenger seat.

"You must be Rose," said Rafe. He reached for her hand.

The tattooed passenger turned and aimed a gun at Rafe. Rose took hold of Rafe's hand.

"It's all right, Rafe. Tandor isn't going to shoot you. He's being cautious. You were quite reckless tonight. You're lucky we were in the right place at the right time or we wouldn't have been able to help you. Aldarik isn't someone you want to meet."

"Please tell Tandor to lower his weapon."

Rose nodded at Tandor. The vampire lowered his weapon and faced forward, but it was Rose's smile that made Rafe feel at ease.

"The Shadowguard are dangerous, Rafe. So is their leader, the Kaiser. Tandor, Picasso, and I are with the Dark Angels. We're a small organization that doesn't agree with the Kaiser's plans, so we left Denver and came to Colorado Springs. The Kaiser must have sent Lieutenant Aldarik after us. When the lights came on tonight, it was the Kaiser's official announcement that he's taken over this city. The Kaiser has been rounding up human survivors for months. Some he turns and the rest are either eaten or forced to fight in his arena for sport. You certainly put the word out tonight. Hopefully, any humans in this area will hide."

Rafe wondered how much he should tell Rose about Cadence and her camp. Rose seemed too good to be true. Beautiful, pleasant, and civil. There had to be a catch.

"There might be a few humans around. They're my friends. I'm not going to let anything happen to them, either."

"I understand, Rafe. You have no reason to trust us, but Dark Angels have vowed to protect humans. We're on your side." Rose gave Rafe's hand a gentle squeeze. "Of course you must have many questions. I'll answer everything once we arrive at the hotel."

Rafe noticed she possessed a gun with a laser on her lap.

"Let me introduce my companions."

"I've met the guy with the gun. Tandor, right? Nice manners."

Rose laughed. "Tandor takes his job seriously. He's saved my life many times. Picasso is a former Ranger. Both are reliable and proficient at killing. We mean you no harm, Rafe, or we wouldn't have bothered picking you up. However, you need to know the Kaiser has been around longer than you can imagine. After your little display tonight, you'll need to take extra precaution if you intend to survive on your own."

"I'm doing okay," said Rafe. "Can the Kaiser make other vampires? I can do it. I know of two others who can, but anyone else who tried only made zombies."

"The Kaiser is a Maker. There are other Makers, Rafe. He's going city to city, collecting them, and relocating them to Denver. All Makers must either bow to his authority or be executed. I don't think you realize just how far his empire extends. Colorado Springs isn't the first city he's taken, nor will it be the last."

Rafe leaned back, still holding her hand. It was a small comfort and she didn't seem to mind. He wasn't sure where they were going, but Picasso had no problem running down zombies as they traveled. The city still had a good number of zombies milling around and he assumed whatever hotel the Dark Angels had claimed was clear and secure.

"Cinder and Cerberus live at Miramont Castle in Manitou Springs," said Rafe. "I suppose this Kaiser will be picking them up. You guys are a lot nicer than those two little monsters. I was starting to think all vampires were evil."

Tandor and Picasso both started laughing.

"Are you on your own, Rafe? If you want a family, I suggest you join the Dark Angels," said Rose. "You said you wanted vampires who want to help restore law and order. We want to do more than that. We find vampires like you and bring them into our fold, but our main purpose is to protect the human race."

"Are you the leader of the Dark Angels?" said Rafe.

"Yes, but it's not a dictatorship. We vote on everything. You should know that vampires have been around longer than you think. At the rate the Kaiser and his Makers are turning people, humans won't be around for much longer. If you join us, we can offer you protection and perhaps help protect your human friends."

Rose pulled her hand from his and Rafe reached into his coat for a pack of cigarettes. He lit up and Rose rolled the window down an inch on her side.

"I guess I'm a lucky guy," said Rafe, puffing his cigarette. "You're telling the truth, right? I've killed one vampire already. I'm not afraid of you guys."

"Yeah, we're telling the truth," said Picasso in a deep, scratchy voice. "The Dark Angels are good guys. The Shadowguard are bad guys. Only Makers can turn humans into vampires. I think that's simple enough for a guy like you to understand."

"It's okay, Rafe," said Rose. "I know you don't trust us yet. I'll tell you what we've learned since coming here. The survivors' camp at the Peak was overrun by zombies and they've relocated to Seven Falls. It's a logical place to select and one that can be defended against zombies. But it will be impossible to keep the Shadowguard out, unless the Dark Angels offer their protection. It's why we've taken up residency close to their camp."

"Our scouts have been watching the humans for some time," said Tandor, turning to take a better look at Rafe. "Word spread fast about the zombie attack on the Peak. Your friends were seen traveling to Seven Falls. The Kaiser knows they are there and he knows about the vampires at Miramont. They'll send someone to their camp to check it out and then they'll start taking your people."

"Perhaps you haven't noticed us, Rafe, but we've been watching you," said Picasso. "And now the Shadowguard know about you. You can't survive on your own. No vampire can. If Aldarik picks you up, you'll be taken before the Kaiser and forced to swear your allegiance or be killed."

Rafe didn't like the thought of being watched. It meant they'd been in town a while and had not attempted to meet him, but were spying on Cadence's camp. He had taken the time to remove all of Cadence's signs, instructing survivors to come to Seven Falls, but he shouldn't have bothered. The word was out.

"So, are any of you Makers?" probed Rafe. "I'd ask you how we were created, but I'm sure you don't know. I figure the virus is always mutating. I swallowed zombie blood a few days ago."

"I'm a doctor," said Rose. "I know a little about it. We barely made it out of Denver alive. None of us are Makers, but we know you are. You are lucky, very lucky, we got to you first."

"Your eyes glow violet, but mine glow blue. What's up with that?" Rafe finished his cigarette and tossed it out the window. "Are we even vampires? The way I see it, we're just infected with the virus and rank right up there with zombies."

Picasso slammed into a zombie, sending the body flying across the hood. He swerved around a corner, and headed south. Rafe stared out the window, amazed most of the street lights still worked and laughed when Picasso ran a red light. He wasn't going to get tired of that, ever.

"The color of a vampire's eyes depends on who made them," said Rose. "Most of the Dark Angels are the offspring of Salustra, but not all. The Kaiser doesn't want anyone making vampires unless he approves it. We don't know how many he has killed, but we do know who joined him."

"Anyone turned by the Kaiser is easy to recognize," said Tandor. "They all have big, glowing, yellow eyes. You meet anyone with gold eyes, they're not your friends."

Rafe thought about Cadence. When he told her what was going on, she would want to know specifics. He needed to know more about the Kaiser and the Shadowguard. Joining the Dark Angels might be the best thing to happen to him since he went to the Peak. If they really meant to protect humans, then Rafe would be able to provide Cadence with a vampire security guard. He knew his own abilities were far superior to any human. He assumed the Dark Angels and Shadowguard were just as strong and fast, and as lethal.

"How many vampires are we talking about?" asked Rafe.

"Thousands," said Rose, "and they are everywhere, in every city worldwide. I was a doctor and worked in a research lab trying to find a cure for cancer. From what I have learned about the H1N1z virus it will continue to mutate and create other species. I was working on a cure when I left Denver. The zombies were the first stage of the virus. Their DNA is fragmenting, disintegrating, and from what I can tell they will all die off in time. As for vampires, our DNA is strengthened by the virus. We will continue evolving as long as there is a supply of blood. Without it our cells will begin to disintegrate as well."

"What other species are we talking about?"

"It's a recent event. Animals are contracting the virus. If a Maker is in desperate need of food and feeds on, say, a wolf, the wolf becomes infected. If that wolf bites a human, the lupine-altered virus is transferred to the prey. The infected human becomes hardier, with increased senses and abilities, and new energy processes. They are able to change into a wolf-like form, but they aren't wolves and retain their human personalities. But there are far more than just werewolves out there, Rafe. Fortunately, werewolves generally feed on other animals and rarely attack humans. Some werewolves run in packs, some are loners, but a rare few like the Cheyenne Mountain Wolf Tribe are more civilized."

"That means they don't have a wolf pack mentality," said Tandor. "They consider themselves humans who can morph into a wolf at will. Humans who can morph into animals are called therianthropes. The wolf tribe we're talking about doesn't want anything to do with the Kaiser or humans. We're not sure where they're hiding, and they are constantly on the move."

Rafe gazed out the window and spotted the Broadmoor Hotel ahead. He looked at Rose and saw a kindness about her that eased his fears. For some reason he felt he could trust Rose, and if she was the leader of the Dark Angels, maybe he could trust them.

"You've given me a lot to think about," said Rafe.

Rose leaned toward him. "I told you I was a doctor. I haven't lost my desire to help people. That's what makes us different from other vampires. We want to help humans because we hope to be human again one day."

As the limo pulled into the hotel, Rafe sat up straight, glancing at his watch. He had less than thirty minutes to reach Cadence and was anxious.

"This is our temporary residence," she said. "You are more than welcome to stay here, Rafe. The Dark Angels don't feed on humans. We feed on animals and kill them afterward, but we're working on creating a synthetic blood."

"You've got this all figured out," said Rafe. "I'm impressed."

Once parked, Rafe opened the door and climbed out. He held out his hand and helped Rose to her feet. Picasso and Tandor were at her side in an instant. More vampires exited the front door of the hotel. Rafe noticed an enormous pile of dead bodies being burned in the parking lot. The stench was overpowering.

"Fire is the best way to get rid of the virus," said Rose. "We always burn their bodies. Afterward, the ashes will be buried."

"Yeah, that's what we did with them at the Peak."

The Dark Angels returned to the hotel. Rafe followed, but knew he was running out of time and needed to leave. Tandor and Picasso shook his hand. The vampires seemed friendly, but so had Savannah at first.

"Look, I'd like to stay," said Rafe, "but I need to be somewhere in a few minutes. If all goes well, I'll come back and tell you about it. Thanks, Rose. I'm glad we met."

"We'll be waiting."

Rafe held out his hand, but Rose ignored it. The ravishing blonde was in his embrace and before he realized what was happening, she granted him a tender kiss. When she slipped away, Rafe smelled like roses. His head buzzed as he ran to reach Midnight Falls at his appointed time.

Chapter Twenty-Three

A soft wind filtered through the trees, sending the first leaves of autumn scattering in every direction. The moon was full and majestic in the clear sky.

Cadence stood at the side of the stream at Midnight Falls. It was a small cascade of water flowing over the rocks to her left. The Fighting Tigers and China Six were like shadows in the darkness. Logan and Nomad had not returned to camp and Cadence was worried. Knowing Luna was running through the forest on all fours with her pride presented a big problem. Cadence imagined seeing glowing eyes in the bushes each time a leaf rustled or a twig snapped, raising the hairs on the back of her neck. Armed with a sword and her handgun, she was resolved to use whatever means was necessary if attacked.

Looking at her watch, she read 12:00 a.m.

She lifted her head at the sound of rustling in the bushes across the stream. A figure stepped forward, moving slow, but she couldn't make out its form. Clouds wisped across the moon, blocking its silver rays for a moment. In the distance, the howl of a wolf carried through the air and she shivered.

"Is that you, Rafe?"

The figure continued to approach, stepping into the stream with a splash. She moved closer to the stream. The clouds passed and moonlight revealed a forest ranger ravaged from exposure and disease. He was close enough for her to see flesh hanging from his brow and his lower lip missing. The zombie lunged, grabbing her by the shoulders. His body bore the harsh odors of decay, feces, and kerosene.

Cadence drew her pistol, but his grip was fierce. He had been strong in life and shook Cadence hard, causing her to drop her gun. She was frantic and tried to push him away. His rancid breath assaulted her face as he lowered his head. A scream froze in her throat as his teeth sank and ripped away a portion of her exposed neck, releasing a stream of hot, red blood.

"Get off her!" shouted Rafe.

He pulled the zombie away from Cadence. She pressed a hand to her throat, watching as Rafe raised the creature high. He snapped it backward, breaking its spine, and tore its head off before the body hit dirt. Cadence sank to the ground as her legs collapsed under her. She could feel the life rushing out of her body. A burning pain spread through her entire being and she sagged forward, watching her blood flow over her hands and to the ground, mixing with the stream.

Rafe knelt and lifted her head. His eyes were aglow with the most beautiful shade of blue she had ever seen. A hard cough forced a foul taste from the pit of her stomach. Panic set in and Cadence fought back tears as Rafe folded her into his arms.

"We don't have much time, Cadence. The bleeding won't stop. You know what's going to happen to you," said Rafe. "But I can save you. I can make you a vampire."

Cadence turned her head as a mouthful of bile bubbled from her throat. He wiped her lips. Her tears stopped as Rafe's face began to blur. Rafe pulled her fevered body close to his and pressed his face to her cheek.

"Is that what you want? Do you want me to save you?"

"Yes," she gasped.

Cadence felt the pinch of fangs sink into her neck. He moved quickly, slicing open his wrist with his own teeth and held the open wound to her lips. Without hesitation, Cadence drank from Rafe, finding pleasure in this consummation. Thoughts of murder flashed her mind. Highbrow drained of blood, Freeborn missing chunks of flesh, Smack and the others, dead, the camp in flames . . .

Cadence shook her head, fighting the images, unsure of what they meant. In a sudden rush, she raised her head and nourished the vision of the full moon.

"How do you feel? Answer me, Cadence. Have I lost you?"

"I'm here," said Cadence, meeting Rafe's stare. His eyes were bright blue. She wondered if hers glowed as well. "I'm dizzy and I feel . . ."

Looking at the moon again, she listened to the wind and heard strange cries of animals in the dark. She could sense her team nearby, chasing a certain werepuma. A scent on the breeze turned her thoughts to Highbrow and she focused, able to grasp a vision of him in her mind. He was racing through the brush and trees toward her, panicked.

"Cadence!" Highbrow emerged from the trees. He saw Rafe and raised his rifle. "You bit her, didn't you? Get away from her, you soulless bastard."

Still clinging to Rafe, Cadence looked at Highbrow. Her fangs extended and she opened her mouth lusting for his blood. Turning away, she concentrated on the heartbeat of the forest, smelled its primal earthiness and felt her skin tingle as the leaves rustled in the breeze. Cadence detected more humans approaching. Had it not been for Rafe holding her firm, she would have attacked Highbrow and the others.

"I can't let go or she'll kill you to feed," said Rafe. "A zombie slipped through. He was on her when I arrived. The only way to save Cadence was to turn her. I didn't want this for her, Highbrow. This is your fault. What the hell were you doing? Why weren't you here?"

"Luna," said Highbrow. "We saw her in the trees. I was only gone a moment. The Tigers and China Six are right behind me."

Cadence heard the two teams crashing through the underbrush

like elephants. She looked away from Highbrow and begged Rafe to go with her into the night.

"I'm so sorry, Cadence," pleaded Highbrow, his voice ridden with guilt. "I promised to protect you and I failed you. Please forgive me." He lifted his rifle.

The scent coming from Highbrow turned from guilt to fear. Cadence smelled the change as if smelling sunshine and then night. Rafe put his body between Highbrow's aim and Cadence.

"Just let go of her, Rafe," said Highbrow. "Let me do what I can to make her comfortable. I'll . . . take care of her. And then you."

"If by that you mean kill us, I think I'll decline." Rafe held Cadence back. "You're not safe, pal. She's hungry. I might not be able to hold her much longer. Return to camp. I'll take it from here. There's a place we can go that's safe for us."

Cadence watched as Highbrow lowered his weapon. She broke free from Rafe and grabbed hold of Highbrow. As she leaned in to feast, the howl of a werepuma echoed in the distance. Turning, she threw him to the ground.

"This wasn't supposed to happen," said Highbrow, sobbing. "I love her. I love her, Rafe. It's my fault this happened. What am I supposed to do?"

Spinning to face Highbrow once more, Cadence regarded him with glowing blue eyes. He seemed so young and stupid that all she could do was smile at him, as she would a child. Another cry from the werepuma filled her with excitement. She sniffed the wind, picking up the scent of cat and took a step in its direction.

"She understands me?" asked Highbrow.

"Cadence isn't dead, you idiot," Rafe said. "But I doubt your proclamation of love makes her feel any better knowing you also want to kill her. I hear the cat, too. She's calling to you, Cadence. Go to her. Go chase the moonlight."

Cadence lingered beside the stream, smelling the rich, brown earth and feeling the silver light of the moon on her face. There was so much to see. A brand new world beckoned her. She wanted to race the wind. Cadence moved forward, feeling the ground soft beneath her feet. She didn't look back, but kept running, answering Luna's call.

Chapter Twenty-Four

*L*una's scent was strong. Cadence scaled a rocky ledge to its peak, gravity holding less sway than before. She was not surprised to find a large white cat waiting when she reached the top. Luna peered at her with luminous violet eyes. Cadence stood transfixed by Luna's eyes and the silver light dancing on her white fur. A sudden ripple crept down Luna's spine, transforming her into a human girl.

"Hello, Cadence," said Luna. "I'm sorry I didn't reach you first. I knew you were at the stream and I smelled the zombie and the vampire. When I knew the bloodlust was upon you, I called to you so we could talk."

"Am I a zombie or a vampire?"

"You smell like a vampire," said Luna. "Rafe reached you in time, at least I think he did. When I died and came back, all I could think about was killing everything around me. I took my pride into the mountains, thinking we'd never return. I sensed you were in trouble so I came back to find you."

Cadence sat back against the cliff so she could stretch her legs out in front of her. She could not feel the chill in the air, nor did Luna. Luna didn't seem real, so she reached out for her hand. Shen needed to touch her to believe.

"When the sun comes, I'll return to the mountains," said Luna. "Don't vampires turn into dust in the sun? Aren't you afraid?"

"I don't think I'm that kind of vampire," said Cadence. "This feels like a dream to me. It didn't really hurt. I knew I was dying when the zombie bit my neck, but when Rafe gave me his blood everything changed. I can run for miles and never tire. Everything is so beautiful. And you're beautiful, Luna."

"I'm happier this way. I don't know how or why it works, but when I'm in my animal form everything feels right with the world. I'm not scared of zombies or vampires or others like me. Don't you see? No matter what happens, I'm not afraid anymore. This is the cure. At least for me."

Cadence released Luna's hand and stood. Luna rose with her. They gazed across pine-covered mountains and silently breathed in the scent of all that was alive and beautiful. It was strange, but Cadence no longer felt afraid either. She finally felt free.

"I don't know what I want," said Cadence. "But I feel like I can have anything."

"Why don't you come with us?" Luna looked over the edge. "This is all new to me, too. I'm not sure what I can and can't do, but I know I'm going to jump down. A normal cat couldn't make that jump and maybe I'll break my legs, but I have to find out. Come with me and let's run until the sun rises."

"Maybe I'll go back to camp. Should I go back?"

"If you want to. I'll come back for a visit sometime. But if you ever need me, Cadence, simply call. I'll hear you and come running."

In the wisp of a breath, Luna jumped over the ledge. Cadence didn't look to see if she landed as a cat. She heard no sound, and assumed Luna was fine. Everything was going to be fine.

Returning to Seven Falls, Cadence marveled at how still the morning was and how wonderful it all smelled. From the last of the summer flowers to the decaying leaves on the ground, rich and strong, they reminded her that she was bound to the earth in a way she had never considered before. She was reborn. It was strange, scary, and fantastic.

Two pairs of footsteps walked the path behind her. She paused to sniff the air. Logan's fragrance was clean, but the rank odor of Nomad begged for a bath. She caught a deer during the night and fed, yet the desire for human blood was difficult to ignore. Cadence wrapped her arms around her body and turned to face the hunters. Neither noticed she had changed.

"How did you fair?" asked Cadence. "Did you find Luna?"

Nomad coughed a gruff 'no.' He limped as he walked past, a sour expression on his face. Cadence marveled Nomad didn't notice any difference in her and kept marching, the smell of blood wafting by. She turned to Logan, who was in much better shape than his companion. He was dirty and looked tired, but had the strength to go another ten miles if necessary.

"Nomad's injured," said Logan. "He took a hard fall. The gash in his leg is still bleeding. It's pretty deep and will need some stitches."

"You should both go back to camp."

Logan grasped Cadence by the arm. His eyes scrutinized her face and lowered to her neck. "My lesser evolved friend didn't notice, but you've changed. Those are two sets of bite marks on your neck. My guess is that Rafe bit you, but that other mark, well, that's not from a vampire."

Cadence jerked her arm loose and threw herself around Logan. He tried to break free, but she laughed and held him tighter. He didn't call Nomad back to help.

"I wonder if I'm a Maker?" said Cadence. "Does it have to be blood or is it any fluid transfer that spreads the virus?"

"Blood. Only the blood," said Logan. "Frankly, I don't want to find out what I'd turn into if you bite me, Cadence. My suggestion is let's not find out."

Still wrapped in her arms, Logan managed to reach inside his coat pocket. Cadence wondered what he was doing and looked down. The mist from a bottle of bug repellent absorbed into her eyes. The sting was rapid and fierce. She released him and rubbed her eyes with her fists.

"Sorry," said Logan. "I don't like taking chances."

"I should kill you for that, jerk! It burns!"

Cadence sank to the ground, expecting Logan to shoot her in the head. Rubbing her eyes only made it worse, so she stopped. It didn't take long for the burning to stop. Her body healed fast, but it made her hungry. She looked up at Logan to find his rifle pointing at her head. It would not have been difficult to take him, but she resisted the urge.

"What were you doing out here anyway? Hunting Luna? Hunting me?"

"Actually," said Cadence, "I was running with the pride. Luna, Barbarella, Skye, and Sheena are adapting very well to their new lives. I'm a bit envious. I can't decide if I like being a vampire or if I miss being human. You smell really good, Logan."

"I'm not your next meal," said Logan. He let her stand up, keeping his barrel trained on her head. "Now, should I kill you or be stupid and trust you? You're a strong person and should be able to fight the urge to feed on me." He lowered his gun and extended his hand.

"What's that for? Are you being gallant now?"

"Come on, Cadence. I feel compassion for you right now and that's not normal. So, while I'm under your thrall, let's go talk to the kiddos and figure this out."

Reaching out for his hand, Cadence glimpsed something whiz by her cheek. Logan's fingers coiled around her hand, but she yanked it back. A small buzzing made her flip her head around. A bumble bee landed on her bottom lip. Cadence turned toward Logan. His eyes widened as he spotted the bee. The back end of the yellow and black bee wiggled, revealing its stinger. Cadence narrowed her eyes in an attempt to look past her nose at the insect. Logan started to laugh and she grinned. At the movement, the bee stung and Cadence swatted it away.

It hit the ground and writhed for a moment, then stilled.

"You okay?" Logan said. He reached out as she puckered her lips and removed the tiny stinger from her swelling bottom lip.

She licked the wound.

Cadence licked again, tasting something sweet. It was like honey and her body shuddered. She reached for Logan to steady herself, but missed and fell forward onto her face as a spasm seized her entire body. A deep, painful cough twisted from her lungs and caused her to writhe with pain. Her tongue flicked across her bottom lip again. It was inflamed and searing with pain. She tasted fetid mucous and a shiver coursed through her body. The morning air was chilly, but that couldn't be right. She had been out all night and not felt cold.

She thought to sniff at Logan, and leaned toward him to breathe him in. He shoved her back and raised his aim at her once more. Cadence fell to her side, laughing, crying, and experiencing a full spectrum of emotions.

A crushing wave of torment hit Cadence without warning. One after another, spasms ripped through her body, setting every nerve on fire. Her muscles strained, agonizing, and her joints ached like hell. If this was death, it was horrible. A final shudder clutched her body and she lay motionless, mouth gaping and eyes wide open.

"You okay?" said Logan. "You're as white as a ghost."

Cadence gasped, sucking in air. Blood rushed to her checks and tears fell from the corners of her eyes. She stared up at Logan. He looked worried as she drew in deep breaths.

Everything had changed, again.

"What's wrong with you? Are you allergic to bees?"

Logan took a hesitant step toward her. Cadence remained on the ground, fatigued and too worried to speak. He knelt beside her, studying her face.

"If I didn't know better, and I don't, I'd say you just died and came back to life. Only you look healthy. In fact, you look better than you did a few minutes ago. You've lost that pale vampire look and your body temperature is up. You don't feel like a corpse. Still want to bite me?"

"Yes, but not because I want to suck your blood."

Cadence lifted her arms and stared at her hands as she spread her fingers. The warmth of the sunlight on her hands and face felt wonderful. She tried to sit up. Logan steadied her with his hands and helped her stand. Their eyes locked.

"There was so much pain. I thought I was dying again. And now . . ."

"Now?" Logan was excited. He squeezed her shoulders.

"I feel human. I can't smell the wind or feel the leaves moving. It's weird, but all I want is a big, juicy hamburger with fries. And a chocolate shake."

Logan gave her a hug. Cadence remained very still in his arms. She could smell him, but she didn't want to sink her teeth into him. Moments ago she felt like she could do anything. Now, she felt embarrassed and clumsy.

"Maybe you're allergic to bees," said Logan. "Your bottom lip is as big as a slice of lemon, which it wouldn't be if you were a vampire. It would be falling off if you were a zombie."

She raised her hand to her lip. It was huge and it still hurt. If she was vampire, it should have healed. Logan was right. She licked her lips again and started to laugh.

She sneezed, and then sneezed again.

"I wouldn't think it possible, but that bee may have cured you."

Cadence wiped her hand across her nose and looked at the ground. "We've got to find the bumble bee. Look for it, Logan. If I was a vampire or a zombie, I wouldn't be having an allergic reaction at all. I have to be cured!"

He scrambled forward, looking for the insect. "I've seen a lot of strange things in my life, but I never counted on a bee curing a plague. Where'd the damn thing go?"

"I'm cured, Logan. I'm too sore and tired to be anything but human."

"Maybe it's an act of God," said Logan. "I believe you. I think you are cured."

It was possible. Anything seemed possible at this point.

"Do you think I could cure Rafe? What about Luna and the others? What about zombies?"

"Let's not try to find out until we figure this out," said Logan. "We need a way to run some blood tests. As for curing everyone else, we'll need someone a little more knowledgeable than me, but it's good to have you back, commander."

Cadence waved at Logan to follow her as she skipped to the stairs. He followed close. She paused when she spotted Highbrow and Rafe standing together at the side of the pool. They saw her and she waved at them. She glanced at Logan, smiling even wider.

"We can do this, Logan. We can make things right."

"You'll cause a lot of confusion down there," said Logan. "Coming back as a human is going to require answers we just don't have yet. Tell them it was a bee sting and they'll turn this place upside down looking for one."

"Because it's the flower, the nectar the bee gathered, that's the cure. Right?"

Logan's eyes narrowed. "Maybe, but tell them it was your own immune system that makes you a bit of a freak. Let's keep a lid on things for now. I'll get to work on figuring this out."

Cadence looked at the sky. "Highbrow's father is in a think tank in Florida. If we can get word to him that we may have found a cure, then maybe we can save the human race."

"Slow down," said Logan. "One step at a time. I'll help you figure it out, Cadence. Everything happens for a reason. But you're right, we can do this. As a team."

Cadence thought about the possibilities. Her future seemed brighter. As long as there was hope left in the world, anything might happen. Reaching the bottom of the stairs, Cadence ran into the waiting arms of Highbrow. He yelped in fright, but was unable to turn her away.

She laughed as she kissed him, delighting in his confusion and surprise.

"You don't have to be scared anymore. None of us do. I'm cured."

Highbrow frowned. "How is that possible?"

Behind him, Rafe frowned even harder.

Cadence turned toward Logan and smiled. "I'm not sure yet. But I'm back. Join me in my quarters, gentlemen, we've much to discuss."

The sun was setting once more.

From the fifth floor of the Broadmoor Hotel, Rose looked over the destruction of Colorado Springs. Dusk cast an apocalyptic backdrop of spikes, ruined buildings, and imperceptible alleys. The Dark Angels were making plans behind her. Supply runs, surveillance, and scouting all needed to happen, and happen fast. Sensing a change in the air, she looked down.

Through the window, she watched Rafe walking across the parking lot. He stopped in his tracks, looking up at Rose. Picasso laughed at one of Lachlan's mischievous jokes, the Irish vampire mocking the Kaiser with pantomime.

She cleared her throat and the room quieted. "Tandor?"

"Yes?"

"We have a visitor. Be a dear and make sure he finds his way up?"

Tandor peered out the window, grunted, and exited the room.

Rose looked back down at Rafe. The time was at hand for the Dark

Angels to make their move. If they were going to shift the tide of this war, they had to act, now.

Cadence walked through the trees with Luna, the moonlight painting them with moving palettes of blacks and pale whites. She couldn't remember how she got here, but knew they were hunting deer. For food, for sport, and for the communion of friendship.

Luna tensed and stopped in her tracks. Her long teeth bared, paws clutching the dirt.

"What? What is it?" asked Cadence. Luna nodded her head, and Cadence looked further into the woods. A large shadow stood ahead of them, yellow eyes penetrating the moonlight. The shadow stretched out its hand and Cadence heard Luna howl with pain. But when she looked down for her friend, Luna had disappeared, a pool of blood in her place.

Enraged, Cadence pointed her gun at the shadow. "Who are you?"

With a gasp of her breath, the shadow closed the distance between them and swatted the gun from her hand. Its yellow eyes danced with malicious delight as it wrapped its cold hands around her throat.

Experiencing a surge of emotion, Cadence grabbed the arms of the shadow and without effort, ripped them from its shoulders. She leapt, and in a feral rage, shredded the image of the shadow. The piercing, yellow eyes squinted with amusement and a deep laugh filled the air.

Cadence woke up in her cabin in a fit of sweat and rage. She heaved for breath, grasping remnants of cloth in her hands. She had shredded her sheets and blanket during her sleep.

The need for fresh air forced her outside. She shivered, but not from any sense of being cold.

Near her cabin, a man cloaked under the shadow of the night watched as Cadence paced back and forth. He grinned, his yellow eyes flashing with momentary delight. The Kaiser was right. This little camp is fertile ground for new fighters to be acquired for use in the annual Death Games.

Shadows grew long over Seven Falls.

About The Author

S usanne L. Lambdin is the author of the *Dead Hearts* series of novels. A "trekkie" at heart, she received a "based in part" screen credit for writing a portion of *Star Trek: The Next Generation:* Season 4, Episode 76, titled *Family*. She is passionate about all things science fiction, horror, and high fantasy. Susanne is an expert on the subject of zombies, and is affectionately known by many of her fans as "The Zombie Lady."

She lives in Kansas with her family and two dogs. To contact Susanne and to learn more about her current and upcoming projects, visit www.SusanneLambdin.com.

CPSIA information can be obtained
at www.ICGtesting.com
Printed in the USA
FFOW04n0058110515
13198FF